PRAISE FOR *TIME OFF*

"...sparkling debut, full of punch... ...moments."

—Sue Margolis, author of *Apocalipstick*

"Delightful . . . hilarious . . . Any woman who is trying to make a change in her life will be able to relate to this book . . . We look forward to more books by this author!"

—BestsellersWorld.com

"Highly engaging. I recommend *Time Off for Good Behavior* for anyone looking for a good, at-times hilarious and meaningful chick-lit read. Don't miss it!"

—Chicklitbooks.com

"A warm and funny story. A perfect read for a rainy afternoon. Or *any* afternoon."

—Karen Brichoux, author of *Coffee and Kung Fu*

"This effervescent debut novel will strike a chord with every woman who has ever been tempted to give her life an extreme makeover."

—Wendy Markham, author of *Suddenly Single*

"Terrific and absolutely hilarious . . . with a thoroughly original and delightful heroine.

—Melissa Senate, author of *See Jane Date*

"Rich deftly crafts an unpredictable plot that charts Wanda's emotional growth without letting the character lose her edge. The novel's freshness and humor prove this author is one to watch."

—*Romantic Times BOOKclub Magazine*

"Rich has managed to skillfully blend serious topics with humor, and readers will love her for it."

—*Booklist*

books by lani diane rich

Maybe Baby
Time Off for Good Behavior

ex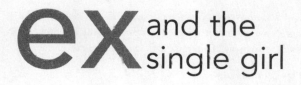and the single girl

lani diane rich

NEW YORK   BOSTON

This book is a work of fiction. Names, characters, places, and incidents are the product of the author's imagination or are used fictitiously. Any resemblance to actual events, locales, or persons, living or dead, is coincidental.

Copyright © 2005 by Lani Diane Rich
All rights reserved.

A 5 Spot Book
Warner Books

Time Warner Book Group
1271 Avenue of the Americas, New York, NY 10020
Visit our Web site at www.twbookmark.com.

The 5 Spot logo is a trademark of Warner Books.

Printed in the United States of America

First Edition: November 2005

10 9 8 7 6 5 4 3 2 1

Library of Congress Cataloging-in-Publication Data

Rich, Lani Diane.
    Ex and the single girl / Lani Diane Rich.—1st ed.
        p. cm.
    ISBN 0-446-69307-3
    1. Georgia—Fiction. I. Title.
    PS3618.I333E98 2005
    813'.6—dc22

                                                                      2005000378

Book design and text composition by Nancy Singer Olaguera/ISPN
Cover design by Brigid Pearson
Cover photo by Leland Bobbe/Taxi

To my mother, Joyce Rich, who taught me everything
I need to know about facing life with strength, integrity,
and courage.

Oh, and who—for the record—is *nothing* like Mags.
Love you, Mom.

acknowledgments

First and foremost, I'd like to thank my husband, whose endless support, love, and patience make it possible for me to live my dream, both professionally and personally. I'd also like to thank my two daughters for giving me a new angle on that particular brand of love-induced crazy that happens to mothers. I think I get it now.

Special thanks to Wanda, who taught me everything I ever wanted to know about Catoosa County, and to Monica, who got excited about this story before it was ever written. Now *that's* fandom.

Thanks also to Cate Diede and Rebecca Rohan, who somehow find the strength to wade through my written muck when it's really mucky; to the UK Cherries for graciously checking my dialogue for British authenticity; to Eileen Connell for reading, commenting, and always encouraging; and to my fellow literary chicks Michelle Cunnah and Alesia Holliday for being such fine, fine company.

A deep, heartfelt, and humble bow to the dream team of publishing, my agent Stephanie Kip Rostan and my editor Beth de Guzman. I'm a lucky, lucky girl. Don't think I don't know it.

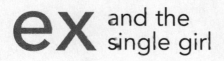

chapter one

Fat white flakes clustered around the edges of my living room window as another Syracuse winter flipped late March the bird. I sat with my feet curled under me on the cheap futon in my tiny one-bedroom, lit by the flickering colors of the BBC version of *Pride and Prejudice*, which I was watching for what was probably around the eighteenth time. My hand was draped casually over a bag of Cheetos, which I planned on trading in for the chilled chardonnay in my fridge as soon as I could locate the motivation to get up.

". . . allow me to tell you how ardently I admire and love you."

I sighed. I couldn't help myself. Nobody knows how to do lovers in a snit like Austen. Darcy paced, lecturing to Elizabeth all the reasons she was unworthy of him. Her eyes widened, then narrowed.

Things were just about to get good.

Ring.

Damnit. I exhaled heavily, shooting my bangs up off my forehead, and glared at the phone, which hung at a defiant angle on my kitchen wall. Almost three years I'd been living here, and I'd never drummed up the wherewithal to straighten it.

"In such cases as these, I believe the established mode is to express a sense of obligation." Elizabeth's eyes lifted and met Darcy's. They were cold. "But I cannot."

Ring.

"Shit, piss, and corruption," I grumbled, searching around for the remote control, even though I hadn't seen the thing in weeks. "I sat through three hours of parties and pianofortes for this scene."

Beep. My voice crackled through my garage-sale answering machine, creaking with the cold I'd had when I recorded the outgoing message in February. "Not here. Do your thing."

I'm a big fan of brevity. My mother, however, is not.

"Portia, darlin'." Mags's voice was like honey, sweet and slow to move. I never noticed her accent until I moved to upstate New York, where words that start out as one syllable tend to stay that way. I shed my own drawl on the train ride out of town, although I'm told it comes out when I've been drinking.

"Are you there, baby? You should answer the phone. It's not right to sit and listen to people talking and not answer the phone. Vera says that sort of thing absolutely ruins your karma."

"Vera thinks hairspray ruins your karma," I muttered, hopping off the futon and sweeping my arm underneath the mammoth cushion for the twentieth time that week, as though repetition of the ritual would make the damn remote magically reappear.

Mags released a stage sigh, the kind regular people only hear during plays by Tennessee Williams. "I guess I can assume you're not there. Well, please, baby, call me the second you get this message. It's *urgent.*"

Urgent. The word didn't have the same meaning for Mags

as it did for most people. *Urgent* could have meant that she had misplaced her unholy red pumps and needed me to talk her through the search. It could have meant that one of her favorite movie stars from the forties had died, and the entire family needed to lift a glass in unison to the Great One's memory. One *urgent* call resulted in my losing two hours of my life to gossip about Felicia Callahan getting fired from the Catoosa County Chamber of Commerce for stealing four staplers and thirty-eight dollars in petty cash.

"I need you to call me tonight, baby, the very moment you get home."

I tossed the futon cushion back down and got up to hit the PAUSE button on my tiny TV/VCR. On an average day, I spent more time looking for the stupid remote than it'd take for me to get up and walk over to the TV, but it was the principle of the thing. It had disappeared around the same time Peter left, and having it at large meant Peter might find it in his things and return it. The very thought of him showing up on the doorstep with nothing to say but "Here's your remote" was the stuff of which nightmares are made.

The machine beeped again, and I released a breath I hadn't realized I was holding. I wandered into the kitchen, curling the top of the bag of Cheetos and tossing it onto the counter where it began its determined work of uncurling. I didn't care. I'd done my part. I grabbed the corkscrew with one hand as I opened the fridge with the other.

Tick tock. Darcy's waiting.

Freeze frame.

This is the pre-epiphany moment, the mental snapshot of myself that I revisit on occasion, mystified at how much I failed to notice. There I was, wearing the oldest flannel robe in existence, my unwashed hair sticking up in all directions out of a lazy ponytail, my glasses smudged and crooked, a bottle of wine in hand with little splotches of Cheeto residue on the neck, and I had no earthly idea that anything was wrong.

It hadn't been that bad when Peter'd been around. I'd been clean, lively, happy. I smelled good. I flossed. But then one day—Valentine's Day, if you can stand the irony—I came home to a half-emptied apartment and a half-assed good-bye note scribbled in the title page of a book. And not just *any* book. *Peter's* book. The one he'd written during two years of late nights and early mornings while I encouraged him, making coffee and providing sexual diversions. The one that had hit the shelves and stayed there, neglected, while Steels and Koontzes flew from either side. The one that I read over and over, gushing over his talent every time.

I'd found it lying on the bed, the front cover held open with my itty bitty booklight, the title page etched with his deliberate handwriting.

I'm sorry. I wish you all the best. Love, Peter.

A simple note, vague as hell, fodder for hours and hours of painful dissection. What did it *mean*? Why would he sign a "Later, Babe" note with *Love, Peter*? Isn't love pretty much a moot point when one is being dumped? And where had he gone? Had he run off with another woman? Another man? Had he simply decided that he would rather be alone than with me? Which was worse?

For six weeks, these were the questions that haunted me as I plummeted into a cavern of self-pity. In six short weeks, I'd mutated from a normal individual pursuing a Ph.D. and a reasonable future to a wild-haired social phobic, rationalizing my obsession with *Pride and Prejudice* by linking it with my dissertation topic, 'The Retelling of Austen in Post-Feminist Women's Literature." Forget that I hadn't written a word since the day Peter left. Forget that I'd left the house only to teach my classes and to grab Cheetos and chardonnay at Wegmans. Forget that I had just earlier that very day briefly considered getting a cat. If nothing else, I should have been tipped off by the fact that when Peter and I were together, I'd more than once caught myself fantasizing about coming home one day to an empty apartment, leaving me blameless and beatified. And free. Now that my dream had come true, it begged the question: What, exactly, was I mourning?

Continue action

I carried the bottle of wine and the glass with me to the living room, kicking a path through the notebooks and pens on the floor as I settled back on the futon. The tape had stopped, and a blond sitcom star from the seventies was hawking diet pills. I debated internally on whether the energy would be better spent getting up and hitting the PLAY button or continuing my futile search for the remote when the phone rang.

Again.

Two calls in the span of fifteen minutes greatly increased the probability that whatever she was calling about was actually urgent. I pulled myself up off the futon and headed into the kitchen, flicking on the light and grabbing the receiver off its crooked base. "Yeah?"

"Portia, darlin', I knew you were home."

"In the shower." I took a sip of my wine. "I heard the phone ring. Was that you?"

"Yes, baby," she said. Her voice sounded tired. I wondered why I hadn't noticed it before. I rifled through the junk drawer in the kitchen. Remotes have turned up in stranger places.

"Baby, I need your help. My back has gone out on me, and every moment is acute pain and torture. Doctor Bobby says I need to stay in bed for a few months."

Only in Truly, Georgia, would a grown man who'd earned a medical degree allow himself to be referred to as "Doctor Bobby." I stood up straight and slammed the drawer shut with my hip. "A few *months*? Jesus, Mags. What did you do?"

"I don't know," she said, distress raising her voice an easy octave. "But Doctor Bobby has given me strict orders. Which puts us in a bit of a spot. Vera can't run the store alone, and Bev needs to be slowing down at this time in her life. So, I've been thinking . . ."

I raised my glass of wine to my lips, knowing exactly what was coming. "Thinking? What about?"

"Well, we had a family meeting, and we thought you might come home for a while. To help out."

I knew it. "How long a while?"

"Oh, not too long, I'm sure. If you could come home for the summer, that should be fine."

I choked on a sharp gulp of wine. "The *summer*?"

"I'm sure I'll be up and around by August. September at the latest."

"The *whole* summer?" I glanced around the apartment, my mind whirling in a desperate search for reasons why I could not leave. My dissertation. My shot at getting the assistant professor position opening up next spring. My life . . .

My eyes grazed over the window, then zoomed back. A chunk of ice formed in my throat. I squinted at my reflection in the glass.

Epiphany.

"Oh, my god," I said, and walked closer to the window,

touching my face, straightening my glasses, running my hand over the bird's nest ponytail hanging off my head at a tilt.

"Portia?" I heard Mags's voice come through the line, tinged with concern. I walked over to the mirror by the front door and took a good look. Pale skin. Bags under the eyes. I practically had a neon sign over my head, flashing the same empty message over and over.

Alone.

I swallowed and the ice shifted to the back of my neck. I blinked and looked around my apartment, seeing fresh the mass of empty junk food wrappers and dirty coffee mugs. My chest tightened.

"Darlin'?" Mags's voice was muffled; I'd let the phone drop against my chest, where it vibrated to the beat of my frantic heart as the neon sign flashed in my imagination.

Alone. Afraid.

Oh, my god, I thought. *I'm four cats and a* Reader's Digest *subscription away from being totally irredeemable.*

"Portia? You still there, baby?"

I shook my head, got control of my breathing. The ice receded. I pulled the phone up to my ear. "Yeah. I'm here."

"Oh, good," she said, apparently missing the panic in my voice. "I thought I'd lost you there for a minute. So, when can we expect you here? You know our busy season starts around mid-May . . ."

"Hold on for a minute, okay, Mags?" I put the phone to my chest again. I breathed deep, turning my back to the mirror, raising my eyes to the ceiling, which was the only place in my apartment showing no evidence of the fact that I'd driven my life into one hell of a ditch.

Use logic. Make a choice. Stay here and recite Austen movies with the actors and never write another word of your dissertation and morph insidiously into the Crazy Cat Lady in the attic apartment . . .

My heart started to pump erratically again. I took another deep breath.

. . . or, spend a summer in the clutches of the Mizzes. Lesser of two evils. Make a choice, Portia.

"Portia?"

"Just a minute, Mags." I grabbed a quarter off the floor and flipped it in the air. Heads—Syracuse. Tails—Truly.

I caught the quarter in the air and slapped it on the back of my hand. Tails.

Best two out of three.

"Portia? Honey?"

I flipped again, then sighed and tossed the quarter back on the floor. I rolled my head on my shoulders. My breathing stabilized. My heart fell into a reasonable rhythm. I squinted at the calendar.

"My last class is May nineteenth," I said, feeling the words stick in my throat as I croaked them out. "I can settle things here and be there by the twenty-second or so. Assuming I can find someone to sublet my apartment. If I can't find someone . . ."

Mags squealed and giggled. I'd have pictured her jumping up and down if it weren't for the acute pain and torture in her back. "Oh, darlin', that's just perfect! I knew you'd come through for us. I just knew it!"

I grabbed a red marker, took the cap off with my teeth, and spit it onto the kitchen counter as I flipped up the pages to August. The panic subsided as resignation flowed in. "I'll have to be back by . . ." I ran a finger over the days. "August twenty-second."

I circled it in red, then put two stars on either side. August 22. Three months. Thirteen weeks. Was it really going to kill me?

Chances were fair to middlin' that it would. But the dismal state of my life had been recognized, and it had to be dealt with. Even though my response was to run far, far away, at least I was doing *something*. At least I wasn't floating around town with open cans of Fancy Feast, trolling for strays. That was good. Wasn't it?

I muddled through a few more niceties and finally shrugged Mags off the phone. I scuffed through the living room, reaching down to flick off the television set as I headed toward the closet, grabbing the last clean towel and revealing the remote, sitting there on the naked shelf.

I stared. All this time, it had been sitting there, waiting for me to hit rock bottom, to get to the place where I'd whittled the laundry down to the last pair of clean underwear, the last clean towel. I raised my fingers to its bumpy, worn surface, then rolled my eyes at myself as my vision started to blur under the tears.

Peter would not be coming back.

I tossed the stupid thing down the hallway, where it skidded to a stop on the living room rug. I longed for a warm, furry kitten snuggling up against my ankles, justifying my existence by needing me. Maybe if I got just one, it would be okay. You have to have more than one to be the Crazy Cat Lady. I tossed the towel over my shoulder and decided to think about it on August 23.

I drove the fourteen hours home for two reasons. One, it allowed for the possibility of changing my mind and turning back, something that's much harder to do on a plane. Two, it gave me a fourteen-hour reprieve from my immersion into the collective bosom of my mother, aunt, and grandmother, known throughout Truly as the Miz Fallons. The nickname stems from the fact that our family has been suspiciously lacking Mr. Fallons. None of us has ever been married, and when we get knocked up, we have girls.

"Men just don't stick to Miz Fallons," Mags had often said throughout my childhood, as though it was simply a fact of life to be accepted and moved past, like having freckles or being color-blind. I hadn't accepted it as fact, but so far, I had to admit the phenomenon was consistent. I've termed it the Penis Teflon Effect. Patent pending.

When I pulled my rattling Mazda sedan past the town limits of Truly, Georgia, population 6,618, I had fourteen hours of self-talk under my belt. I would be gracious. I would be pleasant. I would ignore any quirks, insensitivities, and unintentional offenses. I would enjoy my time with the Mizzes. I might even wear makeup and dresses if it made them happy. After all, how much did it really matter? It was one summer, and I'd be going back to Syracuse at the end of it. I could be gracious for one summer.

I rolled down my window and drew in the clean air, watching the sun set behind the purpling Northwest Georgia Mountains. I was overwhelmed by contentment, even a little nostalgia, as I traded Battlefield Parkway for Truly's Main Street. As I drove past, my eyes clung to the old-fashioned wooden sign that hung over the family bookstore, the Printed Page. I was surprised by the ache I felt, the longing to see once again the shelves of books and random knickknacks, drink the brew from our little coffee bar, inhale the musty wood and pulp.

"God," I said to myself as I waited at Truly's only stoplight and stared at the Page's storefront. "I had no idea how much I missed you."

"Why, Portia Fallon!"

I turned my head to see a large woman in a blue dress waving from the front stoop outside of Whitfield's Pharmacy. I fluttered my fingers at her and laughed.

"Hi, Marge!" I called through the open window, surprised at how quickly she'd recognized me. With the exception of the occasional low-profile holiday visit, I'd been gone twelve years. I didn't know whether to be glad or disturbed that I'd changed so little.

"Good to have you home, baby!" she called as the light turned green and I moved on. It was a short six blocks from the center of town to our old two-story colonial, but I took it slow, remembering every oak tree I'd ever fallen out of, every friend's house I'd ever ducked behind to try on lipstick or smoke a cigarette. They were all there, every last one. How was it possible that a place could be exactly the same after twelve years? Had I been raised in Brigadoon and never even noticed?

By the time I pulled into our driveway, I was feeling pretty good. I chuckled to myself as I stepped out of the car, wondering what all my dread had been about. It was just Truly, and Truly wasn't so bad. It was a place where kids played safely in the streets and neighbors all knew each other, and there were definitely worse things than spending a summer drinking iced tea in pine-scented mountain breezes. The Mizzes would behave themselves, certainly. Hell, Mags would be in bed most of the time. Everything was going to be just fine.

Maybe even fun.

I popped my trunk open and looked up with a smile as I heard the creaky porch door swing open, followed by squeals of excitement.

I heard a pounding and looked up to see Mags bounding down the steps toward me like a Great Dane released from a small pen. My smile froze. She was all energy and verve, and there wasn't even the tiniest evidence of acute pain and torture on her face.

"Good to see you, Mags," I said when she released me from her exuberant hug. "How's your back?"

She gave a dismissive wave as though there was a small fly rather than a huge deception between us. "Oh, my back's fine. That was just to get you here. And now you're here!"

Mags flashed her sparkling white smile at me, and her blue eyes shone under her perfectly lined lids. Not a hint of guilt or shame or anything that anyone with a moral center might show. Either she didn't think it was wrong, or she didn't think I'd be mad.

Or, and this was my vote, she just didn't think.

I lifted my indignant gaze up to the porch. My aunt Vera waved and held up a glass full of clear liquid and clinking ice cubes. I didn't have to taste it to know it was a gin and tonic, the signature drink of the Miz Fallons.

God bless Vera.

"Come on up, darlin'!" she called. "We're fixin' to celebrate!"

Mags easily lifted my heavy duffel bag out of the passenger seat of my car, and I felt my irritation flare up again.

"I don't know why you can't get some proper luggage, Portia. Something with corners, maybe. And wheels. You know they make 'em with wheels nowadays. Isn't that smart?"

I slung my laptop bag over my shoulder and snatched the duffel from her, slamming the car door shut and hearing a small, fading voice in my head calling, *Gracious!* as though from a great distance.

"Acute pain and torture," I said. "I seem to recall those exact words."

Mags sighed and turned to me, grabbing the duffel bag back. "Oh, baby, you're dwelling. It's not attractive. Now come see Vera and Bev; they've missed you so."

She turned her back to me and headed up the steps. That meant the conversation was over. I'd been had, and there was nothing left to discuss. Even if I had it in me to turn around and drive back to Syracuse, which would have served her right, I had sublet my apartment and I wasn't getting it back until August. Best to just let it go, as I eventually did with all my grievances against Mags. She didn't get it, she never would, that's just who she was, and there was simply no point in staying mad.

I followed her up the steps, glaring at the back of her head the whole time. I may talk the talk of a mature adult, but it takes a while to walk the walk. The sooner I got to that gin and tonic, the better.

Vera clapped her hands and jumped up and down when she saw me, running toward me while Mags deposited my duffel bag inside the front door. She gave me a forceful hug, then stepped back to look at me, her hands on my shoulders.

"Beautiful as ever," she said. I could smell the jasmine incense in her hair and clothes. Her long hair trailed down her back in a fluffy braid, and if it wasn't for the gentle streaks of gray in the blond, you'd never guess she was in her fifties. "It's so good to have you back, baby."

"Yes," Bev said, walking over to me and pulling me into a firm hug. Her hugs, like everything about Bev, were always firm. "It's good to see you, girl."

Mags returned, carrying two gin and tonics, handing one to me as she passed by to sit next to Vera on the porch swing. Bev settled herself in the rocking chair, I sat on the old creaky wicker, and we all stared at each other, treading carefully in the familiar unfamiliar.

I watched them in that awkward silence, thinking how they were a lot like the bear beds that Goldilocks had found. Vera was the soft one. Never had a bad thing to say about anyone, always cried when baby birds fell out of the oak that shaded our porch. Bev was the firm one, the one you turned to to fix everything when you'd been wrongly accused of cheating on your math test, but not the person you'd seek out for comfort after, say, you saw Eddie Collier kissing Pamie Scott at the school dance. And Mags—well, you could say Mags was just right. She was sensitive enough to know when to ask what was bothering you, smart enough to know when to leave you alone, and kind enough not to say she told you so. She was beautiful, had impeccable taste, and her feet never seemed to hurt, no matter how cute her shoes were. She would be just right, in fact, if she wasn't just a hair shy of being certifiably nuts.

"So," Vera ventured, leaning forward with a broad smile, "tell us about your dissertation. Mags says you finished it?"

"I finished the rough draft," I lied. It had been half-done and gathering dust since February, while my tab of *Pride and Prejudice* viewings was approaching twenty-five. Epiphany be damned, old habits die hard.

"That's so exciting," Vera said.

"Yes, we are so proud," Bev said. I thought I caught an edge in her tone, but when I looked her way, her smile was as bright as ever.

"When Mary Alice Rainey comes in talking about her Son the Doctor, I just tell her all about my Daughter the Ph.D." Mags grinned at me and sipped her drink. I let out a small *I don't believe this* chuckle. Bev coughed into her hand, a warning.

I cut my eyes at her and noticed her smile had faded. She settled her glass on the table and sat back.

"It'll be nice for you to be home again after working so hard for so long," Bev said, her eyes driving the *shut up and be pleasant* message home. "Maybe you can attend to . . . other things."

Vera and Mags exchanged conspiratorial grins. I sipped my gin and tonic, then leaned forward and placed it on the coffee table, indicating the end of the small talk.

"All right, ladies. Spill it. What's going on?"

"I'm sure I don't know what you're talking about," Bev said, in a tone that said she knew exactly what I was talking about. I crossed my arms and rolled my eyes, one door slam short of being fourteen again.

"This. The summer. Mags calls me, all about the pain and torture in her back—"

Mags gave a short laugh. "Well, I'm sure I never said *pain and torture*—"

I pointed my index finger at her, shutting her up. "Don't push it, lady. You're already on my short list."

Vera waved her hand at me, grabbing my attention, her face glowing in excitement. "Oh, let's just tell her. I can hardly keep it inside anymore, anyway."

Vera looked at Bev, who nodded. Mags donned a mischievous grin and sipped her drink. Vera leaned forward, all bubbles. "Oh, honey, we've found you a *Flyer*."

I froze, my drink hovering in the air on its way down to the table. "You what?"

"Oh, he's so perfect for you, darlin'," Mags said. "He's a writer."

"Ahhh," I said, turning my raised eyebrows at Bev. "How perfect."

Bev gave me a subdued smile, and our eyes had a short exchange.

You're serious?

Yes, we are.

And you expect me to go along with this?

Yes, we do.

And then, out loud, Bev said, "His name is Ian Beckett."

Mags leaned forward. "He's renting the old Babb farm down at the end of Reddy Road. And he's only here for the summer. Then he's going back to London."

"He's British!" Vera added, in case I didn't make that connection on my own.

Mags batted her eyes at me as she laid down the final stroke. "And he'll be at your welcome home party tomorrow night."

I rubbed my fingers over my eyes, listening to my internal chorus singing, *shoulda known, shoulda known, shoulda known.*

"Portia?" I heard Mags saying, "I thought you'd be happy. He's a *novelist.*"

There was a moment of silence in which everyone thought about, but did not mention, the last novelist in my life.

Vera raised her drink, waving it at me for attention. "And I did your cards. You got the Ten of Cups—celebration and contentment—as your final outcome."

"Did I, really? No Tower this time, then?" The Tower was the card that symbolized the storm before the calm, and it usually capped every reading Vera did for me.

Vera shrugged. "Not as the final outcome."

I shook my head and looked from one Miz to the next, each of them smiling back at me as though they were doing me a great favor. "None of you sees anything wrong with this?"

"No," Mags said, then gave Vera a playful nudge. "And neither will you when you see him."

She waved her hand in front of her face as though she was in the middle of a hot flash, and the two of them fell into girlish giggles. I sighed. I couldn't believe I ever thought for a minute that this summer was going to be all iced teas and mountain breezes. How had I allowed myself to give in to the delusion? Wasn't that the definition of insanity? Doing the same thing over and over and expecting a different result?

"Look," I said, "I appreciate that you girls are trying to make sure I have a memorable summer, but you have to stop. Now."

The giggling subsided and all three looked at me.

"Stop?" Mags asked. "Why would you want us to stop? We found you a *Flyer*, darlin'. A sexy British Flyer. That kind of man doesn't come along every day. We thought you'd be thrilled."

"Thrilled?" I said, shaking my head, my words coming out in a sputter of frustration and incredulity. "You lie to me to trick me into coming here for the summer. You act like that is no big deal. You pick out a *Flyer* for me . . ."

I inserted a dramatic pause, in which I imagined they might realize the error of their ways and beg my forgiveness. All I got was blank stares. I wasn't just the definition of insanity; I was the damn poster child.

"It's *wrong*," I said. I turned to Vera. "Surely you know this is bad for your karma."

Vera shrugged. "The cards said it was meant to be."

"Oh, hell, Vera, if the cards told you to jump off a bridge, would you do it?"

Vera was silent. *Right. Don't ask a question you don't want the answer to.* I threw my hands up in the air.

"You're all nuts," I said. "I don't think you know what you're doing."

"Sure we do, honey," Mags said, as though confirming the obvious. "We're fixing you."

"Fixing me?" I blinked. "What am I now? A stray cat?"

Vera and Mags looked at each other. Bev rocked backward. My eyes flicked from one to the other, looking for a clue as to what was going on.

"I don't need to be fixed," I said finally.

"Of course you don't, sweetie," Vera said.

"The hell she doesn't," Bev grumbled. Vera shot her a look. Bev rocked back again. This time, the edge was undeniable.

"Have I done something to offend you, Bev?" I asked.

"Of course not, darlin'," Mags chimed in. As I transferred my gaze back to her, I caught the fringe end of a warning look to Bev. "We're just worried about you is all. You haven't been the same since you and Peter broke up."

I sighed. Yeesh. I must have been bad off, if even Mags noticed. Of course, that realization only intensified my need to deny everything.

"I don't need to be fixed. I'm fine. I like my life. I'm not depressed. I don't even miss Peter all that much anymore, and I do not need to Fly."

Silence. Three pairs of eyes stared at me. A bird chirped in the distance. I heard a kid ring the bell on his bike a block down the street. The thing about silence is that if I'm not in charge of it, I end up talking, typically not to my benefit.

"Everything is fine. I enjoy my work. I have friends." I swallowed. "I . . . I . . . I go out for pizza on Fridays with the rest of the English department. I'm thinking about getting a cat . . ."

One toke over the line. Vera's eyes widened measurably. Bev shifted victoriously in her seat; the prosecution rests. Mags sighed, her face registering deep concern.

"Portia," she said, leaning forward, her hands clasped together over her knees like a guidance counselor trying to get through to the most hopeless case in the graduating class. "Sometimes a person might think she's okay when really she's not, and she needs a family who loves her to tell her what she needs."

I stared at her, my face contorting. "What the hell are you talking about?"

Vera leaned forward and put her hand on my arm. "I think what she's saying is that we love you, and if we think this Flyer might be good for you, then maybe you could just try it to see if it helps you some. What have you got to lose, really?"

"My dignity. My sense of self-respect. My autonomy over my own life." They stared at me.

Bev rocked back in her chair, impatient. "You been up north too long, child."

I sighed. "I'm fine. I don't need to be fixed."

"Yes. You've said that." Bev stood up, the rocker creaking behind her. "I, for one, am almost certain it won't kill you to have a damn drink with this Flyer. And it occurs to me that between your mother, your aunt, and myself, we have a fair amount of life experience and just might understand some things you don't." She walked to the front door and opened it before turning back to me to give her final word. "And you're *not* getting a cat."

chapter two

"Portia Fallon!"

I stepped one strappy-shoed foot on the back lawn and fell right into the waiting arms of Marge Whitfield. The stiletto heels sank into the soft ground, and I wondered how Mags could stand the damn things. I'd argued against wearing them, but after a day of coercive primping, the only battles I'd won were against sparkly eye shadow and contact lenses that would have made my understated hazel eyes a neck-throttling shade of green.

"It is so good to have you back home," Marge said, linking her arm enthusiastically through mine. "I hear you'll be running the Page now? I'm so glad. We'll have to get you and Freddie together for lunch sometime."

Ah. Marge's son, Freddie. Lost a leg drinking and driving in the tenth grade. The last report I'd gotten about Freddie was that he hurt the good leg trying to kick a Three Musketeers bar out of the vending machine at the Truly Laundro-Matic. I smiled diplomatically.

"Well, I'm just out here for the summer, and you know how busy the summers are." I glanced around. The lawn was filled with people I hadn't seen in ages. My high school math teacher, Mr. Ryan. The Feeney twins, who ran the Gas 'n Sip out on River Road. Pearl McGee, who had cut my hair every six weeks from birth to high school graduation. All smiling, all with a little more gray or a little more belly, but otherwise contributing to the Brigadoon mystique. There was only one face I didn't recognize, a tall man standing near the maple tree toward the back, flanked on either side by Mags and Vera. He was wearing a white button-down shirt with tan pants and smiled benevolently as Mags held him conversational hostage.

Ian Beckett. Had to be.

I sipped the glass of wine Marge had shoved into my hands and listened to her updates. Mark Feeney had gotten married; Greg Feeney had gotten divorced. Pearl McGee's cousin died and left her a small fortune, but she still worked at the salon on Tuesdays and Saturdays. I let my eyes drift over to Ian Beckett. At that same moment, his eyes drifted toward me. We caught each other's gaze for a minute, and each of us smiled before looking away. Seventh grade redux.

"And there's a novelist—"

I held up my hand and silenced Marge. "I know. Trust me. I've heard about the novelist."

Marge linked her arm in mine and leaned her head conspiratorially. "You know, he's very reclusive. Staying at the Babb farm, and people hardly see him except at the Piggly Wiggly, and then only on the rare occasion."

I raised my glass to my lips. "Well, you know writers."

"Not as well as you do, from what I hear." I shot her a glance, and she backpedaled. "Oh, I'm sorry, sweetheart. I wasn't thinking. I just find it . . . interesting . . . that of all the places our mysterious novelist might show up, he shows up here."

I gave her a black look. "Have you ever tried to argue with the Mizzes?"

Marge laughed. "I think you might have a point there, darlin'. Why don't you come on over with me? I'll introduce you."

Mags and Vera had been tossing me anxious glances since I'd stepped out of the house. Bev watched from the liquor table, about twenty feet away from where I stood, eying me as if to say, *Hurry up, darlin', we can't hold him much longer.* I sighed. Time to bite the bullet.

"That's okay, Marge," I said, not wanting my inevitable humiliation to be witnessed at close range by any more people than absolutely necessary. "I'm just going to say a quick hello to appease the Mizzes."

I stepped away and forced myself to hold my head up and smile as I took my tattered dignity and walked it right over to its doom.

"Portia, darlin'," Vera said, linking her arm through mine as though to anchor me to the spot. "You just have to meet our new friend."

"Yes," Mags piped in. "Ian, this is my daughter, Portia Fallon. She's an English professor at Syracuse University."

"Uh, actually, I'm assistant teaching while finishing up my Ph.D.," I corrected tightly.

"Let me get you a fresh beer, Ian," Vera said, snatching his half-empty beer bottle before he could respond. She winked at me and retreated so fast I could almost hear a whistle. I felt my face flush. These two were about as subtle as a train wreck, and Ian's kind smile only fueled my embarrassment.

Mags squeezed my arm, pulling me a touch closer to Ian. "Portia, this is Ian Beckett. He's a novelist. From London."

"Hi, Ian," I said, extending my hand. He took it in his,

which was gloriously cool against the oppressive summer heat. His brown eyes locked on mine, and his smile had a flavor of camaraderie to it. *Don't worry*, it said. *We're in this together.*

"Nice to meet you," he said. His voice was like coarse sandpaper, softened and complemented by the accent. *Hoo boy.* I released my grip on his hand and tilted my head, putting my back up against the plan I'd been mapping out all day while the Mizzes fluttered around me with mascara wands and curling irons. There was a brief moment of weakness, when I thought about actually buying into the Mizzes' theory on Flying, but I took a deep breath and stiffened my resolve. Soft brown eyes be damned. Sweet British accent, get thee gone. If I'd learned anything during my time with the Mizzes, it was that following their advice was a bad idea.

"Ian Beckett," I said thoughtfully. "I'm afraid I haven't heard the name. What kind of novels do you write?"

He paused before responding. "You don't know?"

I shook my head. "I'm sorry, no. But that doesn't mean much. I'm a Lit geek. Most of the people I read are dead."

I gave a choppy laugh at the tired joke. It was the socially inept laugh of an academic, and to my horror, it came out accompanied by a small snort. Ian raised one eyebrow and I felt my face flare up. I could only hope that Mags's generous application of rouge would disguise the real flush.

"Oh, Portia, honey," Mags said, checking her watch with a flourish. "I need to check on the food, make sure we're not running out of anything." She winked at Ian. "You two should have plenty to talk about."

She turned and headed away toward the food table, which was stocked to the hilt. I looked over at Bev, who widened her eyes in exasperation and gave me a subtle shoofly wave with her fingers. *Get on with it, girl.* I turned back to Ian.

"So, you're renting the Babb farm, I hear?"

"Yes," he said. "The seclusion makes it much easier for me to write."

"You're writing a book this summer?"

"That was the idea."

Silence. Then Ian inhaled sharply and said, "You really don't know me, then?"

I shook my head. "No. I'm sorry. Should I?"

"No," he said. His smile relaxed. "If death is your prerequisite for reading someone, I'm quite happy to be off that list."

I laughed; a nice normal laugh. "It's not exactly a prerequisite. I mean, my ex-boyfriend was a novelist, and I read his stuff, and he's very much alive."

"I'm glad to hear it."

Our eyes locked. His smile snaked up on one side before the other and it drew my attention away from holding my balance in the damned heels. My ankle flipped inward and I stumbled to the side. Ian's hand was on my elbow in an instant.

Hmmm. Elbows are an erogenous zone. Who knew? My cheeks flared up again. Cripes.

"Excuse me," I said, reaching down and unstrapping the strappy shoes, hanging them from one hand as I sighed with relief.

Ian laughed. "I've often wondered how women get around in those things."

"They're the instruments of Satan," I said, tossing them at the base of the magnolia tree. "Well, now that I've made a startling first impression . . ."

"Don't concern yourself. I enjoy startling first impressions." He smiled again and the muscles in my neck relaxed.

"You're too kind," I said, noticing that the lines that marked the edges of his eyes were smile lines. Great. As if the gorgeous eyes and the killer accent weren't enough, it appeared he had a great disposition, too. I sipped my wine, trying to drown out the sneaking feeling that a crush was forming.

"So, this ex of yours," he said, "would I have read him?"

"Probably not. He's one of those severe literary writers that critics love but no one wants to read."

Ian kept his eyes on me. "What's his name?"

"Peter Miller."

Ian nodded. "*Coffee Table Memoirs,* was it?"

"*Memoirs from the China Hutch,*" I said, unable to hide my surprise. The book had sold about five copies, and I'd bought two of them.

"Ah, yes, sorry," he said quickly. "It was . . ." He paused, as though searching for something complimentary to say. I jumped in.

"It's okay if you thought it was bad. We're not together anymore." I paused. "As a matter of fact, feel free to say as many bad things as you'd like."

Ian gave a short chuckle. "I take it things didn't end well."

I shook my head. "Do they ever?"

Ian nodded. "Point taken. Well, I'm sorry to disappoint, but I didn't think it was bad at all. As I recall, it had a strong philosophical undercurrent. I sensed a deep regard for Kant."

My eyes widened. "You really did read it."

He crossed his arms and looked at me, his eyes searching, connecting. "You're Eloise, aren't you?"

I lifted my wine, draining the last drop. "No. That's ridiculous."

He grinned, shaking an index finger at me. "You are. You're Eloise."

I shook my head and stared at my toes, bare and dirty, digging holes in the grass. "Eloise is an amalgam of many women Peter has known . . ."

"But predominantly you."

I gave him a long stare. "Are you telling me I remind you of a stuttering prostitute with an inability to walk in a northerly direction?"

He laughed. "No. It's the tendency you have to tuck your hair behind your ear. You've done it about five times since we started talking. I put it together when you mentioned the book."

My hand froze in midair as it flew to swoop hair behind my ear. I hadn't realized I was doing it. I stared at my hand hanging in front of me, feeling like an idiot, until Ian gently guided it to the side of my head, running his rough fingertips over mine as he tucked the hair behind my ear for me.

Oh. Man. Crush. Gah.

"There's nothing to be ashamed of," he said. "I thought Eloise was quite charming."

He dropped his hand, but maintained eye contact. I had no idea how to respond. Was he saying *I* was charming? No one had ever called me charming before. Articulate, yes. Driven, absolutely. I'd even gotten a slightly inappropriate *intriguing* from a professor once. But I couldn't recall a single charming. I smiled. I didn't know if it was the wine or Ian Beckett, but for the first time since Mags had bounded down the porch stairs the day before, I felt calm and at ease. I inhaled, enjoying the sensation for a moment, knowing it had to be brief.

After all, I had a plan to stick to.

"This is going to sound crazy, but . . ." I began. At the same moment, Ian also spoke.

"She's not coming back with a beer for me, is she?"

I laughed and shook my head, remembering Vera's excuse for making herself scarce. "No, she's not."

He grinned and leaned toward me a bit. "Your family isn't terribly subtle."

"No." I could feel my face growing warm. *Again.* "They're not."

For a moment I considered abandoning the plan, running away, telling the Mizzes I couldn't do it and resigning myself to a summer of harassment. But it wasn't just me in this. Ian would be harassed as well, invited to endless Sunday dinners and various contrived social situations until we either slept together or died of natural causes. No, the plan was the only way out. For both of us.

"So," he said after a moment, breaking into my thoughts. "What's going to sound crazy?"

I held up one index finger. "I'll be right back."

I turned and took a few steps, then looked back to see if he was watching me. He was, but he wasn't watching my backside or my legs, the way men usually did when you walked away. His eyes were set on mine, as though he was trying to read me. I paused there, looking at him with probably the same expression of curiosity and surprise that he had. I held up my index finger again and continued over to Bev at the alcohol table.

"Gimme the Love Kit, lady," I said, grinning at her. She raised an eyebrow at me and reached under the table, pulling out an oblong nylon pack and handing it to me.

"Moving fast with the Flyer, are we?" she asked.

I smiled. "Daylight's burning."

She nodded. "That it is, darlin'. That it is."

I headed back to Ian, being sure to make meaningful eye contact with both Mags and Vera as I closed the space between us. Ian watched me as I walked toward him, and when I smiled, he returned volley. I stepped close to him and tucked my hand in his elbow, leading him through the throng of partygoers. I leaned my head toward his shoulder, speaking to him in muted tones as we walked toward the house.

"I have a favor to ask you," I began. "My family is a little on the eccentric side, as you might have guessed, and . . ."

I swallowed. This had been much easier in front of the mirror this morning.

Ian raised his eyebrows. "And?"

"And . . . they actually tricked me into coming down here this summer for the express purpose of . . ." I paused, suddenly unhappy with the phrasing I'd rehearsed. I was only now realizing that it made me look just as crazy as the Mizzes. *Crap.* There was no saving my dignity now. I plowed on.

"They want me to sleep with you."

We both stopped walking and looked at each other. I swooped hair behind my ear, consciously recognizing it as a nervous habit for the first time.

"Don't worry," I said. "We don't have to . . . I mean, that's not what I'm proposing. I just need a favor."

His eyebrows knit as his smile quirked. He opened his mouth, closed it, shook his head. "I'm not sure I understand what you're asking."

I moved closer and lowered my voice. Ian's dark eyes were locked on mine, darting back and forth, watching me intently as I spoke.

"See, they think I'm depressed over my breakup with Peter, and . . . well . . ." I sighed, regrouped, started again. "You know how some women, when they're depressed, they eat . . . or drink, or shop?"

He nodded. I moved closer, unable to keep eye contact. His hand was on my elbow, pulling me to him, sending heat rushing to my spine.

"Well, the women in my family Fly." I squinched my eyes shut and barreled through the next part. "That's the term they use. It just means having great sex with a temporary man. And they picked you. For me. And all I need is for you to go inside with me and we can just talk or whatever, just long enough to . . . They just, they won't leave me alone if they don't think . . ." I trailed off, fighting an urge to burst into tears of fury. As bad as the epiphany had been, asking Ian Beckett to pretend to have sex with me was worse. Much, much worse.

He pulled back from me, and when I got the courage to look in his eyes, he was smiling. He held out his elbow. "Shall we?"

I released a deep breath. "Are you sure you don't mind?"

"Not in the least," he said, cupping my hand in the crook of his arm and leading me toward the house. "It's the best offer I've had in a long while."

We stepped into the house and I shut the back door behind us, pushing the curtain aside with my finger and seeing all eyes drift in our direction. *Perfect.*

"So, are all American women crazy, or is it just the Fallon women?" Ian asked. I bristled at first, but then considered what we were doing, and shrugged. *Fair enough.*

"No, it's mostly just us."

I was sitting at the head of the bed with Ian at the foot, our legs stretching over the middle next to each other. The room was lit only by a series of small, rose-scented candles on my dresser, the mirror reflecting the gentle flickering light over the eighties heartthrob posters covering the pink walls. The room was kept like a shrine to myself as a teenager, and whenever I walked in, I always ran my tongue over my teeth, expecting to feel braces.

The first wine bottle was empty, and the second—which I'd snagged from the basement about an hour after Ian and I first shut my bedroom door behind us—had maybe one more round left.

I took a sip of my wine and dropped my head back against the headboard. The cool night breeze flowed through my window screen, carrying the smell of fresh pine and the hint of someone's car exhaust. I was feeling softened around the edges and I liked it. Teaching at a university doesn't give a girl much chance to be soft around the edges.

"The thing about the Mizzes is that they're not bad people," I said. "They're good people. They just do stupid things. Sometimes. I mean . . ." I sighed, briefly wondered what my point was, and kept going. "They're not bad people . . ."

"Don't feel you have to defend them to me. I think they're delightful. Barmy, but delightful." Ian looked at his wineglass, then back up at me. "Do you mind if I ask you a question?"

"Of course."

"Of course you mind, or—"

"Fire away. I'm an open book."

"Where's your father?"

I blinked. "Gone."

He raised an eyebrow. "Gone? Did he die, or . . . ?"

"No. Just gone. Long time ago. I barely remember him. Anyway, did I tell you that Marlowe is the real Shakespeare?"

Ian gave a small nod. *Point taken, topic dropped.*

"Yes, you told me," he said. "It's an interesting theory."

"It's not theory. It's fact."

"It's theory until you prove it, which no one has done."

He crawled over on the bed until he was sitting next to me, then reached over me and grabbed the bottle of wine on the nightstand, attending to each of our glasses until the last drop had been shed. I watched him, enjoying everything about him. His soft hair. The five o'clock shadow running roughly over his jaw and neck. The way he kept asking me questions and listening to the answers.

"How can you listen to all this and not die of boredom?" I slurred as he placed the empty bottle on the other side of the bed. He settled back next to me. Our legs were touching. He shrugged and smiled.

"I like to listen to people. That's how I get my characters. And apparently, I'm not the only one who does that, Eloise."

"I can walk north," I said, hearing a snap in my voice that I hadn't intended. I still didn't understand what the hell that was supposed to mean. Peter had told me it was symbolic, but he had spoken around the meaning—something about magnetic forces that repel each other, blah blah blah. I pretended to understand, but I never did. It still irritated me, and I was glad the book didn't sell well, making it easily forgettable. Until now.

"All right." Ian sighed. "Let's not talk about Peter. I've learned my lesson on that one."

My head shot up and wobbled a bit. "What do you mean? I can talk about Peter. I'm fine talking about Peter."

"You tense up the moment his name comes into the conversation, and I enjoy you more when you're relaxed. Let's move on, shall we? Tell me about your . . . favorite book."

I decided not to lay into him for the tense remark. He was doing me a favor, after all, and he'd earned a little slack.

"We've been talking about me all night. What's *your* favorite book?"

"You're much more interesting than I am," he said.

"To you, maybe. I already know me. Now answer the question."

He sighed. "I don't have a favorite book. Whatever I'm reading at the time is usually my favorite book."

"Ahhhh," I said, rolling my head back to rest against the headboard as I tilted my face toward him. "Noncommittal answer. Future politician potential. And your favorite color?"

He rested his head back and looked up at the ceiling. "Blue."

"Oh, God, boring," I said.

His head pivoted to look at me. "How is blue boring?"

"Because every man's favorite color is blue."

"That's not true. My father's favorite color was red."

"Have you ever been married?"

Ian froze for a second, then tilted his head at me. "Why would you ask that?"

"Why would you ask me about my father?"

"Because I was curious."

"And so am I."

He was silent for a moment, then gave a slow nod. "Yes, I was married. A long time ago. I hardly remember it. Did I ever tell you Marlowe is the real Shakespeare?"

I laughed. "Rebuff duly noted, I will not bring it up again."

"I'm sorry, I didn't mean to make you feel—"

"Tell me about your favorite . . ." I said, talking over him with a hint of a smile so he'd know I wasn't really offended. I paused, turning my face toward his. Our noses were inches apart. I could smell the wine on his breath.

"My favorite . . . ?" He was still smiling, but the amusement in his eyes was waning as we looked at each other. I thought about the other items tucked in the pack Bev had given me. I felt my cheeks grow warm again and rolled my eyes at myself.

"What?" he said, eyebrows knitting.

"Remember what I told you about Flying?" I asked.

"Yes." His smile quirked up on one side. "I hardly think I'll forget it."

I put my hand on his cheek. It was warm sandpaper. He inhaled sharply at my touch. I liked that.

"We could . . . Fly for real if you'd like," I said, barely whispering. *Kiss me kiss me kiss me* reeled around in my head, like a drunk trying to find a place to lie down.

Ian turned his face, kissed the palm of my hand, and got up, taking both of our wineglasses.

"I think we've had enough," he said, settling the wineglasses on the dresser top as he blew out the candles.

"It's okay. I've got condoms in the pack right here, if that's what you're worried about."

He laughed and sat down on the bed next to me, putting his hands on either side of my waist as he leaned over me.

"I have very few rules but one of them involves future English professors who've had too much to drink."

"Oh." I thought about arguing over whether I'd had too much, but since I was struggling not to slur my words, I figured I'd just let it go.

"Don't be hurt," he said. His voice was soft and he was leaning in closer. "It's not personal."

"Rejection is always personal."

"I haven't rejected you . . ." he began, pulling back.

"Whatever." I flicked my hand at him, shooing him away. I snatched the covers, pulling them up to my chin and flopping on my side, trying to pretend that I wasn't reliving a thousand rejections, both real and imagined. "All right. Off with you, then. 'Night."

He pushed himself up off the bed. I heard him moving around in the room, and right when I expected to hear the door closing quietly behind him, I instead caught the distinctive sound of a zipper. I shot up in bed in time to see him taking off his pants.

"Offer's off the table, Sir Ian. Back to the farm with you."

He laughed, stepping out of his pants and flipping his T-shirt over his head. He was wearing a pair of flannel boxer shorts. I withheld my sigh. He looked good.

"I've never left a woman in the middle of the night," he said, pulling the covers up and hopping into bed next to me, "and I don't intend to start now. You're not the only one with a reputation to protect. Or sully, as the case may be." He lay down on his side, propping his head up on his palm. "You're a very complicated woman, Eloise."

I put a glare in my voice. "Don't call me that."

"Right," he said. "Bad form. I apologize. Would you set the alarm for six? I write in the mornings."

I gave a frustrated sigh, then reached for the alarm clock and set it for six. I could feel him settle on his side, his back to me. I huffed, pulling myself up out of bed and over to the dresser.

"Can you keep your eyes closed for a minute, please?" I asked.

"My back is to you," he said.

"I know," I said. "Humor me."

He chuckled. "Consider yourself humored."

I stepped out of the sundress and into a T-shirt—Huey Lewis, *Sports* Tour, 1983—and a pair of sweats cut into shorts. I sneaked into bed next to him, flat on my back, arms tight at my sides over the covers.

"Can I open my eyes now?" he asked.

"Yes."

He rolled over until he was facing me, his head perched up on his hand. There was just enough light coming in through the window for me to see he was smiling.

"You are a highly unusual woman," he said in a rough whisper.

I locked my eyes on the ceiling. "Can I ask you a question?"

"Absolutely."

I swallowed and forced myself to look into his eyes. "This is going to sound suggestive, but the offer to Fly for real is still officially off the table. Understood?"

He smiled and nodded. "Understood."

I closed my eyes, letting the room spin around me. "Do I . . . repulse you?"

He drew back, as though he'd just touched something sharp. "What?"

Am I the kind of woman who will drive every man away screaming? I thought. *Am I made of Penis Teflon?*

"Let me put it another way," I said out loud, my voice stretching tight and thin. "Do you think I'm . . . attractive? You know, as a woman?"

I felt him plop back down on his pillow. "Bollocks."

I opened my eyes and looked at him. "What's that supposed to mean?"

"It means that out of a barmy lot, you're the barmiest."

"You keep saying that word. *Barmy.* What the hell is that supposed to mean?"

He rolled back to face me, leveraging one elbow under him to elevate his upper body. "It means you're all crazy."

"We've already covered that," I said. "Now answer the question."

"You know damn well I can't answer that question."

"Why not?"

"If I answer yes, you'll think I'm lying. If I answer no, the whole barmy lot of you will beat me senseless." He fell back on his pillow. "Either way, I lose."

I could hear the subdued sounds of partygoers saying their good-byes outside. We were both still and silent for a minute, staring at the ceiling, until I spoke again.

"It's okay," I said. "It's okay if you lie to me. I just . . . I need to hear the words."

A heavy sigh escaped, whistling through his lips. "If you don't know you're beautiful, then there's nothing I can say to convince you."

The tears started on "beautiful." I kept them a secret for a minute, but one quiet sob caught in my throat, and I felt Ian's head turn toward me. A moment later, the back of a rough finger brushed against my wet cheek. I tightened my eyes shut and swabbed at my face, rolling onto my side with my back to him, too mortified to chance seeing his expression. Worse than the Crazy Cat Lady, worse than the Girly Giggler, I had now sunk to being a Bed Weeper.

I don't know how long we stayed like that, me on my side, him on his back, but it was long enough that I was almost asleep when I felt him spoon himself behind me, one hand resting lightly on my hip.

"Whoever neglected to tell you you're beautiful is a complete sod," he whispered in my ear. "And if you see him again, you can tell him I said so."

He reached over and smoothed some hair away from my face, then relaxed next to me. I heard his breathing grow ragged, and a few moments later I felt a small lurch where his crotch was snuggled against my backside. He pulled away from me, flopping on his back again with a rough exhale. I feigned sleep as a small smile spread across my face.

chapter three

Thump-thump-thump.

I opened one eye. 8:17. *Good God.*

"Go away," I whined into the pillow. Must have sounded like "Come on in," because a half second later, Mags was poking her head through the door.

"Are you alone?"

I flipped over and looked at the empty space next to me, then back at her.

"Unless he's under the bed, I'd say so, yes." I had a vague memory of the alarm going off, of Ian's soft lips bussing my cheek, of the sound of the bedroom door clicking shut behind him.

Mags bounded in and bounced on the edge of the bed.

"Well?" she said, her eyes dancing. "How was it?"

I sat up, rubbing my eyes. "How was what?"

She grabbed a pillow and threw it at me. "Oh, you are the most impossible child that ever did walk the planet. Don't make me tell you again about giving birth to you, which was so painful that Vera had to take morphine. Is it too much to ask to be rewarded with the occasional bit of girl talk?"

I groaned. "Is it that you don't know it's wrong for a mother to want to know about her daughter's sex life, or is it that you just don't care?"

She grinned and leaned forward. "Is he a gentleman in bed? He seems the type who'd be concerned about your pleasure."

"Ah!" I said, cringing and waving my hands at her, trying to shake off the whole conversation. "Stop! I can't afford enough therapy to cover this."

Mags sighed dramatically. "How did a daughter of mine grow up to be such a prude? I'm sure I don't know."

"I'm not a prude. I just don't want to discuss my sex life with my mother. That's not prudish. It's normal."

"I don't understand what your problem is. Vera and Bev and I talk about sex all the time. How can you live your life without girl talk? What fun is it?" She looked at me and grinned. "At least tell me if you got a good orgasm out of it. You know that's all I wanted for you, baby."

I sighed and spoke loudly upon her apparently deaf ears. "I am not discussing this with you. Is there coffee downstairs?"

She gave my leg a playful pat and stood up. "Yes, that's what I came to tell you. And you'd better get a move on. You're helping Vera run the bookstore today."

"Me?" I said. "Why? Your back's fine."

"Because it's the family business and you're family." She looked in the mirror and poked at her hair, smoothed out her lipstick. "And I have plans today."

"Plans?" I got up and nudged her away from my dresser as I pulled out a pair of jeans and a T-shirt. "Since when did you start making plans outside of running the store and torturing me?"

She turned away from the mirror and leaned against my dresser, crossing her arms over her midsection. "Well, I must

say I'm disappointed. For such a promising Flyer, I see no
change in your demeanor whatsoever. Maybe we should try for
Greg Feeney. Didn't he used to do gymnastics?"

"Enough!" I forced on a smile. "I'm great. I'm fine. Happier
than I've ever been. Best sex of my life. And you're avoiding the
question."

"Oh? And what's the question?"

"What's so important today that you can't go to the Page?"

She gave me a wry smile. "Is it that you don't know it's
wrong to interrogate your mother, or that you just don't care?"

I smiled. "Don't be a wiseass, darlin'," I said in my best
honey drawl. "It's not attractive."

"Now there's my smart-mouthed girl." She gave me a sharp
pat on my behind. "It's good to have you home, baby.'

Then the woman who hadn't missed a day at the bookstore
since she was sixteen flitted out of my bedroom, leaving a wisp
of perfume hanging in the air behind her like a big lilac question mark.

At 8:45, Vera and I were out the door and on our way to the
Page. Jimmy the mailman waved as we passed him, the same
way he did when I was fifteen.

And sixteen.

And seventeen.

I looked down at my feet and mindlessly stepped over the
cracks, a habit I picked up at the age of seven when I felt a certain responsibility for the health of my mother's back. Even the
cracks hadn't changed.

"Brigadoon," I muttered with a laugh.

"What, baby?" Vera waved across Pine Mountain Road to

Bella Thomas, who sat knitting in her rocker the way she had since the beginning of time.

"Nothing," I said quickly, hopping over some cracks to catch up with her. My mind was on Mags's weirdness, but I thought I'd edge in with a softball first. "So, tell me, Vera. What's up with Bev?"

"Bev? Nothing. Why? Did she say something to you?"

I shook my head. "No. That's just the thing. She's been weird. Distant. Pissy."

Vera smirked. "That's not weird, baby. That's Bev. You've just been away from home too long. But you know she doesn't mean anything by it. She's just got a little vinegar in her, that's all."

I shrugged. "Maybe." We turned the corner on Main just as Marge Whitfield was pushing up the awnings over the pharmacy. Pearl McGee waved to us as she unlocked the front door of the salon, pointing a mock-accusatory finger at me. I waved, then put an instinctively protective hand to my ponytail as Vera stepped up on the stoop to the Page.

"So, what about Mags?"

I caught a momentary stiffness in Vera's shoulders. I was right. Something *was* going on with Mags.

"What about her?"

"Oh, please. It's been you and Mags every day at the Page since I can remember. And today she's not coming in. Why?"

Vera rummaged around in her humongous macramé purse. "Well, it's hardly something to make a federal case over," she said. "Sometimes people take days off."

"Not Mags."

She gave me a tight smile. "Well, today she did. Now tell me about your Flyer. You haven't given us any details and I think that's just rude."

I shrugged. "I don't kiss and tell."

"Oh, honey, everybody tells." She pulled out the keys and stuck them in the front door. "Some take more time than others, but eventually, everybody tells." She pushed the door open, and we stepped inside.

I inhaled deeply and smiled. As a little girl, I spent every day after school roaming through the shelves, touching the books, flipping through them, living in the scent of fresh pulp and ink. Whenever I needed to lighten a black mood, a trip to a bookstore or library would almost always work, but the Page was still something special. I turned and gave Vera a wry smile.

"Okay. I'll give you one detail."

She grinned. "Do tell."

"He said we were a barmy lot."

"Barmy." She tucked her purse under the counter. "What does that mean, exactly?"

"It means we're all crazy."

"Honey, there's no such thing as crazy. There's just degrees of interesting." The phone rang in the back office, and Vera sighed. "I'm gonna go answer that, but don't you think I'm done with you yet. I won't rest until I know how a British Flyer kisses."

I shooed her away, stepping around the mismatched easy chairs and simple swivel-topped barstools that huddled around the coffee bar. I went into autopilot, scooping the coffee into the filtered basket, filling up the hot water carafe for tea. My mind drifted elsewhere, back to my room the night before and to Ian Beckett's lightly dimpled smile.

I stepped out from behind the coffee bar and listened. Vera was still on the phone. I could tell by the tone of her voice that it wasn't anyone from Truly. That probably gave me about five more minutes; someone from Truly would have taken a good twenty. I stepped out from behind the bar and made a beeline for the fiction section. My finger ran quickly along the B's, my eyes popping up to the office door to make sure Vera wasn't going to catch me.

Barnes. Baxter. Beals. Bebey. Bederman.

No Ian Beckett, which was fine by me. The Page was a small bookstore, which meant we could afford shelf space only for the stuff that was selling well, and literary fiction wasn't always on that list. I smiled again. Maybe I'd look up his books later and special order them. Set up a book signing for later that summer. After all, it was the neighborly thing to do, and the Miz Fallons were nothing if not neighborly.

The bell jingled, followed by an excited wail. I turned around and saw a pregnant belly waddling toward me, arms outstretched, followed by the round, freckled face that had smiled at me through many guilty trips to the principal's office.

"Portia, baby!" Beauji's belly hit me in the gut, bending me into her embrace. I wrapped my arms around her shoulders and we wagged from side to side as a single, excited unit.

"What did you do to your hair?" I said, running my fingers over the half-inch or so of red that puffed out of her head. It was shocking to see, as Beauji had always kept her hair in long, fiery locks. Well. At least something in Truly had changed.

She pulled away and swept one hand on her scalp. "I'm gonna be bald during every pregnancy," she said. "Even hair irritates me now. Pearl almost cried when I made her take out the clippers."

"I don't know why. You're gorgeous. As always." I stepped back, holding her arms out, staring at her smiling face, her bright blue eyes, her ruddy cheeks. Beauji had always been what you'd call a natural beauty, the one the boys notice in the sixth grade but then pass over for the made-up Barbie types in the ninth grade. Somehow, it never fazed her. She was the only woman I'd ever known who really never gave a rat's ass how she looked.

"Yeah, yeah, yeah, well, I need to sit my gorgeous self down," she said, turning from me and waddling over to the comfy chairs surrounding the bar. "I hope motherhood is pleasant, because pregnancy is a right pain in the ass."

I followed her, tucking myself behind the bar to make some herbal tea. In Truly, there was always a pregnant woman in the general populace requiring entertainment at the Page. We had a special store of teas set aside, organized by touted effects: peppermint tea to mitigate nausea, red raspberry leaf to encourage labor.

"How far along are you?" I asked, poking my fingers through the sweet-smelling box.

"Thirty-four weeks and counting," she said.

"I just can't believe—"

"Ow!"

I looked up, my eyes wide and my heart beating like a jackhammer. "Beau? You okay?"

She winced and pushed at the top of her big lump of a belly, shouting downward. "I told you! Get your damn foot out of my ribs!" She shifted in her seat, sighed, and leaned her head back, talking to the ceiling. "I hate my life!"

I tucked my finger behind an index card marked "irritability" and pulled out a bag, then stood up and set the full teakettle on the hot plate.

Beauji whistled out a breath of air and shifted again, her legs and arms splaying out so that she looked like a spider squashed by a tremendous, spherical rock. "I'm not very good at being pregnant," she said after a moment.

I smiled. "I think you're doing fine."

"You're a big fat liar, but I love you for it." She shifted in her seat again. "By the way, I would have come to your party last night but the idea of standing around with everyone feeling my stomach all night long . . ." She rolled her eyes. I smiled and dropped the tea bag in a mug.

"You're forgiven," I said. I leaned my elbows on the counter and grinned at her. "How's Davey doing?"

"He's fine," she said. "Of course, he's not carrying seven pounds of wriggling baby on his bladder."

"I still can't believe he's a cop."

"Yeah, well, if he wasn't, I'd still be a size six." I raised my eyebrows at her. She patted her stomach. "First night with the new uniform. He can't wait to see you, by the way. You're coming over for dinner Friday, I suppose I should tell you."

"Good to know," I said, laughing. "Should I bring anything?"

She grinned. "A British Flyer, perhaps?"

"Good God," I said. "You heard about that already?"

"You kidding me?" she said. The teakettle began to whistle and I grabbed it off the hot plate. "You're back in Truly now, darlin'. You fart in the tub in this town and the news will be marching down Main Street within the hour." I brought her mug over and she watched me with interest as I sat down in a sinfully comfortable but inarguably hideous orange easy chair next to her.

"Anyway, word has it you paraded that Brit straight out of the back lawn and up to your bedroom in front of half the town. You're a Miz Fallon and he's a famous writer. Don't even pretend to be surprised that people are talkin'."

"He's hardly famous," I said.

"You don't consider Alistair Barnes famous?" she said, now raising an eyebrow at me and taking in my blank expression. The other eyebrow went up, and she laughed. "You did know you were sleeping with Alistair Barnes, didn't you?"

I leaned closer to her, and spoke in a low voice. "Lock, first of all, I didn't *actually* sleep with him . . ."

Beauji waved her hand at me. "Oh, please."

" . . . and second of all, his name is Ian Beckett."

I paused, and a memory from the night before flashed through my head.

So, you really don't know me?

I'm sorry. Should I?

If death is your prerequisite for reading someone, I'm quite happy to be off that list.

"Alistair Barnes?" I asked. "The guy who writes the Tan Carpenter spy novels?"

"They say Brad Pitt is gonna play Tan in the movie. Pearl and the girls are hoping he'll drop in for a visit this summer, but I doubt it. And while we're on the subject, what kind of name is Pitt for a man who looks like that?"

"Drink your tea," I said. Beauji took a sip. I sat back in my chair and gave an incredulous huff, then sat forward again almost immediately. "He can't be Alistair Barnes."

"Go look at his picture on the books if you don't believe me," she said, shooing me away with one hand. "I'll be right here to pick your chin up off the floor when you get back."

I stood up and headed back to the B's.

"He can't be Alistair Barnes," I repeated. It was running through my head like a mantra.

"You keep telling yourself that, girl."

I flicked my fingers over the B's and pulled out the latest Barnes hardcover.

"I know you're all into the classics and everything," Beauji called from her chair, "but he's not bad. You should read one. I recommend *Clean Sweep*, to start."

I flipped the book over. Ian Beckett's lopsided smile jumped out at me from a full-size color picture. I looked at the front cover, running my fingers over "Nonstop action!" and "High-Octane Excitement!" embossed above the "#1 *New York Times* Bestselling Author" at the top. I tucked the book back onto the shelf and returned to Beauji, who was smiling from ear to ear.

"You look like you need to sit down."

"I can't believe he didn't tell me he's Alistair Barnes."

"I can't believe you didn't know. What kind of rock have you been living under, anyway?"

The rock of Peter Miller. The rock of the Syracuse English Department. Shakespeare. Austen. Marlowe. Take your pick. Lots of rocks. I sank down into the hideous orange chair and pushed the heels of my hands into my eyes.

"Poor baby," she said. "You've been dallying between the sheets with a famous millionaire and you didn't even know it."

"Dallying between the sheets?"

She grinned and took a sip of her tea. "How was he?"

I smiled. Her grin widened.

"That good, huh?"

I leaned over and put my face between my knees. "No."

"Oh, Portia. I've missed you, baby." She took another sip of her tea. "I don't know if it's you or the tea, but I'm feeling so much better."

"Well, I live to amuse you," I said.

Beauji grinned. "Welcome home, darlin'. Welcome home."

"So," Mags said, leaning her chin on one hand, her bangle bracelets dangling precariously over the glob of mashed potatoes on her plate, "how are you feeling today, Portia?"

I stabbed at the roast, avoiding her gaze. "Fine. And you?"

"I'm fine. I was just wondering how *you* were doing."

I put my fork down and glanced from Miz to Miz, all watching me over the steaming spread of hearty Southern food. I smiled.

"I'm great, thank you." I took a sip of my iced tea. They were still staring. "What? What do you want me to say?"

"We're just curious, baby," Mags said. "A few details won't kill you."

I raised one eyebrow. "They might kill *you*."

She leaned forward, her eyes gleeful. "Now that's more like it."

"I'll bet he was a wonderful kisser, wasn't he, Portia?" Vera asked, refilling my iced tea. "I hear that men from England do this fabulous twisty thing with their tongues."

I stared at Vera. "Where'd you hear that?"

She shrugged. "We stock *Cosmopolitan* magazine."

"Well, I think a girl who'd been kissed all twisty last night would be smiling more today, don't you, Vera?" Mags said. She and Vera erupted into giggles. I shook my head and looked at Bev, who raised one eyebrow and took a sip of iced tea.

"What exactly did you girls think?" I asked. "That one night with Ian Beckett was going to turn me into a giggly little teenager? It doesn't work that way."

"Sometimes it does." Vera said with a grin. "Why, there was this one time, when I was twenty-two . . ."

Mags pointed her fork at Vera. "Marcus the banjo player!"

"Yes!" Vera said, her eyes drifting heavenward at the memory. "He did this one thing with his toes—"

I held up my hand. "Ah-ah-ah-ah. No. Please. Vera. I love you, but please. No."

Mags and Vera giggled again. Bev handed me the basket of warm rolls.

"Surely you must feel a little different," she said. "Every man a woman sleeps with changes her a little, whether she wants to admit it or not."

I took a roll and Bev withdrew the basket.

"Not me," I said. "I am unchanged. I was fine before our little dalliance, and I'm fine now. So y'all can stop with the Flyers and stop with the fixing and just hand me some of those potatoes."

"I don't know, baby," Mags said. "I think Bev is right. About the men changing you, a little bit at least. There was that man I met in Bermuda, Rory Munroe. I only slept with him once, and I've walked a little different ever since."

Vera and Mags descended once again into a fit of giggles. I tossed my fork down on my plate and looked at Bev.

"Doesn't that bother you? To hear your daughters talk like that?"

Bev shrugged. "Why should it? They're just being *honest*."

I stared at her. She stared back.

She knew I'd faked the Flight.

I didn't know how she knew, but she knew. I picked up my wineglass and hoped she'd keep it our little secret. Mags and Vera would have me Flying with every unattached man in Truly before they'd admit defeat, and that's a prospect that could get very, very scary very, very quickly.

"So, are you going to see him again?" Vera asked.

"Of course not," Mags said before I had a chance to answer. "What's the point of Flying if you have to see him again?"

"I don't know," I said with a shrug, my eyes on the bit of roast I was sawing into. "He's a pretty big deal as authors go. I was thinking it might not be a bad idea to do a book signing or something."

Vera smiled and leaned forward. "Really?"

I rolled my eyes. "Yes, really, Vera. This hadn't occurred to you? We own a bookstore, for crying out loud."

"I think it's a wonderful idea," Vera said, practically glowing with satisfaction as she sat back and reached for her iced tea.

"It's a horrible idea," Bev said. "He lives in London."

I looked at them. "What does that have to do with a book signing?"

Bev stabbed at her green beans. "Why don't you call up that nice Greg Feeney?"

I spoke to the ceiling. "Because Greg Feeney hasn't written a book."

"Oh, Portia." Mags raised her glass in my direction to get my attention. "I think you should go see Pearl McGee."

I looked at her. "For what?"

She grinned. "Well, surely you know that ponytail has got to go."

My hand flew to my ponytail. "No. I don't."

"I think if you cut it shoulder length, maybe added a little flip to it? Some highlights, maybe? It'd be real pretty. Not that you're not pretty now, baby, but you know we all have to put our best foot forward."

I stared at her. She smiled back and patted my hand, standing up from the table. "Who wants more sweet potatoes?"

My eyes flew open on the edge of a dream I couldn't quite remember. I pulled on my glasses and looked at the clock. 2:34. I rolled onto my back and stared at the ceiling, wide awake. I knew myself well enough to know it was hopeless. The back-home insomnia had set in.

I sat up in my bed and looked around at all the items from my youth. The field hockey trophy I'd gotten during freshman year. The shelf with all the copies of my favorite books from high school. William Goldman's *The Princess Bride*. Tolkien's *The Lord of the Rings*. *The Compleat Shakespeare*. A collection of Melville's short stories, my favorite of which was "Bartleby the Scrivener," about a clerk who got out of work simply by telling his boss "I prefer not to" whenever he was given a task. Obviously a man who'd never lived with a Miz Fallon.

I got up and ran my fingers along the worn spines of the books, smiling. I moved over to the dresser, touching the candles that had remained unlit since Ian had blown them out. I opened the wooden jewelry/music box that Vera had given me when I turned sixteen, and it creaked out a few strands of "Sunshine on My Shoulder" before petering out.

I walked over to my closet and opened it. I hadn't unpacked my duffel bag, so all that was in there were my prom dresses, encased in dusty dry cleaning bags. I laughed and ran my hand over the rip I'd made in the mauve taffeta when Beauji and I got caught drinking beer in the elementary school playground. That was probably the fastest I'd ever run in my life.

I looked up to the top shelf of my closet and my smile disappeared as I saw the faded red shoebox peeking over the shelf. I think originally it had held a pair of Mary Janes I'd had in the first grade, but since then, I'd been using it to store letters.

I reached up and pulled it down, walking over to the bed and settling in. For a moment I just stared at it, then finally forced myself to pluck off the top.

They were there, a series of fat envelopes stuffed with letters and pictures. The return addresses were written in my handwriting, which flowed from the scratchy print of my childhood to the fat cursive of my teenage years. Miss Portia Fallon, 1232 Sweet Tree Lane, Truly, Georgia. The addressee was always one line: Lyle Jackson Tripplehorn. I'd never had an address to put under the name.

I pulled one out and opened it. A picture of me from the sixth grade fell on top of the pile. The writing was round and fat. I dotted my i's with tiny circles.

Dear Jack,
I turned twelve last week. I got a Walkman from Mags, a Billy Joel tape from Bev. Vera gave me a stuffed polar bear. She's nice and everything, but she still thinks I'm a kid or something. I'm getting all A's in school and I'm especially good in English and Social Studies. I hope you are doing well and maybe someday you will come see me. I'm a good kid, and I'm getting my braces off in three months.
Love,
Portia

I put the cover back on the box and stuck it back on the top shelf, then got dressed and headed the six blocks toward the Printed Page.

"Portia? Portia baby?"

I swatted lazily at the hand on my arm and opened my eyes. I looked up. Vera. I blinked, and shifted in the hideous orange chair. "Hmmm. I must have fallen asleep."

"We were worried about you, sweetie. I wish you had left us a note." Vera walked over to the coffee bar and put down the big platter of muffins she'd been carrying. "Although we all figured you'd come here to read. You having trouble sleeping again?"

I pushed myself up in the chair. "Sorry. I didn't mean for you to worry."

"Oh, don't you think twice about it." She stepped around the bar and stood next to me, a small smile spreading over her face. "Good reading?"

I looked down at the book in my arms, and the itty bitty booklight that was glowing all over the handsome face of Mr. Ian Beckett, otherwise known as Alistair Barnes. I turned off the itty bitty and tossed the book onto a side table.

"He's not bad," I said, getting up and stretching. "I really think we should have him come in for a book signing."

"You know what, baby?" Vera said, smirking. "I think that's a wonderful idea. Why don't you go out to the Babb farm and see if Ian has any time for us?"

I blinked at her. "Why can't we just call?"

"Oh, that phone hasn't been hooked up for ages. You'll have to go out there yourself."

"I can't," I said. "I haven't showered."

She jerked her head toward the ceiling. "Use the shower in the apartment upstairs. We haven't used it in a while, but it should still work."

"Don't you need my help here?"

She pulled a small basket out from under the coffee bar, lined it with a linen towel, and filled it with muffins from the big tray.

"Oh, I can get by for an hour or two. Bev said she'd come in for a little while this morning." She held the basket out for me with a smile. "Now go. Be neighborly."

When I was a kid, I spent one summer selling eggs for Morris Babb at the farmers' market, working a table in the high school parking lot every Sunday afternoon until I could afford the ten-speed bike I'd had my eye on. Working at the Page after school contributed to the family income, and as part of the family, I never saw an actual paycheck. Morris gave me five dollars a week, and at the end of that summer I rode my new bike out to the Babb farm to show it off to Morris and his wife, Trudy. She invited me in and made cornbread. He gave me iced tea and sat on the porch with me, telling stories about Trudy when she was young.

"Now Miss Trudy Bates was the prettiest gal in Catoosa County, and there were plenty of fellas tryin' to catch her eye, you know." He laughed and winked at me. "Now, how do you suppose the upstart son of a dairy farmer got that beauty for himself?"

I smiled and shrugged. He leaned forward.

"Well, I knew the only way I'd get a chance with Trudy was to get her attention. So I got me up at four in the morning one Sunday and dragged Butter, the crankiest milk cow ever to exist anywhere, all the way into town, and I left that ornery cow right there on her daddy's lawn. Then I went to hide across the street, waiting for the family to wake up and get all ruffled so I could come in looking for my lost cow and save the day. Be the big hero, don't you know."

Trudy had come out of the house at that moment, crossing her arms and leaning against the doorjamb. She smiled at Morris, then looked down at me.

"He telling the story of how he won my heart?" She and Morris exchanged looks, and she smiled at him as she finished the story. "Fool puts a cow on my lawn, what did he think was gonna happen? My daddy saw that beast eating up his grass, and he got his shotgun, of course. The first time I noticed Mr. Morris Babb was when my mama was pulling buckshot outta his backside."

They laughed together, her chipper giggle harmonizing with his rough bark, almost as if they'd been practicing it. I watched them, wondering at this strange world where a man fell in love with one woman and stuck long enough to harmonize a laugh. I made a quick excuse and rode my bike out to Beauji's.

The next time I saw Trudy was at Morris's funeral during my senior year of high school. I told her how sorry I was, and she stared at the funeral home wallpaper and said blankly that they'd had fifty-two years together; who could ask for more than that? I squeezed her hand, my mind unable to wrap itself around a man who'd stick for fifty-two years.

Now, I stepped out of my car in front of the Babb farmhouse and looked around. The cows were gone. The chicken coop was empty. The big red barn still stood, but the color was dulled by years of inattention. A side door was open and seemed to be hanging a little crooked, as if the top hinge had given up hope. The farmhouse, however, looked just as it had the day I'd ridden up to show the Babbs my pink ten-speed. I'd heard some rumbles about Bridge Wilkins keeping the place up and renting it out, but since we weren't allowed to discuss Bridge Wilkins in our house, I never did get the full story. At any rate, whoever had been taking care of the house had done a great job.

I grabbed the muffins from my passenger seat, walked up to the front door, and rang the bell. Moments later, the door opened, and there was Ian Beckett, wearing a pair of blue sweatpants and a plain white T-shirt, leaning one hip against the doorway and sipping from a mug that read WORLD'S GREATEST GRANDMA.

"This is a pleasant surprise," he said, smiling down at me. "Would you like to come in? We could pretend to have coffee."

I smiled at him, swinging my left arm out and presenting him with the basket of muffins. "I'm being neighborly."

He took the basket from me. "Thank you. That's very thoughtful." He stepped back, holding his body against the inside door while stretching out one arm to pin the screen door back for me. "Please. Come in."

I slid past him and turned around to face him as he stepped inside, letting the doors shut behind him. He caught my eyes and smiled. I smiled back and held up a hardcover copy of *Clean Sweep*.

"I just was wondering if you could sign this for me. I'm a huge fan."

chapter four

"I'm sorry I don't have any coffee," Ian said, coming up behind me and putting a mug of steaming tea on the end table next to my side of the couch. "I will have to get some soon."

"Don't feel you have to give in to cultural pressure on my account," I said, looking at the writing on the side of the mug before taking a sip. GRANDMA'S KITCHEN. "I like tea just fine."

Ian shrugged. "When in Rome . . ."

We were quiet for a moment. Ian's eyes dropped to the book sitting on the kitchen table between us.

"Sorry about that, by the way."

"No big deal," I said with a shrug. "As lies go, it's not so bad."

"Well, I didn't exactly lie . . ."

"Yes, you exactly did. I asked if I should know you. You said no."

He held up one pedantic finger. "That's not a lie. Why should you know me?"

"Because you're Mr. Tan Carpenter. That's a big deal." He opened his mouth and I held up my hand. "I come in peace, Tonto. It's okay. I'm not angry."

He smiled and sipped his tea, placing it gently back down on the table.

"Sometimes it's nice when I meet someone who doesn't know who I am," he said quietly. "Not that I'm mobbed everywhere I go, but there are times when it matters, and I'd rather it didn't. Does that make any sense?"

I nodded. "I understand. And it's really not a big deal. I mean, it's not like we actually . . ." I made an awkward gesture in the space between us and we both chuckled a little.

"So, how's your dissertation coming along?" he asked.

I smiled. "Great. Good. Almost done."

"It was about Austen, wasn't it?"

Don't know. Been so long since I've touched it I can hardly remember. "Yeah. I've always had something of a fascination with her work. But lately . . . I don't know."

A light smile played on his face. "What don't you know?"

I shrugged. "I don't know. I'm up for a faculty position. If I finish my dissertation in time, I've got a real shot at it."

He lifted his mug. "So what's the problem?"

"I don't know."

He smiled. "Well, I'm sure you'll figure it out. At any rate, you should be proud of yourself. Getting a Ph.D. is a tremendous accomplishment."

"Yeah," I said lamely. "I know. It's just . . ."

I stared down at the table for a moment, then looked up to find him watching me, waiting for me to finish. He seemed genuinely interested. Maybe someday he'd write about a half-hearted bookstore clerk. Maybe the ambivalence I typically kept to myself would be helpful.

"I envy people who know what they want," I said, finally. "I've been quarter-owner in a bookstore since I was born. It seemed to make sense to go to college and study literature. And then, I just kept going to college. And now it's the end of the line."

"And you don't know what you want to do."

I didn't answer. He reached over and tapped two fingers on the back of my hand.

"You'll figure it out."

I met his eyes, and my heart kicked up a notch. *Time to go.* I stood up.

"Thanks for the tea," I said.

"You're quite welcome." He stood up as well. "Thank you for the muffins."

We smiled at each other for a moment, then I turned and walked to the door. He held it open for me and I walked out to my car without looking back. I parked in front of the Page before I realized I'd completely forgotten to ask him about the book signing.

"So, you never had sex with Ian Beckett?" Beauji said, resting her glass of ginger ale on her stomach. We'd finished dinner over an hour earlier, and she and Davey had used a good meal and a bottle of wine to crack me wide open about Ian Beckett. "Honey, if I had that man in my bed, there's no way either of us would have gotten any sleep."

"Surprisingly, that kind of comment doesn't bother me as much as it should," Davey said. He stood up and grabbed the bottle of wine. "The third-trimester hormones are making her horny as hell. You should have seen the way she looked at the pizza guy the other night."

"I did not!" Beauji said as she smacked his knee, the only

part of him she could reach without moving. Davey grabbed my glass and emptied the bottle into it, then headed into the kitchen, throwing a wink at me over his shoulder.

"All I know is that if that kid comes out in thirty minutes or less, I'm ordering a paternity test."

"It's not just that we didn't sleep together," I said, covering my eyes with my hand.

Beauji leaned back and shouted into the kitchen, "Davey, there's more, get in here!"

Davey skidded out of the kitchen and hopped onto the couch, still working the corkscrew into the bottle of wine.

"I can't believe I'm telling you this," I said.

"Confession," Beauji began.

"Good for the soul," Davey finished.

I clamped my eyes tight. "I cried."

Beauji gasped. Davey sighed. I opened my eyes, and both of them were handing me compassionate looks.

"Why?" Beauji's voice tightened. "What did he do to you?"

I looked at the ceiling, too annoyed with myself to make eye contact. "He said I was beautiful."

"Bastard," Davey said, popping the cork out.

"Did he know you cried?" Beauji asked. She, like all women, understood how being told you're beautiful can make you cry. It's a sure sign you're in a bad place, and every woman has been there, even Beauji, who'd always been loved. Even Beauji, whose men had stuck.

"Yes," I said, taking another sip of my wine. "It only lasted for a few minutes. He handled it well. I mean, he didn't run screaming from the room."

"I've done that," Davey said, nodding.

Beauji cut her eyes at him. "Once."

I sat up. "But enough about me. Tell me about the baby. Have you picked out a name?"

This was a stupid question, as Beauji's name had been a result of her father's dogged determination to name whatever came out of the chute Beau Jr., and as such she had sworn never to name a child before he or she was born, but I thought it would at least be an effective way to change the subject.

I was mistaken.

"We still have to talk about you a little more," Beauji said.

Davey gave her a warning look. "Beauji . . ."

She cut him a look back. "Davey, she has a right to know. Mags has probably already told her, anyway."

"My wife," Davey said, turning to me as he stood up, "doesn't have any sense for what's her business and what is not."

He leaned over and kissed me on the forehead. "Good to have you back, baby," he said. He leaned over Beauji and kissed her on the lips. "Stay out of it."

Davey headed up the stairs and I kept my eye on Beauji, my heart beating a little too hard and a little too fast. I knew something was up with Mags. I could smell it. Judging by the look on Beauji's face, whatever the news was, she wasn't expecting a positive response from me.

"What is it, Beau?" I asked. "You have to tell me now. Is Mags sick? Is Bev sick? Who's sick?"

She waved her hand at me. "Nobody's sick. But I think Mags tricked you into coming down this summer for a reason. Has she told you why?"

My eyebrows knit. "Nothing aside from getting extracurricular with the Englishman. Is that what you're talking about?"

She shook her head. I waited a few seconds, then spit out an impatient, "Well, what is it, then?"

"It's Jack," she said. "He's coming to town."

It doesn't matter who your parents are or how healthy or sick or ambivalent your relationship with them is, they will always be the most powerful people in your life. They will be the ones whose approval you will always crave. They will be the ones who hold the power to elate or crush you with a word. No matter what you tell yourself—that your father wasn't worth your time anyway, or that your mother was too batty to really know what she was doing to you—your parents will always be the people who juggle knives over your heart. If you're lucky, they'll know it and will juggle carefully.

If you're unlucky, you'll be born to Mags Fallon.

"Wake up, lady!" I said, flicking on the light in Mags's room. It was one o'clock in the morning. She was lying on her stomach with curlers in her hair, as she had during every night of her adult life. She was wearing an old T-shirt from a Lynyrd Skynyrd concert she'd gone to in the mid-eighties during a brief flirtation with recapturing her youth.

"Mags!" I said, louder. She didn't move. I reached over and pulled the blanket off of her and shook her shoulder. "Up, up, up!"

One eye creaked open.

"Mmmmmf?"

"Mags, we need to talk."

She flopped over and pulled herself up. "Portia? What's the matter, baby?" She blinked her eyes and squinted up at me. "Is the house on fire?"

"No."

"What's going on?"

"You called Jack, that's what's going on." I crossed my arms over my chest, trying to look intimidating. "You invited him to visit, that's what's going on."

She yawned. "Oh. That."

"Yes. That," I said, getting even angrier at her lack of shock and instant remorse. I was expecting regret, sorrow, chagrin. Something that would confirm how right I was to be upset, how wrong she was to arrange a visit with my father without asking me first. I was expecting all that, which was insane, because yawning and stretching and acting like it wasn't a big deal was what Mags always did, and I should have known.

"Good night, darlin'," Mags said, flicking off the light and pulling the covers around her. "We'll talk about it in the morning."

"Mags—"

"In the morning," she said again, waving her arm limply over her shoulder, shooing me away.

I stood there in the shaft of dim yellow light coming from the hallway, watching as my mother drifted back to sleep. I considered flicking the light back on and demanding to know what the hell she was thinking. I considered wheedling Jack's phone number from her and calling him and telling him not to come. I considered getting a bucket of ice water and dumping it over her head, making a big ruckus until the entire house woke up, until the entire neighborhood woke up.

Instead, as Mags's soft snore gained momentum, I shut the door behind me with a gentle click and headed off to my room.

I have one vague recollection of Lyle Jackson Tripplehorn, in which he plays a classical music album on the record player in our living room. That's all I have: one flickering image of him carefully placing the needle on the record and then smiling at me, walking toward me, arms out, ready to dance. I remember snuggling my head into his neck and smelling his shirt as he waltzed me around the living room. I remember feeling happy and safe and loved.

But what the hell did I know? I was two.

I don't remember much about the letters in the shoebox. I sealed them all immediately after writing them and never looked back. Mostly, they were just stories about me growing up. What happened at the softball game. What kind of trouble Beauji and I had gotten into. What my favorite books and movies were. Some letters contained school pictures. There were some drawings. There were questions about his life. Where did he live? What did he do for a living? Did he ever have any more children? I never asked him why he'd twirl me around a room so lovingly and then leave me without so much as a look back. I never wanted the answer to that question.

I turned on the light in my room and went straight for my closet. I pulled the shoebox out and tossed it on the bed, then paced back and forth, unable to look at it. What was I going to do? Open the letters, torture myself with the ghost of a little girl who was stupid enough to believe her father might come back? What did it matter, anyway? Why did I care? I picked up the box and put it back in the closet, closing the door quietly behind me. I put my hand to my chest, felt my heart banging against it.

Damnit.

I was thirty years old. I hadn't seen him in over twenty-seven years. I could barely remember the man. What did it matter?

I walked over to the bed and sat down. It mattered. And Mags should have known that it mattered. It could have at least occurred to her that it might matter. What the hell was wrong with that woman, anyway?

I tossed my legs up on the bed and pulled the comforter over me. I slept in fits and starts throughout the night, until finally the clock said six, and I got out of bed and put on my sneakers.

It took me an hour to trek the five miles out to the Babb farm. When cars passed, which wasn't too often, I stepped off the road and ducked out of sight, just in case it was the Mizzes looking for me. It never was. A man in his sixties drove by in a Ford pick-up, and my heart rate sped up. It could have been Jack. Would I even recognize him now? All I had was a small handful of old pictures and a faded memory of a smiling man waltzing me around to Bach, or Rachmaninoff, or whoever wrote waltzes.

When I saw the farmhouse, I stopped walking and looked at my watch. 7:05. Ian was probably inside, writing. Doubt began to creep over me. It hadn't occurred to me until that moment how it might look, me showing up two mornings in a row. On the other hand, I had forgotten to ask about the book signing, so there was a legitimate reason to return.

But not at seven in the morning.

I turned and started to walk away, then stopped. I'd also left my copy of *Clean Sweep* there for him to sign. I could go back for that. And he knew that I knew he started his days at six, so it's not like the hour was all that outrageous.

And I wanted to see his smile. Just for a second. Just one quick hit of warmth before I went back to face the Mizzes.

I turned around again, took a few more steps toward the farmhouse, then slowed down. I was going to look like an idiot. Like a *stalking* idiot. Like . . .

"Portia?"

I froze. The door swung open and there he was, holding his WORLD'S GREATEST GRANDMA mug.

"I was wondering if you were going to come in and say hi," he said, his smile radiating warmth and good humor. "It was looking doubtful there for a minute."

I winced. "You could see me?"

He jerked his head toward the front window to his left. "I like to write by the window. The view inspires me when I get stuck."

Oh. Good. God.

"I'm sorry," I said, dropping my head and putting my hands over my eyes. "I just . . . I . . ."

I looked up. I had no excuse. There was no way to mitigate the humiliation. Time to face the music.

"Come on in." He raised his mug and winked at me. "I have coffee."

"I'm sorry to interrupt your writing," I said, sitting on the couch with my mug of coffee. Ian sat on a high-backed chair in front of a small table pushed up against the window. His laptop sat on the table, a screen saver drawing random multicolored swirls behind him.

"Not at all," he said. "I needed a break anyway."

"I was just coming by to see . . . Yesterday, I forgot to ask you . . . I was wondering if you might be interested in doing a book signing event at the Page? We couldn't pay you, but there'd be hot coffee and some more of Vera's signature muffins."

He raised an eyebrow. "Blueberry?"

"Anything's possible."

He laughed. "I'd love to. Thank you for asking."

I smiled at him, then looked down at my coffee. I could feel his eyes working on me, checking out my dusty sneakers, my mussed hair, my slept-in clothes. I suddenly wished I'd taken a shower before I'd come.

"Do you want to tell me what's really going on?" he asked after a moment.

"Hmmm?" I'd been enjoying talking in circles around the very obvious fact that I was a woman on the edge. I'd been hoping he would have picked up on that.

"It's okay," he said. "If you want to tell me what's going on, I'm happy to listen. If you'd rather talk about something else, we can talk about something else."

I took a deep breath, willing myself to think of nothing other than Tan Carpenter and the Russian mob that was, at the end of chapter 3, threatening to kill his daughter.

"The book," I said finally, motioning toward the desk where it sat next to the laptop. "It's really good. I especially like the way Tan used the prosthetic leg as a weapon. Very funny."

He cut his eyes at me. "Are you making fun of me?"

"No," I said, although I was, a little. You can take the girl out of the snobby elitist literary program, but you can't take the snobby elitist literary program out of the girl. "I'm just changing the subject. Badly."

He nodded. After a moment, he stood up and walked over to me, holding his hand out for mine.

"Come on," he said. "I want to show you something."

The barn stood back on the property, about fifty yards away from the house. The earthy smell of the summer morning was thick on the grass, and each step we took seemed to make the fragrance stronger. Ian dropped my hand when we got to the barn to pull one of the doors open, then motioned for me to go inside.

I stepped in, my eyes taking a moment to adjust to the darkness. The last time I'd been in the barn was when I was in high school, when Vera sent Bridge Wilkins and me over to help Morris do some repairs on the roof. My role was limited to handing tools to Bridge like a surgical nurse, and keeping Morris, whose body was just starting to fail him, from working too hard.

While the barn still looked the same from the outside, inside was a bit of a shock. All the aging straw and random whatnot that had been stored there over the years was gone. The cement floor had been swept, and fresh planks of wood were piled up next to a table saw and a couple of sawhorses. Two golden X's glowed along the barn's east wall, vibrant against the older, darker wood they supported.

"Have you been doing this?" I asked.

"Bridge mentioned tearing it down when he met me here to show me the place. I thought that would be a shame."

"Bridge Wilkins?"

He nodded. "You know him?"

"You're in Truly now, darlin'," I said, thickening my drawl. "Everyone knows everyone."

"Good point," he said.

I looked around. "How'd you learn how to restore barns?"

Ian shrugged. "My uncle was a carpenter."

"And you've been doing this? All by yourself?"

"Today, as it happens, I think I'll be needing some help." He walked over to the pile of lumber and picked up a limp tool belt that was sitting on top. He grinned at me as he returned, cinching the belt around my waist, his eyes locked on mine. He gave the belt one final tug, dropped his eyes, and pulled a hammer out of a loop on my side. "My father always said that nothing clears a mind like manual labor."

"Sounds like a wise man," I said.

He nodded, not moving. "He was."

My breathing went shallow. He stood perfectly still, two feet away from me, his eyes reading mine. I inhaled as my heart rate quickened, thus making it official: I had me a bona fide crush.

And it was the absolute last thing I needed.

I put my hands on the tool belt and smiled up at him.

"Where do I start?"

It was noon when we broke for the day. I hadn't decided not to go in to work at the Page so much as I hadn't wanted to stop working on the barn, so I played hooky and stayed with Ian, pounding nails into walls and feeling better with each swing of the hammer. We'd managed to put up a few more supporting posts on the east wall, but when we were done, it didn't look like the sweat and dirt that covered us amounted to a whole lot. We went back to the house, and Ian grabbed a clean pair of sweatpants and a T-shirt from his room.

"The shower's across from the master bedroom," he said, pushing me up the stairs. "I'll put something together for lunch."

I headed up to the second floor, looking at the old family photographs. Fading school pictures of gap-toothed kids, family portraits that betrayed their era with wide lapels or excessive shoulder padding, old black-and-whites of Babbs gone by. I traced my fingers over a smiling anniversary picture of Morris and Trudy, taken probably around the time Morris was paying me five dollars a week to hawk his eggs at the farmers' market. I heard the clunk of a kitchen cabinet being shut and tore myself away to get my shower.

Fifteen minutes later, feeling refreshed and calm, I hopped down the stairs, dropping my balled-up clothes by the front door. I pulled my wet hair into a ponytail and turned the corner into the kitchen, my grumbling stomach following the smell of food.

Ian was at the sink, wearing a frilly faded apron that read DON'T MAKE A MESS IN GRAMMA'S KITCHEN. I laughed, picturing Trudy surrounded by grandchildren bearing the Hallmark-sloganed fruits of a hundred Christmases and Mother's Days. Ian smiled back at me and nodded toward the kitchen table, where he had two plates set out, filled with sausages and eggs and toast, accompanied by two glasses of orange juice. I sat down and pulled a napkin into my lap.

"This smells great," I said, digging a fork into the eggs and stuffing in a mouthful. "I'm starving."

"Good," he said, walking over and putting the lid from the skillet over his plate to keep it warm. He pulled the apron off and balled it up, leaving it on the counter. "I'm going to clean up. I'll be back in a minute."

I nodded and watched him walk out, the kitchen door swinging absently in his wake. I took another bite and gulped down some orange juice, then sat back and took in the kitchen. The walls were covered in faded wallpaper with pictures of vegetables that looked like they came straight out of a nineteenth-century newspaper. Shelves at random heights held volumes of knickknacks: plastic plates with children's drawings on them, old lady dolls frozen in the act of sweeping, wooden cats with paws hanging over the edge of the shelf, ready to pounce. I bet if Trudy were there, she could tell me exactly who'd given her each knickknack and what the occasion had been when she'd received it.

The door swung and Ian came back in, his hair still dripping from the shower. He grinned at me as he rounded the table and lifted the lid from his own meal.

"Feeling better?" he asked.

"Good as new," I said, smiling and forking a piece of sausage.

- - -

"Portia."

My eyelids flitted open. The sun was still out. I rolled my eyes up without moving my head to get a look at the clock: 4:38. Ian had driven me back home at about one o'clock, and I could barely remember making my way to the bed before falling asleep. I picked up my head and turned it to the right, where the voice had come from.

Bev was standing next to my bed, her arms crossed over her chest. She didn't look happy. My mind stumbled in a fog, grasping at a sense of unrest that huddled in the back of my head.

"Hey, Bev." I pushed myself up on my elbows and rubbed my fingertips over my closed eyelids, trying to generate some activity in my brain.

"Mags is going to be home soon. She was worried about you when you weren't at the store this morning."

The fog in my head began to clear. I had a flash of Jack, holding his arms out to pick me up while classical music played. A spear of anger shot through me. I sat up.

"Where is she?"

"Still at the store," Bev said. She hadn't moved, was still

looking down at me like I was the bad guy here. "I came back early, hoping I'd find you first."

"Well, you found me. Wanna tell me what the problem is?"

Bev's jaw tightened, a gesture I'd learned to read very carefully when I was a kid, as it usually meant you could get in maybe one more smart-mouth comment before the can of whoop ass was officially opened. "You ran off without telling us where you were going, for one. Mags was worried about you. We all were."

"Then maybe Mags should have talked to me last night," I said, getting up off the bed, trying to minimize my vulnerability to a pissed-off Bev. I had three full inches on her, and I still felt like I was about to get my butt tanned.

"Maybe you should have stayed around like a grown-up, instead of throwing a tantrum like a spoiled little girl." Her voice was sharp. She may have raised two ditzy broads, but Bev was no one to be trifled with. I took my tone down a notch when I answered her.

"She should have told me."

"Told you what?"

"That she found Jack. That he's coming to visit."

Bev narrowed her eyes at me. Instinctively, I straightened my posture.

"And why does she owe you an explanation for that?"

I stared at her. "Are you kidding me? He's my father."

"Did it ever occur to you that *maybe* this has nothing to do with you?"

"Nothing to do with me?" I flapped my arms in lame confusion. "Then why am I here? Why'd she fake a bad back to get me down here? So I could sleep with an Englishman? What the hell is going on, Bev?"

"Let me tell you something, Portia," she said, her voice low and serious. "Your mother loves you. She has always loved you, and she has raised you well. Right now she's doing something she needs to do for her own reasons, and it's time you stopped being her little girl and started being her friend."

"I've always been her friend," I said, anger rising in my throat, can of whoop ass be damned. "Maybe it's time she started being my mother."

Whoosh. The air left the room. Bev and I stared each other down and for the first time since the beginning of time, Bev looked away first. A moment later she was gone, slamming the door behind her. I stood in the room alone, wondering what the hell had just happened.

"You're right," Mags said, staring down at her fingers, which were clasped on the edge of the kitchen table. Vera and Bev sat on either side of her, and me opposite. "I should have told you."

I looked at Vera. She had been the one to let it slip, knowing full well it would get back to me, and while I wasn't going to give her up, her reaction was a point of interest. Her face was blank, staring at an invisible focal point over Bev's left shoulder. Bev, on the other hand, leaned forward and put one hand on Mags's arm, drawing a clear line on the battlefield.

"So tell me now," I said. "What's going on?"

Mags sighed, gave Bev a helpless look. Bev shook her head.

"I can't tell you yet," Mags said finally, her voice so timid I almost didn't recognize it.

"Why the hell not?" I said, half in fear, half in anger. There'd never been a secret among the Mizzes. This was new territory.

"I just need you to trust me," she said. "I'm sorry; I just need that."

"When were you planning on telling me he was coming? When I came home and saw him drinking lemonade on the front porch?" Eyes darted back and forth. I stared at them defiantly. "What?"

Mags looked up at me. "We've been talking about September."

I thought of August 22, circled and starred on my wall calendar. I felt a coldness swivel down my back and I swallowed, working up the nerve to ask my next question. "Was that his idea or yours?"

Mags was silent. I sat back, feeling my chest close in.

"Are you ever going to tell me what the hell is going on here?"

Mags looked up at me, her face pained. "I can't. Not yet."

Bev's eyes worked on mine, telling me not to make a big deal out of this. Telling me to grow up and be a buddy. I looked away.

"Fine," I said, my voice tight as I pushed up from the table. "I'll go get my things."

Mags shot up. "You're not going back to Syracuse, are you?"

"No," I said. "I can't go back to Syracuse. My apartment is rented. But I'm not going to live here waiting for you to spring the next surprise on me. I'm going to the apartment over the Page."

Bev settled both palms flat on the table, fingers spread wide, her eyes on Mags. Mags looked like she was about to cry. Vera kept staring at the invisible spot over Bev's shoulder.

"That's probably a good idea," Bev said.

I froze. *A good idea?* I looked around the table. Not a one was looking at me. Not a one arguing. I couldn't get a glass of orange juice without inciting an argument from the Mizzes. Now I was moving out and they weren't going to fight me?

"What's going on?" I said. "What are you not telling me?"

Silence. I felt a brief inclination to back down, to give in to a gnawing fear of this secretive, combat-free zone we'd just stepped into.

But a girl can't always rise above her raisin'.

"I'll go get my things," I said quietly, and left the kitchen to go pack up my duffel bag for the second time that summer.

The door creaked as I opened it. The living area was large and open, with one door leading to the bedroom and another to the bathroom. The hardwood floors were dusty, as was every surface: the windows, the counter that separated the kitchen nook from the wider living area, the naked queen-size bed that took up most of the bedroom. I walked over to the kitchen nook and opened the valves under the sink, then turned on the faucet. The water, after a groan of complaint and a few sputters, was good. Clean.

"Okay," I said to the hollow room. "Okay, then."

I dumped my duffel bag on the floor and unzipped it enough to grab some bedding I'd taken from the house. Ian's book was just underneath; he told me he'd signed it while I was in the shower, but I hadn't taken the time to read what he wrote. I flipped open the front cover and looked inside.

Glad to see you can walk in a northerly direction after all.
Hope you'll do it again.

Ian

I smiled and shut the book, placing it on the counter of the kitchenette as I stumbled into the bedroom. Tomorrow I'd make a run to the Wal-Mart in Fort Oglethorpe and get the rest of the stuff I'd need for the apartment. Tonight, there was nothing I wanted more than to fall into a deep, blank sleep.

I opened my eyes, focusing on the blurred movement I could see through the crack in the bedroom door. I floated my hands over the top of my duffel bag and grabbed my glasses, then pulled myself up out of bed and stumbled out into the living area.

"Vera, what are you doing here? What time is it?"

"It's seven-thirty," she said. The kitchen counter was covered in plastic grocery bags. Vera unloaded various food supplies into the cabinets and refrigerator, taking a moment to check the eggs cooking on the stove.

"You didn't have to do this," I said, sitting down on the bar stool by the counter, inhaling the spicy scent of the brew in my new Mr. Coffee. Vera plunked a mug down in front of me.

"I didn't do it for you," she said. "You need to help me in the Page today."

"Where is Mags, Vera? What is she doing?"

Vera stuffed the last of the plastic bags under the sink and shook the griddle with the eggs on it, but didn't say anything.

"I don't get you, Vera. You slipped the Jack thing to Beauji. You knew she would tell me, which means you know it's the right thing to do. So spill."

Her eyes were sad and torn, but I knew it didn't matter. Vera was not a woman who changed her mind once it was made up.

"What?" I said, pouring coffee into the mug. "Did the cards tell you not to tell me?"

She looked away. "You can make fun of me all you like, Portia, but those cards have never steered me wrong."

I huffed. "I think Bridge Wilkins might have something to say about that."

Vera's back straightened, and she gave the eggs one violent

shake before sliding them off the griddle and onto a plate. She put the plate in front of me, slid the salt and pepper my way, and nodded toward the toaster oven sitting on the counter.

"Your toast should be ready in a minute," she said. Her eyes were watery, and I realized I'd taken it too far.

I released a breath. "Vera . . ."

Without looking at me, she turned her back and headed toward the door.

"I'll see you downstairs."

I watched her leave, then sat down at the counter and stared at my eggs for fifteen minutes before abandoning them to hop in the shower.

chapter five

"Oh, please," Beauji said, tossing a bright pink alarm clock in my basket as we wandered through Wal-Mart's home furnishings section. "She and Bridge split up like, what, ten years ago?"

"Eleven." I put the clock back on the shelf and grabbed a plain black one. Beauji shook her head and waddled ahead of me, her yellow shirt making her look like a mama duck.

"You need color in your life," she said.

"You *are* the color in my life, darlin'." I batted my eyes at her.

"Then you're much worse off than I thought." Beauji gave me a bright grin and kept moving. "What are you doing for furniture?"

I shrugged. "There's a couch and coffee table and a bed in there, under about eight years of dust, and anything else I need I can pull up from the basement."

Beauji made a better-you-than-me face. "At least it's just temporary. Anyway, it was one little comment. You shouldn't be beating yourself up about it like this."

"She hardly talked to me at all today. And you know Vera—she never stops talking."

"Why did they break up, anyway?" She held up a neon pink and yellow daisy-shaped bath mat. I allowed it. I'm not particular about bath mats.

I sighed, surprised that I suddenly felt a small impulse to cry. "I don't know."

Beauji rested her hands on the top of her stomach and narrowed her eyes in thought.

"You should go see him," she declared finally.

"Oh. No. I couldn't." I picked up the most hideous, neon-colored shower curtain I could find, sure Beauji would love it. She scrunched her nose at me and shook her head, pulling out one with the same daisy scheme as the bath mat and tossing it in the cart.

"Y'all were pretty close, though, weren't you? I remember he was always at your house, telling those bad jokes. He taught you to drive, God help him. You really should—"

"No," I said firmly, taking a few steps away and pulling a pillow out from a huge bin. I turned around and saw Beauji standing right where she was, one hand on her belly, the other on the cart. I walked over and put the pillow in the cart.

"I'm sorry," I said. She crossed her arms over her belly and gave me The Eye. I sighed. "Look, that's just not how it is with my family. The Mizzes stick together, and that's that."

She twisted her mouth and stared at me. "Mmmm-hmmm. Just don't stick so close that y'all squeeze out everyone else."

She turned around and headed back down the aisle. I watched her waddle for a minute, thinking about what she'd said, until she turned back and waved one arm at me.

"Well, come on," she said. "You still need a bedspread and I'm surely not gonna let you pick one out on your own."

I smiled and pushed the cart, following along like the obedient baby duck.

I managed to keep up my Mizzes avoidance for another eight days, finishing off six of the seven Tan Carpenter novels in the process. I sat on the old sofa, staring at the seventh installment in the series just lying there on my coffee table. I could dive right into it, but then I'd finish it in a day or so, and I'd have to find another author. Or, and here was a thought, actually work on my dissertation.

Or, possibly, come to terms with the fact that a grown woman of thirty years should not be hiding away in a dank attic apartment to avoid her family.

I got up, walked over to the kitchen, and checked the clock on the bottom of my coffeemaker.

3:17.

My eyes drifted to the remote control for my little TV/VCR, which I'd picked up at a garage sale just in case I needed a fix of Darcy and Elizabeth. Sitting on the kitchen counter. Right where I'd left it. I opened the fridge. One bottle of chardonnay. Half of a deli sandwich I'd gotten a week earlier.

On top of the fridge. A bag of Cheetos.

It was time. I headed to the shower, deliberately keeping my eyes averted from any reflective surfaces. I could feel another epiphany chasing me as I cleaned up, got dressed, and grabbed my keys. I shut the door behind me, clean and ready to do something, anything, other than have another epiphany. Even if it meant taking Mags's advice. I traipsed down the steps, hooked a left, and headed to Pearl McGee's salon.

"I like your hair," Ian said as we walked toward the table saw at the back of the barn. I self-consciously tucked a piece of hair behind my ear. I still hadn't gotten used to the lighter weight of it, the flippy ends. And every time I caught the blondish high-lights in a mirror, I did a double take. I was sure I'd get used to it after a few days, but for the moment, it was full-on weird.

"Thank you," I said, running my fingers over it. "I just felt like a change."

"Here." Ian handed me a pair of hideous clear plastic gog-gles. "You'll have to wear these."

I put them over my eyes and laughed. "I feel silly."

Ian lifted a long two-by-four and put it on the table. "You'll feel sillier with a big splinter of wood sticking out of your eye."

"Oh, come on. Like that ever happens."

"Fine. Don't wear them. Lots of men find eye patches ter-ribly attractive." He tossed a wry smile over his shoulder and slid the wood down the table, situating it under the circular blade. He showed me how to measure and mark the wood to cut at a specific angle. I watched over his shoulder and tried not to let the smell of the soap on his skin distract me. He turned the saw on and the blade whirred as he effortlessly lowered it onto the wood. When he was done, he turned off the saw and lifted the blade, removing his glasses, which left little marks below his eyes.

"There. Think you can do that?"

I shrugged toward the wall. "Can't I just hammer the hell out of the wall over there and leave all this power-tool stuff to the big strong man?"

He laughed and slid the cut two-by-four onto the floor. "We need to cut the wood or we won't have anything to ham-mer the hell out of."

"I don't know," I said, moving in front of him and grabbing a piece of wood, trying to look graceful as I wrestled the thing onto the table. "I'm not sure the goggles are really a good look for me."

I put the wood on the table and turned to him, smiling. He reached over and moved a strand of hair away from the goggles.

"I think it's a great look for you," he said softly. I could feel my skin tingle as he spoke. I turned back toward the saw and measured the wood.

"Thanks for letting me come here and work," I said. "It's cheered me up a lot this past week."

"Thank you for coming. It's a nice diversion for me."

I stepped back so he could review my work.

"Looks great," he said.

"Okay," I said, looking at the goggles around his neck. "Safety first, mister."

He smiled and pulled the goggles back on. I hesitated, almost forgetting about the wood I was about to cut as I contemplated doing other things.

"Portia? You in there?"

I looked toward the barn door. A man in a sheriff's uniform stepped into the barn.

Davey.

I gasped and pulled my goggles off, moving toward him. "Davey? Oh, God. Is Beauji okay? Is she having the baby?"

"Beauji's fine." He met us in the middle of the barn, holding his hand out to Ian. "David Chapman. I'm a deputy with the sheriff's department."

Ian shook his hand. "Ian Beckett. Nice to meet you."

Davey gave Ian a surrogate-older-brother once-over, then turned back to me. "I need to talk to you about something, Portia."

"Why?" I asked. "Is everything all right?"

Davey's eyes went from Ian's face to mine. "It's Mags."

My hand flew to my mouth. "Oh, my god. She's sick, isn't she? Is she . . . She's not . . . ?"

Davey shook his head. "She's fine. I mean, relatively fine. She . . . uh . . ." His eyes went from Ian to me again.

I gestured toward Ian. "It's okay. You can tell me in front of Ian."

Davey nodded. "Mags is in jail."

I blinked. "In jail? For what?"

Davey touched his upper lip, and I could tell he was trying not to smile. "She let a bunch of dairy cows loose."

"I'm sorry, what?"

Davey straightened his posture, but I could see the amusement in his eyes. "It appears she went to Carl Raimi's farm and released all his livestock."

"That's impossible," I said. "You're saying Mags Fallon let *animals* loose?

Davey rocked back on his heels. "Yep."

"My mother?" I said. "With the big hair and the art deco nails and the strappy shoes?"

"Do you need to sit down, Portia?" Davey asked.

"The woman who never let me have a dog when I was a kid because it might jump on her and spill her drink? This woman went on a farm and let animals loose?"

"I don't know what to tell you, Portia," Davey said, smile in his eyes. "She gave us a full confession."

I tried to picture it. I couldn't. Mags was the type of woman who was appalled by both animals and dirt. She openly mocked the "no animal testing" labels on makeup and swore if it weren't so warm in Georgia she'd buy a fur made from every fluffy scampering mammal on the planet. Veal parmigiana was her favorite dish.

So what the hell was she doing setting cows loose and getting arrested like some sort of throwback sixties hippie? Was she crazy?

Oh, my god. That had to be it. That was what Bev and Vera didn't want to tell me.

Mags had finally gone certifiable.

"Portia?" Ian touched my arm at the elbow. "Would you like to go see your mother?"

"Yeah," I said, reaching down to unhook my tool belt. "I don't think I can miss this one."

I handed Ian the tool belt. Davey put his hand on my elbow and started to guide me out of the barn. After a few steps, I turned back and looked at Ian, who was standing there with the tool belt in hand, watching us.

"Do you want to come with me?" I asked. Ian's smile twitched and he tilted his head a bit.

"Do you want me to go with you?"

"Yes," I said quickly. "I mean, unless you need to stay here."

He shook his head and tossed the tool belt on a pile of wood as we headed out of the barn.

Ian and I followed Davey's squad car in Ian's rented SUV. We passed three sheriff's deputies trying to wrangle a stubborn milk cow into a trailer on the corner of Loralee and Main. Based on the sporadic piles of poop that Ian and I had to step around as we crossed the street to the police station, I guessed we'd missed most of the good stuff.

"What did you call us?" I asked as we pushed through the front door. "Barmy?"

Ian opened his mouth, but anything he might have said was overwhelmed by gruff shouting.

"What do you mean, you're gonna let her go?"

We froze and let the door shut behind us. Carl Raimi, a big, grimy hulk of worn jeans and torn flannel, spit on the floor of the police station. I exchanged a look with Ian. *Welcome to Truly.*

"Carl, I understand your frustration, but she's posted her bond and is free to go until the hearing." Davey tapped a folder in his hand and nodded at me. "Hey, Portia. Ian. I'll be back in just a minute."

"And what good does a goddamn hearing do me, when I still got eight cows on the loose?" Carl hollered after Davey, then turned and saw me. He pointed a finger at me and moved closer. "You'd better keep an eye on that crazy mama of yours, afore she messes with the wrong person."

Ian stepped in front of me. He had an easy eight inches on Carl, who stopped and looked up.

"And who the fuck you think you are?"

Ian crossed his arms. "My name is Ian Beckett. I'm a friend of the family."

Carl gave Ian the once-over, then turned his head and spat again. "Poking the daughter don't make you no friend of the family."

I could see Ian's hand clenching into a fist. I wedged between them, putting myself up in Raimi's face, my eyes level with his, and spoke in my harshest down-home tones.

"You best watch yourself now, Carl. Where this man comes from, people get their teeth knocked out for talking like that. Now you go on back to your farm, and don't you worry about your cows. You'll get 'em all back."

Raimi's cold, black gaze bored into mine. For a moment I thought he might go for the fight. Instead, he just grunted at me, shot one harsh glance at Ian, and backed off, grumbling to himself as he pushed through the front door, slamming it behind him. I sighed. Of all the people to cross, why the hell did Mags have to pick Carl Raimi? The guy was the biggest asshole this side of the Mason-Dixon line.

I felt Ian's hand touch my shoulder. "Well done."

I shrugged. "Guys like that, you just have to get in their face and call them out, is all." I could hear the drawl linger in my voice and gave a small cough, hoping to expel it.

He squeezed my shoulder and pulled his hand away just as the door opened and Davey stepped out.

"Mags should be out in a minute."

"Have you talked to her?" I said, stepping around Ian and walking over to Davey. "Did she tell you anything about why she did this?"

Davey shrugged. "Not a word. Just that she'll accept responsibility for the consequences."

My stomach clenched. "Tell me about the consequences."

Davey sighed. "Well, there was a hell of a dust-up in town for a while. There will be some financial restitution for the cleanup crews and the guys who wrangled most of the livestock back to the farm. Legally, it's a misdemeanor. Criminal trespass."

I pinched at the headache forming at the bridge of my nose. "Could she go to jail?"

Davey was quiet. I dropped my hand and stared at him. Davey gently touched my arm. "Don't panic. It's her first offense, and most of the property has been returned unharmed, so it isn't likely she'll do time for it. Raimi's an asshole, but he's got nothing to gain from pushing this. He'll probably drop the charges once he cools off, if y'all agree to reimburse him for his losses."

I sighed at the thought of further dealings with Carl Raimi, but there was nothing to be done. "Okay. We can handle that."

"I'm gonna go back and get her now. You wait here." He squeezed my hand and nodded at Ian, then disappeared through the door again.

"It's going to be all right," Ian said.

I turned and looked up at him. "Thanks for coming with me."

He smiled. "Not at all. I'm happy to be here for you."

We held eye contact for a moment, and Ian's hand reached up to brush a strand of hair away from my eyes, tucking it behind my ear. My breath whooshed out of me at the feel of his rough fingertips against the side of my face, and I didn't start to breathe again until his glance flicked up over my shoulder. I turned.

And there was Mags. Her hair was a mess. Her strappy black shoes, covered in mud and God knew what else, hung from one hand as Davey escorted her into the lobby, with Vera and Bev not far behind. Her feet were speckled with dried mud, as was her dress. Davey handed her a clipboard and she signed a piece of paper. A moment later, she looked up and saw us.

"Portia, darlin'!" She gave a big smile and walked over to me, running her fingers through my hair. "You've had your hair done! Oh, baby, I *love* it. Doesn't she look just beautiful, Vera?"

Vera smiled and nodded. Mags turned back to me. "So, how are you doing, baby?"

"How am I doing?" I gasped. "I'm springing my mother from the can, how do you think I am?"

"Now, that's a little dramatic. Technically, it was Bev who sprung me." She winked at me. "Really, baby, you didn't have to come all the way down here. Everything's just fine. It's all a big misunderstanding."

I looked at Vera, who looked away, and then at Bev, who gave me a starched smile.

"A misunderstanding?" I said. "Mags, there's a cow running loose in the Piggly Wiggly parking lot."

She smiled up at Ian. "Why, Ian Beckett. It's good to see you again. How's that novel coming along?"

"Quite well. Thank you, Mags."

"Good, that's good." She handed me a classic it's-all-good smile. "I need to get home and clean up. You take care, baby."

I gave a slow nod. She grinned at Ian.

"It was good to see you again, Ian."

She winked at me and strolled out of the police station, head held high despite the mud. Vera and Bev looked at each other, then at me.

"Okay, you two," I said. "You have to tell me what's going on here."

Ian gave me a gentle touch on the shoulder. "I'll wait for you outside." He nodded at Vera and Bev. "Good evening, ladies."

Vera watched Ian leave, then opened her mouth.

"Honey, don't you worry none, it's just that Mags—"

She stopped as Bev put her hand on Vera's arm. "It's not our place, Vera."

Vera shot a look at Bev, then turned back to me.

"Come to dinner Sunday, darlin'," she said. "We'll talk then."

I felt my stomach turn and grabbed Vera's arm. "Look, at least tell me . . . Is she okay? Is it early senility? Is she on medication? Because this is not Mags."

Vera patted my hand. "It's not like that, Portia. I know it looks bad, but it's just a . . . thing. See you Sunday? Okay?"

I nodded. "Okay."

I watched through the windows as Bev and Vera crossed

the street to our old red Jeep Cherokee. Mags sat in the back, waiting to be taken home. I couldn't see much of her expression from the distance, but I knew something was different. I knew it. I just couldn't figure out what.

"So he . . . tucked your hair behind your ear?" Beauji pumped her arms as she walked. I was more than a little discouraged by the fact that a woman who was about to explode with baby was clocking me at six in the morning, but I was trying not to dwell.

"Yeah. I know it sounds like nothing . . ." I puffed. "How are you walking so fast?"

"Walking induces labor," she said. "I've been walking a few miles every day during the rest of pregnancy, but I had to take it easy then. I kicked it up to five power miles a day last week."

Oh. God. Five. Miles. I dropped it down a notch.

"Well, slow it down," I said, taking a pull from my water bottle. "That baby's not due for another two weeks, and it might not even come on time. Don't people go late all the time?"

Beauji stopped walking and gasped, horrified. "I can't believe you just said that to me."

I turned to face her, trying to pretend I wasn't struggling for breath. "So, what do you think? I mean, it's just a hair tuck. It's not like he . . ."

" . . . kissed you."

"Exactly. But there was definitely a . . ."

" . . . moment."

"Right." I stared at her. "Am I making too much out of this?"

Beauji shrugged. "I have no idea. I mean, maybe it's an English thing. But, gun to my head, I'd say he's hot to get you between the sheets."

"Ah!" I held up a hand, turning and walking away. "Stop! I can't deal with that right now."

"Why not?" Beauji caught up with me. "I really don't understand this whole, 'Oh, drat, the sexy millionaire likes me' bit you keep playing."

"I don't care about his money." What I cared about was the rough softness of his voice, and the way his eyes seemed to dive into mine whenever he looked at me. The way I felt so much happier when I was with him. "I just enjoy his company."

"So where exactly is the problem here?"

"He lives in London."

"Perfect for a summer fling, then."

"He's already rejected me once."

"He was being a gentleman."

I cringed. "I *cried* in bed with him."

Beauji paused, then started walking again. "I'll give you that one as a definite mood spoiler, but he seems to like you anyway, so what's the problem?"

I caught up with her and debated answering the question before finally coming out with it. "Penis Teflon."

"Tell me you're kidding," she said. I shook my head.

"You mean you're going to throw away a perfectly good famous millionaire writer because of *Penis Teflon?* It's imaginary, Portia."

"That's easy for you to say," I grumbled.

I got a few feet ahead before I realized Beauji had stopped. I turned to face her.

"What? Your water break or something?"

She stared at me. "Why? Why would it be any easier for me than it would for you?"

I shrugged, trying to come up with something that

wouldn't make me sound stupid and petty. I couldn't, so I said what I was thinking.

"Your men stick. Your father stayed. Your boyfriend became your husband and he's still around. You've got brothers. Me . . . I'm Penis Teflon. If I learned anything from Peter, it's that it's a waste of energy to invest in a man emotionally."

She studied me with sharp eyes and crossed her arms over her tremendous belly. "Well, that's about the stupidest thing I've ever heard."

I kicked a stone and sent it flying off the side of the road. "Thanks for your support."

"The truth is better for you than blind support," she said, "and the truth is that you can't know if something's a waste of energy if you've never tried it."

"What's that supposed to mean?"

"Name a man you've invested in."

I stared at her. *Duh.* "Peter."

"How? You never brought him home. I never met him. The Mizzes never met him."

I stared at her. I never invested in Peter? What was she talking about? Of course I invested in Peter.

Didn't I?

"I slept next to the man for two years." My words limped out, lame at the gate.

"Whatever." She gave a dismissive wave of her hand. "Anyone can be roommates."

"We were more than roommates."

"Did you ever tell him about the Penis Teflon?" She paused. "Did you ever tell him that you have this insane idea that every man you ever care about will desert you?"

I stared at her. "What the hell does that have to do with anything?"

Beauji eyed me for a minute, then gave a brief nod and started down the road again. I looked at my watch and headed after her.

"Shouldn't we be turning around?"

"No. It's only two more miles to the Babb farm. Ian can drive us back."

"Whoa, whoa, whoa," I said, grabbing her by the arm. "Hold on there, cupcake. What do you think you're doing?"

"I am not going to sit here and listen to you ramble on about Penis Teflon for the rest of your damn life," she said, jerking her arm out of my grip and pumping down the road. "You can come with me or you can go home, but I'm paying a visit to Mr. Writer Man."

"To what exactly do I owe this unexpected—and very early— pleasure?"

Ian sat down at the kitchen table after supplying us with tea and muffins. His hair was disheveled and his eyes bleary, but he'd been awake and writing when we barged in on him, despite the fact that it was 6:45 in the morning.

"I want to know what your intentions are toward Portia," Beauji said. Both of my hands slapped flat against the table.

"Beauji. Stop."

Beauji picked off a small chunk of muffin and popped it into her mouth. "What? He's leaving at the end of the summer. You two need to shit or get off the pot." She waved the muffin at Ian. "These are very good. Where'd you get these?"

Ian rubbed his eyes. "Um. Sue Ann's Bakery, I believe."

Beauji nodded, popping another bit in her mouth. "Sue Ann's? Really? Wow. You know, they're right? Everything does taste better in the third trimester. So what's your answer?"

"Beauji . . ." I grumbled.

Ian glanced from me to Beauji, looking heartily confused. "I apologize. It's early and I haven't gotten much sleep. Did you ask me a question?"

Beauji motioned toward me. "Your intentions toward Portia. What are they?"

Ian sat back. He opened his mouth, closed it, and looked at me with a confused smile. Beauji tapped her fingers on the table. "Come on. I don't have all day. I could go into labor at any minute. Tick tock."

Oh, god, oh, god, oh, god. I felt a sheet of ice run over my body. Ian rubbed his forehead.

"Forgive Beauji," I said. "She's temporarily insane. I think it's the pregnancy. The hormones." I gave her a hard look. "Isn't that right, Beau?"

Beauji stood up. "Well, my work here is done. Talk amongst yourselves. I have to go pee."

Ian stood, motioning toward the hallway. "It's just down the hall on the left . . ."

She waved him off. "I know, I know, I've been coming out here since I was a baby." She waddled out of the kitchen, leaving the door swinging in her wake.

Ian sat back down. There was a year of excruciating silence packed into about five seconds. I put my face in my hands.

"I got arrested for running naked on campus once," I said.

"Excuse me?"

I pulled my face out of my hands and forced a sardonic smile. "Just searching for a moment more humiliating than this one."

He laughed, then leaned forward. "Look, Portia . . ."

I stood up. "Beauji's crazy, and I shouldn't ever have mentioned the hair tucking, so is there any way we can just forget all of this and go on with our lives like none of it ever happened?"

He stood up, too, and took a step toward me. "The hair tucking?"

"The hair. Tucking. Ear. Thing." I gave a sharp exhale. He reached over and pushed some hair away from my face and tucked it behind my ear.

"You mean this?"

I jumped back.

"Yes. That. Stop doing that, okay?"

His posture straightened and he pulled his hand back. "I'm sorry. I didn't mean to—"

"I know, you didn't mean to send me . . . wrong signals and please understand that I don't mean to send you . . . wrong signals." I pushed my chair in, hoping Beauji had faked the pee and was standing outside the door and would take the sound as a signal to come in and save me from myself, because I was heading into a full-tilt ramble.

"I'm going through a lot of weird stuff right now. My mother is running around town setting farm animals free like some sort of Greenpeace wacko. My father—who abandoned me at the age of two, by the way—is coming to town."

Ian's eyes widened. "Portia. Christ. Why didn't you mention—?"

"He doesn't want to see me," I said, feeling my throat begin to tighten. Ian's eyebrows contorted in concern, and he touched my arm.

"Are you all right?"

"I'm fine." I held my hand up, gently shrugging off his touch. The last thing I wanted to do was get started on the whole Jack thing. "It's just that my family is nuts and Beauji is trying to help and I know that, but she's making things worse." I took a deep breath and looked up at him. *Oh, hell. Might as well keep going.* "You're the only nonexplosive thing in my life right now. And I don't want anything to mess that up."

Ian was quiet for a second, then gave a brief nod.

"I wish you'd told me about what was going on with your father," he said.

"I come here to get away from all that," I said quietly.

Ian smiled. "Good. I'm glad coming here makes you feel better. But if you ever need to talk about anything, I want you to know I'd be happy to listen."

"I know that. Thank you."

Our eyes held. I looked away first.

"Beauji is usually not this crazy. I mean, she's crazy, but not like this, not like . . ." I sighed and put my hand to my forehead. "I am really, really sorry."

Ian smiled and rocked back on his heels. "It's all right, Portia. It's actually made for a very interesting morning." He moved forward, then stopped and placed one hand awkwardly on the back of a kitchen chair. "I'm sorry if I've been making you uncomfortable."

I gave him a weak smile. "You haven't."

He tucked his hands in his pockets. "Yes. I have."

"No," I said, playing with my watch, unable to meet his eye. "I like it. It's just . . ."

My eyes darted up and caught on his.

I'm afraid I'm going to be alone forever.

He smiled that little sincere smile, the smile that refused to be distracted by shiny conversational objects.

I'm afraid every man I care about is going to leave me.

He was supposed to be laughing at me, or annoyed with me, or something aside from unbearably sincere.

I'm afraid.

But I couldn't say any of that. Instead, I said, "She really is crazy, you know."

Ian grinned. "I gathered."

There was another brief silence. Just as Ian opened his mouth to speak again, the kitchen door swung into the room and Beauji reappeared.

"Everything settled?"

I pulled on a forced smile. "Yes."

"Good." She grinned. If she wasn't supporting the life of an innocent party, I would have strangled her right there. She looked up at Ian. "I'm glad we had this talk. Any chance you could give us a lift back into town?"

Ian smiled, stepped around her, and pushed the kitchen door open, holding it for both of us. I tried not to look at him, but I did notice his hand move instinctively toward the small of my back as I passed, and I also noticed him jerking it away before he touched me. On the ride back to town, I mentally planned a trip to Babies 'R Us, where I intended to buy Beauji a slew of the noisiest damn baby toys ever made.

chapter six

"Sit down, baby."

I had my hand on the doorknob, ready to go inside for Sunday dinner, when I heard Mags's voice. I turned to see her sitting on the porch swing, hands clasped in her lap. I glanced inside at the apparently empty house, then looked back at Mags.

"Where are Vera and Bev?"

"At a movie." In the muted glow of seven o'clock, Mags looked young. Vibrant. Her makeup flawless, her dress perfectly smooth, every strand of her hair in place. It was hard to believe that the last time I'd seen her, she'd been covered in mud and cow pies.

She patted the space next to her. "We need to talk."

I sat down. There were two sweating glasses of gin and tonic sitting on the coffee table in front of us. I reached for mine. She reached for hers. We both drank.

Silence.

"Well?" I said after a minute. "Are you going to tell me what's going on or what?"

Mags sighed and stared down the street, but didn't say anything.

"Mags?" I said. "You're scaring me. I'm worried about you. Vera won't tell me much, and Bev won't tell me anything. I just want to know that you're okay. That's all."

Mags smiled and patted my hand. "I'm gonna go refresh my drink." She gave a furtive glance at my glass, which was almost full, but Southern women draw comfort from hospitality, so I took a large gulp and handed it to her.

"Thanks."

She smiled and headed inside with our glasses. I stared down the street and remembered riding my first bike down that bumpy sidewalk when I was six, the Mizzes cheering me on from the porch. I remembered looking back at them and waving, not seeing that I was headed straight toward the fire hydrant until it was too late. I knocked into it and got a good scratch on my leg. I played up the crying as the Mizzes played up the rescue, passing me between them as they carried me back to the house until I began to giggle with each pass.

Mags returned, handed me my drink, and sat down. More silence. A car engine started a block down. A baby cried in the house across the street. Mags sighed.

"I'm not sure where to start."

"Why don't you start with Jack?" I said. My voice cracked on his name. I took another drink. "You could tell me what that's all about."

Mags stared at her bright red fingernails. "No, I don't think I can start there."

I heaved a sigh. "Fine. Start with the animals. What possessed you to break into Carl Raimi's farm and set his cows free?"

Mags put her drink down and stood up. "I can't talk to you if you're going to be angry."

"Well, then, we've got a problem because you can't expect me to be anything else if you won't talk to me."

She glanced at me and walked over to the porch railing, her arms crossed over her abdomen as she stared out at the fire hydrant where I'd fallen all those ages ago.

"It's just a thing, really."

"A thing." I paused, gave her the opportunity to speak. She didn't take it. Her back was still to me. "What kind of thing?"

"A thing." She waved her arm around in the air, her fingers making delicate circles. "I've been . . . thinking. A lot. About things. I've been . . ." She sighed. "I've been sad."

My eyes widened. Sad? *Mags* had been *sad*?

"That's impossible," I said. Two gin and tonics and my thoughts were going straight to my lips. I took another sip. In for a penny, in for a pound.

"Well, it's the truth. I've been sad," Mags said. More silence.

"Is that it?" I said. I wondered how much energy I had left for conversations like this. It was just so much work trying to understand her. "That's how you explain all of this? The finding me a Flyer, the mysterious morning activities, the letting farm animals loose through the streets of Truly? It's because you're sad?"

Mags kept her eyes on the fire hydrant. "There comes a time in a woman's life when she has to look at herself and fix the things that need fixin'."

I tried to process that and failed. "I don't understand."

"I know, I know." She turned around to face me, leaning against the railing. "So, tell me what happened with you and Peter."

I blinked. "That's it? We're done talking about you and your sad thing?"

"Yes, we're done." She sat down in the wicker chair next to the porch swing and leaned forward. "You and Peter were together for a while."

"Two years."

"So what happened?"

"Why do you want to know about Peter?"

"Because I do."

"Why?"

"Because I do."

Well, that line of questioning was obviously going nowhere. I shrugged. *What the hell?*

"We were perfectly happy until one day I came home and found all his stuff gone."

She sipped her drink. "Were you happy? *Really* happy? I mean, people who are happy don't just up and leave, right?"

"I guess not," I said. It made sense, but I'd put a lot of hard work into not delving into what happened with me and Peter, and I liked it that way.

"It just seems to me," Mags went on, "that people who really love each other find a way to work it out, no matter what." There was an intensity in her voice that made me unsure if we were actually talking about me. She turned her head to look at me. "Did you love him?"

I leaned back. "I don't know. Maybe. I think I did." I squelched a burp. "I was sad when he was gone."

She nodded. I took another drink. It was one of the first times in my life Mags had shown a genuine interest in how I felt, and whether it was about me or not, I sopped up the attention like a dry sponge.

"To be honest, there were times when I wished he would leave, but once he was gone, I wanted him back. And I don't know why. Maybe because it was love. Maybe because I thought he was my last chance."

"Your last chance? At what?"

"I don't know, Mags. Marriage. Children. A man who sticks."

Mags looked out at some indistinct point down the street and took a sip of her drink. "Do you think that would make you happy? A man who sticks?"

"Does it matter? Men don't stick to Miz Fallons, do they?"

Our eyes locked. I was right. We weren't talking about me. But before I could focus my gin-scattered thoughts enough to figure out exactly what we were talking about, she changed the subject.

"I'm sorry, darlin'," she said, touching the corners of her eyes. "I was wrong to get you involved with that Flyer. I don't think it's done you any good at all."

I gaped at her. "Did you just apologize to me?"

"Don't get me wrong. He's a very attractive man. But I think what you need is—"

I held up my hand. "Stop. Stop, stop, stop. I'm thirty years old. It's time for you to stop telling me what I need."

She sat back and stared at the drink she held in her lap, and as I watched her I was amazed, not for the first time, at what a mystery my own mother was to me. I've struck up conversations with strangers on planes who made more sense to me than this woman.

And yet, I loved her. I loved her and I hated seeing her sad and if whatever she was doing was going to take that sadness away, then I was going to have to just shut up and accept it.

I reached over and put my hand on hers. She blinked in surprise and looked at me.

"Mags, are you okay?"

"Oh, I'll be fine," she said, throwing a smile my way. "Really, you're making a bigger deal out of this than it needs to be—"

"No," I interrupted. "I mean, are you *okay*? This . . . thing you're going through. It's not . . . medical, or anything? You're not going to die on me, right?"

She waved me off. "No. No, it's not anything like that."

"And you're not going to get arrested again, are you?"

She smiled. "Not if I can help it."

"That's not a comforting answer."

She squeezed my hand. "I won't get arrested again. You have my solemn vow."

"So it's just that you're fixing things that need fixing?"

She nodded. "Yes. Exactly."

I took a deep breath. "How about a truce? I agree not to push you on this whole sad thing you've got going on, and you agree not to try to fix me. Think you can do that?"

She looked at me and grinned. "Yes."

"Okay, then." I lifted my glass. She lifted hers.

"Truce," I said.

"Truce," she said.

We clinked. We drank. As it turned out, we were both lying, but it was a nice mother-daughter moment all the same.

I stepped out of the tiny stall shower in my apartment and squinched my toes in the neon pink and yellow daisy bath mat Beauji made me buy. I had to admit, she was right. Every time I looked down at it, I smiled.

I didn't hear the knocking until I opened the bathroom door, although from the sound of it, whoever was knocking was losing patience. I wrapped my hair in a towel and slipped into my old flannel robe.

"I'm coming!" I yelled as I opened the door. Bev.

"Get dressed." She pushed past me into the apartment. I shut the door and walked around her toward my bedroom.

"That's what I was going to do before you decided to beat the hell out of my door." I tossed the towel on my bed and yanked open the top drawer of the dresser, pulling out socks and underwear. "What's going on?"

Bev stopped at the doorway of the room. "We've got a fondue."

I shut the drawer and turned around to look at her. "A fondue? For who?"

Her eyes traveled around the barren room and then back to me. "Vera."

"Vera? Why? What happened?"

Bev put her hand on her hip. "I'll give you the details in the car. I'm supposed to be out getting the oranges and the chocolate. Now get dressed. I'll wait in the living room."

She shut the door. I grabbed my jeans.

"Oh, y'all are making way too big a deal over this," Vera said, crumpling up another tissue and tossing it in the empty grocery bag at her feet. Her eyes were red, and her face was blotchy, but ever since we'd pulled out the chocolate and the orange slices, she'd at least stopped crying.

"Nonsense," Mags said. She grabbed Vera's fondue fork out of her hand, stabbed a slice of orange, and handed it back. "Dip."

Vera leaned over our old avocado green fondue pot and dipped the slice into the melted chocolate. "I'm fine, really. I just wasn't expecting to see him, is all."

"Of course you weren't, darlin'," Bev said. I sat back in my chair and played absently with an orange slice on my plate. Mags kicked me lightly under the table. When I looked up at her, she whisked her hands at me. It was my turn to comfort.

"Oh." I dropped the orange slice. "Um. Haven't you seen him before? I mean, it's been eleven years. There are only six thousand people in town. The odds—ouch!"

The kick was harder that time. I turned to Mags. "What the hell, Mags?"

Mags gave me a look of mild contrition. Bev opened her mouth and seemed ready to rip me a new one, but Vera held up her hand to stop her, then turned to me.

"Yes, I've seen him a few times. Usually it's at the grocery store, like today. Once I saw him at the movie theater in Fort Oglethorpe. But . . . I don't know . . ." She sighed and dumped her chocolate-dipped orange slice on her plate.

Bev leaned forward. "It's hard, baby. We know that."

Mags leaned over the fondue pot and stirred. "And I think he has a lot of nerve showing up at the Piggly Wiggly on a Tuesday afternoon."

I looked at Mags. "Why would Bridge know she shops there on Tuesday afternoons?"

Bev and Mags gave me glacial stares. Vera put a protective hand on my arm.

"No, she's right." She reached for another tissue. "It's been long enough. I should be able to bump into him and just say hi like any normal person, ask him about his construction work, and help him pick out a ripe honeydew melon without breaking down like a damn old fool." Her face contorted and she blew her nose into a tissue.

"Oh, tell me you didn't help that man pick a melon," Bev said. "I hope you picked one out that was rotted right through."

"No," Mags said, waving her fondue fork in the air as she spoke. "You should have just walked away like you didn't even see him. Like he didn't even register on your radar. Serve him right."

I shifted in my seat and stared at my plate. There was a moment of silence. It was my turn to say something comforting, but I was drawing a blank. I figured Mags's shoe was already aimed for my shin anyway, so I said the first thing that came to mind.

"What exactly happened with you two, Vera?"

Vera raised her eyes slowly to mine. Mags didn't need to kick me; Vera's pained expression was enough to tell me I'd said the exact wrong thing.

"Excuse me," she said, her voice barely a whisper. She grabbed another tissue, skirted around us, and left the dining room. When I looked up, both Bev and Mags were staring at me, their faces a blend of shock and horror.

"What?" I asked. "I don't understand what happened. Did he just leave her? Was he seeing someone else? I don't understand why two people who seem to still love each other aren't together."

"Do you know the point of a fondue?" Bev asked me. I rolled my eyes.

"Of course I know the—"

"*The point of a fondue*," Bev growled over me, "for those of us who have been hiding under the veil of education for twelve years—"

"Excuse me? *Hiding?*"

"—is to provide a soft, safe place for someone who needs comfort. What part of that is too difficult for you to understand, Professor?"

I stood up and grabbed my plate. "It's not difficult for me to understand, Bev, I'm just saying—"

She stood up and grabbed her plate as well. "You don't *just say* anything. You say whatever will make her feel better. If that means saying you believe that little men from Mars are stocking the shelves at the Piggly Wiggly, you say it. Are you really incapable of coming up with a single nice thing to say?"

Anger pricked up the hairs on the back of my neck. "Bev, you know I love Vera as much as anybody, but I mean, come on. It's been eleven years. Maybe if y'all didn't *fondue* her every time she and Bridge Wilkins bumped elbows, she might be over it by now."

Bev raised her index finger at me. "Let me tell you something, little miss—"

Mags shot up between us.

"Hey," she said, grabbing Bev's raised hand and lowering it, "who's in the mood for a gin and tonic? I know I could sure use one right about now."

I put my plate down. My hand was shaking and my stomach felt like it was about to evict the three orange slices I'd eaten. I kissed Mags on the cheek before throwing my napkin on the table and beelining for the front door.

I tossed on my bed and looked at my new alarm clock, blazing 11:45 at me in furious red. I stared at the ceiling.

Hiding under the veil of education? What was that supposed to mean? So I'd gone to school. So I'd gone directly into grad school after undergrad and had stayed for eight more years. I was improving myself. Investing in my future.

"If I was hiding, I wouldn't be here, I can tell you that much," I muttered, throwing back my new quilt and tossing my legs over the side of the bed. "If I was hiding it's a safe bet you people wouldn't know where to find me."

I sat there, staring at my toes against the old hardwood, wondering what Bev's problem was, fearing I had been too hard on Vera. She'd needed a fondue, and I'd given her an inquisition. I'd just wanted to understand the problem. What was so wrong with that?

I got up and walked into the kitchen, flicking on the gas under the teakettle. I leaned against the counter, waiting for the kettle to whistle, staring down at my feet. It was almost midnight. I couldn't stand the thought of another night counting the nail holes in the walls here, but I knew sleep wasn't likely.

"Hiding," I muttered to myself. "What the hell is her problem, anyway?"

I wiggled my toes against the hardwood again, then turned off the gas and went to get my sneakers.

"Stop right where you are!"

I screamed and dropped the hammer in my hand. It clattered to the cement floor, sharp reports echoing through the barn. A light was shining in my face. I held my hand over my eyes and squinted.

"Ian?"

The flashlight lowered. That's when I saw the shotgun.

"Oh, for Christ's . . ." Ian staggered over to the sawhorse and leaned against it, gun at one side, flashlight at the other. I picked up my battery-powered lantern and walked over to him, trying to mask the smile on my face.

"You okay?" I asked.

"No, I'm bloody well not okay," he sputtered at me, accentuating his speech with jerks of the gun. "You scared the bloody hell out of me."

"Careful with that thing," I said, nodding toward the shotgun. He tossed it to the ground.

"It's not loaded. I'd blast my own foot off, I'm sure." He let out a sharp exhale and looked at me. "What the hell are you doing here?"

"Working on the barn."

"Working on the . . ." He huffed. "It's one o'clock in the morning."

"I couldn't sleep, and I thought maybe working on the barn would help. I would have knocked on the door when I got here, but I didn't want to wake you." His eyebrows shot up. I raised my hand, motioning for him to settle down. "I'm sorry. I didn't think the hammering would be loud enough to wake you up."

He ran his hands through his hair, skewing curly brown tufts in all directions. "I wasn't sleeping."

"What were you doing?"

"Writing."

"I thought you wrote in the mornings."

He shrugged. "When I'm writing, I write. All day. All night, if necessary. I've tried to limit it to just mornings, but . . ." He trailed off, ran his hands through his hair again.

"In a bad place with the book?"

He gave me a half-smile. "I'll get past it."

"Well," I said, picking up my lantern, "I'm sorry I scared you. I didn't mean to. I would have called, but . . ."

His smile went from half to full. "Ah, so it's my fault for not having a phone installed out here, is that it?"

"Come to whatever conclusions you'd like." I grinned and picked up the hammer. "Sorry to have bothered you. You can go on back to your book now."

I walked over to the support I'd been assembling and raised the hammer. I saw the beam of the flashlight move behind me, and then I heard Ian pick up a plank of wood. I turned.

"What are you doing?"

"I'm bloody stuck," he said. "I can't get past this one scene, and it's for damn sure I won't be able to sleep now."

I nodded, stuck a few nails in my mouth, and hammered them one by one into the support. Ian walked over to the back wall and flicked a switch. The barn lit up with a series of track lights that huddled on the floor against the back wall.

"Oh," I said, pulling out the last nail. "I didn't even realize you had lights in here."

He plugged in the table saw and put the goggles over his eyes. "You're not the only one who turns to barn restoration when insomnia strikes."

We exchanged smiles. He picked up a plank of wood and marked the angle on it. I watched him as he set it on the table, pulling the whirling blade down to cut. It wasn't until he'd finished and pulled off his goggles that he realized I was still watching him.

"What?"

"Tell me about your block," I said.

He looked at the wood, then back at me. I picked a nail out of the pocket on my tool belt and placed it against the support plank I'd been working on.

"No, your story. Maybe I can help."

I smelled coffee and opened my eyes to see a steaming I'D
RATHER BE FISHING mug sitting on the coffee table. I rolled
onto my back, adjusting my head on the couch pillow and
noticing that at some point, someone had covered me with a
blanket.

Ian.

He was sitting down at the desk facing the front window in
his living room, his back to me. His laptop was blazing, as it
probably had been all night. He placed his mug quietly down
on the table and pulled out the chair, glancing at me over his
shoulder.

"Ah, you're awake." He nodded to the coffee next to me. "I
decided to do as the Romans do. I hope I made it right."

I smiled. "How'd it turn out?"

He sat, still facing me, and sipped his coffee. "I think it
might be a little strong . . ."

"No," I said, laughing. "Tan and the smuggler. Did he jump
in the harbor?"

Ian smiled, glanced quickly over at the laptop, then looked
back at me. "No, actually. The water's too cold that time of year.
He'd die of hypothermia, and then there's the end of my series,
and then I'd have to get a real job, and we can't have that.
But"—he waggled a finger at me—"I did use your idea to
throw the disks on the boat before it explodes."

I sat up, grinning. "Only they're not the real disks?"

He nodded. "Right. It means I'll have to rewrite that bit in
chapter four, but I think it'll work."

I smiled. "Thank you."

He shook his head. "For what? You're the one who was up
all night helping me slog through this mess."

"I had fun," I said, stretching. "What time is it, anyway?"

He checked his watch. "Quarter past seven."

"I'm gonna have to get back soon. The Page opens at nine."

He stood up. "I'll get your jacket."

He walked into the hallway, and I heard the closet door open. I smiled to myself as I slipped my feet into the sneakers I'd kicked off sometime during the night. Ian returned with my windbreaker and draped it over my shoulders, his fingers lingering for a second before he pulled them away.

"Sorry," he said, his smile flickering.

I kept my eyes on his. "No. It's okay."

He raised one eyebrow. "Are you sure? I'd hate to inspire another hostile visit from your little redheaded friend."

I laughed. "I think you could handle it."

He smiled and tucked a strand of hair behind my ear. My heart went into a Sammy Davis, Jr., tap dance number. I felt a smile spread across my face as his hand landed lightly on my shoulder, sending a pleasant zing down my spine. His body was maybe an inch from mine and I was sure he was going to kiss me until he gave a small laugh and looked away.

"All right. Time for you to go."

My face must have registered my disappointment, because he laughed again, and his eyes did a quick self-conscious jig.

"I haven't brushed my teeth this morning, and I'm rather firm on positive first impressions." He picked up my hand and kissed my palm, his eyes on mine. "Come over for dinner tonight?"

"Yes," I said, barely whispering.

"Seven o'clock? I'll pick you up."

"You don't have to . . ."

He put a finger against my lips. The warmth shut me up. I was one touch away from melting into a puddle at his feet.

"First impressions," he said. "Humor me."

I smiled. "Consider yourself humored."

His fingers traveled from my lips to my face. His arms fell around me, pulling me to him, and as I pressed my cheek against his shoulder, I felt that soul-deep comfort that you can usually only get from things like hot tubs and eiderdown. I'd never gotten that from another person before. I liked it. When he finally released me, I let out a small groan of grief.

"Off with you, then."

I stepped back, pulled my windbreaker around me, and walked to the door. When I turned to look back through the front window, I could see him standing right where he was, watching me. I smiled.

It felt good to be watched.

chapter seven

"Vera, I'm sorry about the fondue. I should have been more supportive."

Vera and I sat in the back office at the Page, sharing a lunch of veggie subs, lemon-kissed tonic water, and organic blue corn chips. Mags and Bev were busy gossiping at the coffee bar with Marge Whitfield, giving me and Vera some time alone.

"No, darlin', don't you worry about that." She sipped her water. "You're right. I should be past it by now."

"I didn't mean to make you feel that way," I said. "I just wanted to understand what happened."

Vera looked panicked. I held up my hand. "Not now. Not if you don't want to talk about it. I'm just saying, there are a lot of things I don't understand that I wish I understood."

Vera picked up a chip and broke it in two pieces. "Such as?"

I raised my eyes to her. Technically, pumping Vera for information was a violation of the truce with Mags, but Vera asked. Surely that was a mitigating factor.

"Such as what's going on with Mags. Why she's disappearing in the mornings. Why she's setting farm animals free."

Vera gave me a long look, not justifying my line of questioning with an answer. I huffed and grabbed a chip out of the bag.

"Okay. Fine." I sat back and watched her. "Tell me about Jack, then."

Vera blinked. "Why?"

"He's my father, and I hardly know anything about him. That's why."

Vera looked down and brushed some crumbs off her shirt. "You know I can't talk about that."

"No, I don't. Why not? Because of the Miz Fallon code?"

"Don't be silly. We don't have a code."

I raised an eyebrow at her. She gave me a look and kept going.

"It's not my place, Portia. If you want to know something, ask Mags and leave me out of it."

I widened my eyes in sarcastic surprise. "Ask Mags? Gee, I never thought of that. What a simple solution. How could I have missed it?"

She threw a chip at me. "Don't be a smart mouth."

I picked the chip off my shirt and tossed it in the garbage. "Look, I'm not asking what went on with Mags and Jack. I've given up. I'll probably never know. I just want to know . . ." I picked up my water and put it down again. "What he was like, I guess. What kind of man he was."

Vera studied me for a minute, then sighed. "He was a nice man."

"*Nice*? Nice how? Was he kind to animals and small children? Did he tip big at restaurants? Did he give blood? What?"

Vera's eyes glanced over toward the door as though checking for Mags, and then darted back to me. She grabbed a chip.

"He was smart. He loved classical music. He read a lot. He

was really into Shakespeare. You know he was the one who came up with your name, from that play . . ."

"*Merchant of Venice,* I know." That was one of the small bits of information I'd gleaned from Mags. I looked at Vera impatiently. She tossed the chip down and wiped her hands with a napkin.

"He liked boats and the water. He used to take you down to the pond out off River Road to teach you to swim." A small smile crept over her face. "He'd bring you back all wrapped up in a towel and beaming. He said you were the best little swimmer that Catoosa County would ever see."

I grabbed my tonic and took a sharp sip, blinking my eyes. It was the first compliment I'd ever gotten from my father, and it cut through me harder than any insult I'd ever received.

"I knew we shouldn't be talking about this," Vera said quietly as she watched me wipe at my eyes. There was a long silence. Then, quietly, "He loved you very much. I know he did."

"Oh, really?" I felt the anger surge through me, and I knew none of it was Vera's fault, but I turned a sharp look on her anyway. "Then why'd he leave?"

Vera sighed and bit her lip, but didn't say anything. I got up and shot my water bottle into the garbage.

"You know," I said after a moment of staring at the back of the computer monitor, "I understand why Bev's not talking. That's just Bev. And Mags was born clueless and will always stay that way."

Vera looked up at me over her half-moon reading glasses. I met her eyes dead-on.

"What really gets me is that you're the one who's supposed to know better."

I left without looking at her and sneaked out the back way so that Bev and Mags wouldn't see I was upset. As long as we were keeping secrets, maybe I'd start keeping a few of my own.

"Well, if Mags found him, I probably can. You'd be amazed at what you can find on the Internet." Beauji adjusted herself again on her couch, then pushed into the top of her bulging stomach. "Foot out of the ribs, kid," she grumbled.

I sighed and leaned my head back on her big, fluffy couch. "I don't know."

"Look, just give me everything you know about him and I'll do what I can. Just because I get his number doesn't mean you have to dial it."

I sat forward. She had a point. And it was a sure bet that she wouldn't let up until I agreed. I grabbed a pen and a notepad from the coffee table and jotted down everything I knew about my father.

Lyle Jackson Tripplehorn.
Born February 28th, 1937, in Hastings, Tennessee.

I handed the sheet to Beauji. She read it and sighed, then tossed it on the coffee table. "Okay. That's settled."

She paused, cocking her head to the side as she watched me. "So . . . how are things with the Brit?"

"When is that damn baby due, anyway?"

"Eight days. Don't change the subject. It's rude. How goes it with Sir Ian?"

"Fine, no thanks to you."

She waved her wrist at me. "Oh, please. If it wasn't for me, you two would still be doing the is-you-is-or-is-you-ain't-my-baby shimmy."

I fought a smile. "How do you know we're not?"

"Because I can read your face like a damn newspaper." She reached over and picked up her ice water. "So, spill it, girl. What's going on?"

I looked at my watch. "We have an official date in three hours and twenty-two minutes."

"Great. I like him. You know"—she bit her lip—"I think he's a really good guy."

I glanced up at Beauji. Her face was the picture of sincerity. Her face was never the picture of sincerity. An alarm in my head went off. "What's going on?"

She sighed and paused, watching me. Finally, she came out with it.

"He told you he's divorced, right?"

"Yeah," I said slowly. "How did you know?"

She waved her hand at me dismissively. "I figured he did. I mean, most people are divorced, right?"

She gave me a tight smile. I sat up straighter. There was more.

"What did you find out?"

"Nothing. I just . . . I looked him up on the Internet. I was just curious about him." She pointed to a folded-up piece of paper sitting on the coffee table. "I personally don't think it's a big deal. But I know you will."

I reached over and grabbed the paper and opened it. It was a printout of an article about Ian from *People* magazine. *Spy Master Thrills Booksellers*, the headline read. I glanced up at her.

"Second paragraph from the bottom," she sighed. I turned my eyes back to the article.

Ebullient and gracious during the discussion on craft, Alistair Barnes clams up when asked about his personal life. Although he

won't comment on his divorce three years ago, he did confirm that he
hadn't seen his ex-wife since she was hospitalized in Seattle for com-
plications from childbirth just before the split.

I folded up the paper and tossed it back onto the coffee
table, trying to maintain a normal breathing rhythm. I clasped
my hands together over my knee, disgusted with myself that
they were shaking.

"I'm sorry, Portia," she said. "I shouldn't have shown it to
you. I just didn't feel right knowing something you didn't
know."

Wish more people felt that way, I thought. "No, you did the
right thing."

Beauji skimmed her hand over her head. "I'm a horrible
friend."

She had tears in her eyes. I remembered a story Davey had
told me about how she cried for an hour when the pizza guy
brought ham instead of pepperoni, and decided to tread carefully. "What are you talking about?"

She reached behind her and pulled a tissue out of the box on
the end table. "You really like this guy and I've ruined it. I confronted him on the hair-tucking thing and totally embarrassed
you—Davey reamed me a new one for that, let me tell you. And
now I've shown you this." She motioned to the printout on the
coffee table and blew her nose. "I keep ruining your life."

"You've hardly ruined my life," I said.

She reached over and grabbed my hand. "You know my
intentions are good, right? You know I'm just insane because
I'm about to have a baby, right? On a normal day, I'm okay,
right?"

"Beau, you're fine." I patted her hand. "Thank you for being
concerned, but it's really not a big deal."

She laughed and wiped at her eyes, then squeezed my fingers. "Portia, don't let this ruin anything. I'd feel horrible if I ruined everything for you."

I shook my head. "You haven't ruined anything."

Her eyes darted over my face. "So . . . you're still going to see him tonight?"

"Sure," I said, running my hands over my legs. "Yeah. Why not?"

"It was three years ago, Portia. And you don't know what happened."

"Am I arguing with you?"

"I like this guy," she said. "He's good people. I can tell. I mean, how many guys would put up with a cranky pregnant lady knocking down their door at the crack of dawn?"

I raised an eyebrow at her. "I know of only one."

I took a drink of water, tried to squelch the sinking feeling in my gut.

"He's not like your father."

I smiled as brightly as I could. "You're right. He's not."

Beauji sighed and took another drink from her water. "Don't tell Davey, but I think he's right about me minding my own damn business."

I stepped back and looked at myself in my full-length mirror. I'd pulled my hair back in a twist, done the natural-but-glowing makeup routine, and slipped into a semi-clingy red dress that Beauji loaned me with wistful eyes.

I sighed, pushing away thoughts of a wife and baby sitting alone in a hospital room.

"Just because he left the wife doesn't mean he left the baby,"

I told my reflection. "Give him a chance. Don't assume any-thing."

Hell, it might even be why he was here in the States, to be closer to his kid. I'd only known him a few weeks. There was plenty of time to find out what really happened.

"It's nothing," I said, pointing a scolding finger at myself. "It's not a big deal. Do not overreact."

I pulled on a smile. A little wine and some time in Ian's company, and I was sure it would grow more genuine. I walked out into the kitchen and poured myself a glass of water, debat-ing on whether I should wash the piling dishes or not.

The doorbell rang. I looked at the clock. Six forty-five. Ian was early. I dumped the water in the sink and put the glass on top of the pile. I gave my dress a quick smoothing over, grabbed my jacket off the coatrack and opened the door.

The first thing I saw was the Syracuse English Department T-shirt, the very one I'd resented picking up off the floor for two years. My gaze drifted upward. Blue eyes. Sandy hair. Small scar cutting a thin line through the left eyebrow.

Peter.

"Portia?" He blinked at me. "Is . . . is that you? You look . . ." He shook his head and smiled. "Wow."

I stared at him, somewhat tempted to reach out and poke him in the shoulder to make sure I wasn't hallucinating.

"Peter?" I put my hand up against the doorframe to steady myself. "What are you doing here?"

His Adam's apple bobbed as he swallowed. "I had to see you."

I stared at him. He took a step closer. I moved back, still standing in the doorway, declining access. He stopped.

"I need to talk to you."

"So you came all the way down from . . . ?" I paused, shook my head. "I don't even know where you've been. Where ya been, Peter?"

"Boston."

"Boston. I should have guessed. How's the family?"

He looked over his shoulder and then back at me. He seemed almost wary. Ashamed. Two emotions I'd never seen on Peter. "They're good. Thanks for asking."

"So, they don't have phones in Boston, then?"

He held up his hands in defeat. "You're right. I should have called. I'm sorry."

Oh. Okay. He's sorry. Well, that makes everything all right. I glanced out at the alley and saw Peter's silver hatchback parked by the side door, just below the steps that led up to my apartment.

I turned my eyes back on him. "You drove."

"I drove."

"From Boston."

"From Boston."

I crossed my arms over my chest. "What are you doing here, Peter?"

He inhaled, and his face reddened a shade. "I have something that belongs to you."

"And so you drove nine hundred miles . . ."

"A thousand, actually."

"Is it an elephant? Because UPS will ship just about everything else."

Peter looked around to check if anyone was watching, then turned back to face me. "Can I come in?"

"No."

"It's starting to rain, Portia."

"That's not my problem."

"Okay." He inhaled again. His breathing seemed unusually labored for someone who was not asthmatic. "Okay, then, if it's gotta be here, it's gotta be here."

Then he got down on one knee.

I bent at the waist and hissed at him. "What are you doing, Peter?"

"What I was too stupid to do six months ago."

Oh, you have got to be kidding me. "Good God, Peter, did you fall on your head or something?"

"Portia Fallon, I love you."

"What? Peter, what are you—?"

He talked over me. "I have always loved you, I will always love you."

"You really need to get up now, Peter. Now."

"Will you marry me?"

I shut the door, putting both hands against the hard wood. This wasn't happening. This couldn't be happening. Where was the distant, preoccupied person who got my birthday presents a month late and then forgot how old I was?

This couldn't be happening.

I opened the door. He was still on his knee, staring down at the ring in his hand as though he couldn't believe it, either.

"Get up, Peter."

He looked up. "Are you going to give me an answer?"

"No."

"No, you won't give me an answer or no, you won't marry me?"

My eyes narrowed. He stood up. I stepped back and let him inside, watching as he headed to the couch and sat down. I tossed my jacket over the back of the couch and shut the door behind me.

"How did you find me?"

"Actually, it's a funny story." He put one hand over the back of the couch and smiled. "It was your mother."

Fire shot through my stomach. "What?"

"I was thinking about you. All the time. Every day. But I was too scared to call you after . . . well, you know."

I swallowed. "So Mags . . . How did she find you? I didn't even know where you were."

"She contacted my publisher, and they contacted me."

"I'm going to kill her."

He leaned farther over the back of the couch. "No, don't. It was perfect. It was like a sign, the final thing that told me this is what I need to do."

I crossed my arms over my stomach. "Then I'm definitely going to kill her."

Peter stood up and walked over to me. He put his hands on my elbows and leaned his head into my line of vision. I pulled my head back.

"Portia, I was so stupid. I was so wrapped up in myself, in my failure as a novelist, in my fear of never being a success at anything . . ." His eyes searched mine, darting from pupil to pupil, his breathing still erratic. I pulled my arms out of his hands and stepped back from him.

"Well, gee, Peter. That might have been nice to know a while back. You've been gone for what? Four months?"

He pulled his eyes away from mine. "Twenty-one weeks."

He'd counted the weeks. Why was I not surprised? "Twenty-one weeks. Without a call. Without a letter. Just a note scribbled in the front page of your book. I can't even donate the damn thing to the library now."

"I know. It was awful. I wish I could help you understand . . ."

"Oh, I understand, all right." The shock was in full retreat, and fury approaching the offensive line. "You left. I moved on. There's nothing else to understand."

"Yes, there is." He stepped closer. "I was so stupid. I was jealous. You were so close to finishing your dissertation and being a professor . . . You were so successful . . ."

Wait. *Successful?*

". . . and so smart . . . and so . . ."

His head tilted to the side and he reached up and touched my face. I put my hand on his chest and pushed him away. He straightened up and tucked his hands in his pockets, giving me a pained look.

"I just . . . I had to get away. To think things through. And once I got away . . . I knew."

"Knew? Knew what?"

He took a half-step closer to me. "How much I love you. How much I need you with me. Portia, I'm miserable without you."

"Oh, please," I said, my heart pounding in my chest. "You have no right to come back into my life with no warning and try to give me a ring, Peter."

He squinched his eyes shut. "I know. I thought that might be a bad idea. Your mother—"

"My *mother?*" I shouted, then held my hands up. "No. Don't tell me that was her idea. It's not going to do anybody any good if you tell me this was her idea. This was her idea?"

"Not entirely," he said. "I want to marry you. I want to be with you. Forever."

My throat constricted on *forever.* Peter put his hand back on my arm. I didn't move.

"Portia, I know I totally blew it when I left like that. I know

I don't deserve a second chance. But if you'd give me one . . . just one more chance . . . I'll spend the rest of my life making it up to you."

His hand trailed down my arm and locked onto my fingers. I felt a rush of dizziness ride through me.

Forever.

A year ago, I would have given my right arm for Peter to say these things to me. It had been all I wanted. A promise of forever. A promise to stick. Instead, I'd gotten notes on the fridge telling me he'd be writing at the library and not to wait dinner.

Peter put his palm on my cheek. "I know I screwed up. It's haunted me every minute. All I want is a chance to make it up to you."

No, I thought. But I didn't say it. *Forever* was still ringing in my ears.

Peter stepped back, glanced at the door.

"Are you expecting someone?"

I blinked.

It was the doorbell ringing.

"Oh, holy Christ," I said. I stepped back from Peter and opened the door.

Ian stood there smiling in a navy blue suit jacket with a white button-down shirt and jeans. I felt a small whine rise in my gut at how perfect it all might have been. He held out a bouquet of lilies and kissed me on the cheek as he ducked in out of the rain.

"You look beautiful," he said.

"Thank you, Ian." I stepped back. He shut the door behind him and his smile dimmed as his eyes locked on Peter. Resigned to a ruined evening, I made a gesture toward Peter with my hand.

"Peter Miller, Ian Beckett. Ian Beckett, Peter Miller."

Ian's eyebrows rose a notch with recognition, total recognition, and he held out his hand to Peter. They shook. Then both of them, in unison, rocked back on their heels with their hands clasped behind their backs.

Ian looked at me. "Um, perhaps this is a bad time . . ."

"No." I gave Peter a look. "Peter was just leaving."

Peter met my eye but didn't move. Ian glanced at Peter, then back at me.

"I think another time would be best," Ian said. He turned and put his hand on the doorknob. I grabbed his arm.

"No, Ian." I pressed my fingers into his arm and looked him solidly in the eye. Ian took my hand off his arm and squeezed my fingers briefly before letting go. His face was tight, and his eyes held mine for only a brief moment before trailing away to a point somewhere behind my left shoulder.

"Well. Good night."

He stepped out and shut the door behind him.

Crap, crap, crap.

I glared at Peter. He didn't meet my eye.

"I'm sorry, Portia. I wasn't thinking. I should have known there might be someone else."

I grabbed my purse from the coffee table, rummaging through it for my keys. "There wasn't. Not yet. Now there probably won't be." I pulled my keys out and yanked the door open. "I'm gonna go talk to him."

Peter looked at the floor. His voice was quiet. "Do you want me to be here when you get back?"

I wanted to say no. I needed to say no. Instead, I stepped out into the drizzle and guided my shaking legs down the steps and out to the street, thinking, *Crap, crap, crap* in rhythm with the rain.

I pulled up to the Babb farm. Ian's car was already there. I knocked on the door. No answer. I stepped back off the porch and looked around. I could see light coming from the barn. I took a deep breath and hurried over as the rain started to come down in earnest, soaking my dress.

I stepped inside the barn and saw Ian clearing off a table he'd set up in the middle of the open space. Two candles sat on a plank of wood next to a bottle of champagne tucked in a bucket of melting ice. The sawhorse sported a single rose in a bud vase as Ian pulled a tablecloth off the circular table that usually sat in the Babbs' kitchen. The rain pelting the roof filled the barn with hollow echoes.

"It would have made a great first impression," I said.

He stopped folding for a second and looked at me, then turned his attention back to the tablecloth. I took a few steps forward.

"Ian, I didn't even know he was in town. He showed up literally five minutes before you did."

Ian put the folded tablecloth on the sawhorse, but didn't look at me. "Look, Portia, you don't owe me any explanations. If you and Peter have things to work out, go and work them out."

"We don't have anything to work out." Here with Ian, I felt fairly sure that was the truth. I stepped another foot closer. Ian's eyes shot up to mine.

"I'm sorry, Portia," he said. "I don't think this is going to work."

"Wow," I said. "That was quick."

His jaw muscles twitched. "I'm sorry?"

"This morning you were Mr. First Impressions, and now it's don't-let-the-door-hit-you-in-the-ass-on-your-way-out."

Ian was quiet for a moment. "Perhaps we should wait and talk about this tomorrow."

"No, I'd like to talk about it now." I paused and grabbed the first defense I could think of: deflection of guilt. "The way I see it, I'm still one up on you. At least you knew about Peter."

He crossed his arms and narrowed his eyes at me. "Excuse me?"

"Were you ever going to tell me about the baby you abandoned?"

Ian's eyes widened as though he'd been slapped. "Excuse me?"

"Beauji found an article on you from *People* magazine. It mentioned your ex-wife." I paused as I tried to think of a way to say the important part without saying it, but my mind came up blank, so I choked it out. "And the baby."

He inhaled through his mouth. "Ah. So Beauji pulls up a magazine article and suddenly I'm a deserter, is that it?"

The hurt expression on his face cut right through me, and I wanted nothing more than to run over to him and apologize until he forgave me. Instead, I stood where I was, clinging to my righteous indignation. Ian grabbed the tablecloth off the sawhorse and clutched it in his hand with an iron grip.

"Just to fill in some blanks for you, *she* had a baby; I did not."

I blinked and felt my stomach churn. "What?"

"The baby's father is a fellow from her office," he said, his voice gritty. His eyes shot ice through mine. "Guess the distracted husband is always the last to know."

Crap, crap, crap.

"I'm sorry, Ian," I said. "It never occurred to me—"

"No. I guess it didn't."

I closed my eyes. "I don't know what to say.'

I heard his boots clopping against the cement floor. When they stopped, I opened my eyes to find him standing next to me.

"I'm sorry your father abandoned you, Portia. I really am. But his guilt doesn't automatically transfer to the rest of us."

I looked at him but said nothing. He turned his focus from my face to the open barn door behind me.

"This may come as something of a shock to you, Portia, but you're not the only person in the world who's been left.'

As the sound of his steps faded behind me, I focused on the candles sitting next to the bucket of melting ice. The single rose in the bud vase hung its head to one side, as though it didn't want to look at me. I stamped my foot against the cement, sending a shot of sound careening off the empty barn.

Crap. Crap. Crap.

"Okay, Peter, get out," I said as I opened my front door. It had stopped raining, but my dress was still wet, and I was anxious to get him out and get changed into something I could eat five quarts of Ben & Jerry's in without feeling self-conscious.

The living room was empty. I stepped out onto the porch landing and looked down.

The Hyundai was gone.

Deflated, I settled myself on a bar stool at the kitchen counter, running my fingers through my damp hair.

"Shit," I huffed to myself, and got up. I opened a cabinet and grabbed a glass.

You're not the only person in the world who's been left.

I pushed up the handle on the faucet, filled the glass with

cold water, then put it down on the counter. I looked out the
window into the night, grabbing a streetlight for a focal point.

*It was like a sign, the final thing that told me this is what I
need to do.*

I picked up the water and took a drink, my eyes glazing as
the streetlight blurred in my vision.

I want to be with you. Forever.

I tossed the rest of the water down the sink and plunked the
glass down. That's when I noticed that all my dishes were done.

I turned around. The books and magazines that had been
splayed all over the coffee table were piled neatly on one side.
The jacket I'd thrown over the back of the easy chair was hanging on the rack by the door.

Peter.

I smiled before I could stop myself. Straightening up had
always been Peter's preferred method of apology. I leaned over
the counter and put my head in my hands. That's when I
noticed the little black velvet box sitting between my elbows.

I stood up straight. I wanted to be furious. I wanted to toss
it across the room.

Instead, I opened it.

A half carat shimmered at me, set in a simple platinum setting. Almost exactly like the one I'd shown Peter a year ago,
when I'd gone through a brief hinting phase, before the relationship started its downward spiral into the fifth ring of hell.

Forever.

I shut the box with a snap. I couldn't think about this now.
It was too much. And the fight with Ian was still tearing a hole
in my stomach. It was time to do something else, time to get
out of the apartment, time to distract myself.

And settling a score is often a perfect distraction.

"Mags!" I slammed the front door behind me. "Mags, where the hell are you?"

It was only eight o'clock. The house was empty. I rushed through the living room and kitchen to the back door, where I found all of the Mizzes playing gin rummy at the big umbrella table.

"Portia!" Mags stood up, her smile tremendous. "I'm so glad you came by, darlin'. Sit down, I'll get you a drink."

"Mags," I said, trying to keep my voice calm. "We need to talk."

She patted my arm and kissed my cheek. "Okay. Sit down with the girls, I'll come back with your drink, and we'll talk. G and T all right?"

Mags headed into the house, not waiting for my answer. Bev gave me a wry smile and patted the seat next to her.

"Sit down, Portia," she said. "I have a feeling this is gonna be an interesting discussion."

I crossed my arms. "Did you two know about this?"

Vera forced a smile, but I could see the discomfort in her eyes, although whether it was about our argument that morning or about this Peter thing, I couldn't be sure.

"You mean that Peter's in town?" she asked. "Yes. Isn't it exciting?"

Exciting? My head tilted to the side. Before I could ask the question, Bev glanced up at me over her cards. "He's upstairs sleeping in your old room."

"His room, now." Mags tapped me on the shoulder, forced the drink into my hand, and motioned toward the seat next to Bev.

"*His* room?"

"Sit down, honey," she said, settling herself down opposite

the empty seat. "What do you say, girls, should we start a new game and deal Portia in?"

"Absolutely!" Vera said, tossing her cards on the table. "That was the worst hand of my entire life."

Bev snapped her fan of cards closed and handed them to Mags. She raised an eyebrow at me. "Well, sit down, child."

I didn't move. "*Peter's* sleeping in my *room?*"

Mags nodded as she shuffled the cards. "Well, yes. He looked so tired when he showed up here, poor boy."

"I don't know what you said to him, Portia," Bev said, "but he wasn't in a good state."

"Oh, so what, now I'm the bad guy?"

Vera shook her head. "You're not the bad guy."

Silence. Mags and Bev gave me looks that said in no uncertain terms that I was, indeed, the bad guy.

I shook my head. "I don't believe this."

Mags sighed and put the cards down. "I really don't see what the problem is, Portia. Just the other night you were telling me that all you wanted was a man who would stick."

"Excuse me?" I shook my head as the whole obvious scenario began to sink in. I stared at Mags. "You orchestrated this whole thing, didn't you?"

She answered with one raised eyebrow, and then went on. "And now a perfectly good and might I say easy-on-the-eyes young gentleman comes to town and proposes." She shook her head and picked up the cards again. "I thought you'd be happy."

I swallowed. There was more to this story, I just knew it. "Mags, what have you done?"

She looked at Vera and Bev and smiled, then batted her eyes at me. "Peter didn't tell you?"

I felt like I was going to throw up.

"Well, darlin'," she said. "We've hired ourselves a new business manager."

My stomach heaved. "Oh, my god."

Mags rearranged her hand of cards. "He'll be staying with us for a while until the apartment over the Page opens up." She glanced up at me. "Or someone finds room for him."

"Are you kidding? Are you *kidding* me? You *hired* me a husband?"

"Why not?" Bev asked, her mouth tight. "We had intended for you to be the business manager when you finally decided to return from your endless schooling, but you're not interested, so . . ."

My mouth dropped open. "Are you *kidding* me?"

"Shhh, you'll wake him, poor boy. He's had such a rough day. He didn't say exactly what happened when he saw you, but based on the look on his face, I think you could have been nicer to him." Mags glanced toward the empty seat at the table, then back up at me. "Well, Portia. Are you in or not?"

I stared at them for a minute. Vera looked appropriately contrite. On the opposite end of the scale, I'd never seen Bev so pleased. And Mags just smiled, like it was no big deal.

"Good night, ladies," I said. I went back into the house, slamming the screen door behind me. I was making my way down the front steps when I heard Mags's voice calling after me.

"Portia?"

I turned around to face her. She closed the distance between us.

"He's a nice boy. And he loves you."

"Are you crazy? You're crazy. You cannot run my life any way you see fit, Mags. Things don't work this way."

She smoothed her hand over one silk sleeve and then raised

her eyes to meet mine. "Well, darlin', things don't seem to be working the way you've been doing them, either, now have they?"

I turned around and trudged the six blocks back to the Page, stepping on every sidewalk crack I could find along the way.

chapter eight

"So," Beauji asked as we power-walked, "have you talked to them yet?"

I shook my head. "No."

"What about Peter?"

"He's with the Mizzes. I avoid them all."

"It's been a week," she said. "Not that I don't like having company for these morning walks, but you're a bit of a downer, you know."

"Am I?" I said, kicking a large pebble into a ditch. "I thought I was being pretty cheerful. Considering."

"Hmmm," Beauji said. "What about Ian?"

I shrugged. "I haven't seen him, either. You're officially the only person in my life with whom I have any contact, aside from my faculty adviser, who was nice enough to pretend to believe me when I told her I was almost done with my dissertation."

Beauji gave me a sideways glance but didn't break her stride. "You're not almost done?"

I shrugged and looked toward the east, where the sun was in full bloom. "What time is it, do you think?"

Beauji glanced at her watch. "Seven-eighteen. So, when is the dissertation due?"

"December."

"Are you at least mostly done?"

"Define mostly."

She sighed and shook her head, picking up the pace. "For Christ's sake, Portia, if you throw twelve years of school down the drain—"

"I'm not throwing twelve years of school down the drain. I'm just delaying it. Maybe. I only wanted it done by December so they could consider me for the new faculty position opening up in the spring. But now . . ."

"But now what?"

"I don't know." We started again, in the direction of the Babb farm. "Do we have to walk on this road every day? Couldn't we go through town and down River Road? I really don't want to bump into Ian."

A big fat lie, that. But still. A girl's got to keep up appearances.

"Ian writes in the mornings," Beauji said, arms pumping. "But we can go another way tomorrow. If we do it tomorrow." She grinned at me. "I have a feeling today's the day."

"You have a feeling every day's the day." I tried to keep the irritation out of my voice. Every morning we walked. And walked. And walked. Still no baby. I had my suspicions that she wasn't even pregnant, just fat in a highly abnormal way.

"But today's my due date," she said, taking a swig of her water.

"Yeah, and yesterday was supposed to be the day because no one ever gives birth on their due date. And the day before that was supposed to be the day because it was a full moon, and birth rates climb during a full moon. And—"

"Hey, are you trying to alienate the last friend you got left, or what?"

I didn't say anything. Beauji slowed down a little more.

"We're almost to the farm," she said. "Ready to turn around?"

We stopped and stared northward, silent for a moment. I considered going farther, visiting with Ian, having coffee, chatting, trying to mend that busted-up fence. I'd bet dollars to doughnuts Beauji considered dragging me screaming by my hair to do that very thing. We each sighed on the same note. Nobody beats old friends for clairvoyance and timing.

"I'm sorry," she said. "I didn't mean that about me being your last friend."

I shrugged. "Truth hurts, right?"

She put her hand on my shoulder. I thought it was a comfort gesture, until I saw her face, which was contorted in pain.

"Beauji?"

She bent over, grabbing her thigh with one hand and my shoulder with the other.

"My cell phone," she gasped. "It's in the pack. Call Davey."

"Are you in labor?"

"Call Davey!" She sucked in a breath. I zipped open the fanny pack we'd assembled for just such an occasion, pulled out the cell phone, and hit the power button.

Nothing. I hit it again.

Crap.

"Beauji?"

She whooshed out a breath and straightened up.

"Oh, holy Mother of God, that fucker hurt."

"Are you okay?"

She shook her head. Her eyes were glistening. "I think this is it, Portia."

"Sit down," I said. She looked down at the dirty road under her feet.

"I'm not sitting down here. I'll never get up again. What did Davey say? Is he on his way?"

I sighed. "Have you charged this phone recently?"

She grabbed the phone and punched the power button a few times. Her eyes welled up in tears.

"Oh, my god," she wailed, her voice high-pitched and squeaky, "I'm going to have my baby on the side of the road!"

I put both my hands on her shoulders.

"Beauji, look at me." She did. I put my palms on her face. "You're going to be fine. I'm right here and I will not let you give birth on the side of the road. Do you understand me?"

She nodded slowly. Her expression calmed. Then she bent over again and let go with a stream of obscenities. I put my arm around her, supporting her until the contraction passed.

"Beau?" I asked, when I felt the muscles in her shoulders relax under my hand. "You okay?"

She whimpered. I ran my hand over her hair.

"You might not even be in labor right now. You said yourself that you've been having false contractions."

"No," she said, gasping. "This is different."

As if to make her point, her water broke, gushing over our feet and dribbling down the road. She began to cry. I closed my eyes. We were three miles from town, two miles from the farm, and she wasn't going to budge. I heard what sounded like a car and looked over my shoulder.

"Beau?" I said into her ear. "I'm going to flag down that car, okay?"

Her hand tightened on my arm. "I'm scared."

I kissed the top of her head. "You're gonna be fine, baby.

Don't you worry about a thing. I've got it under control, but I need to step into the road and wave that car down, okay?"

Beauji gave a small nod and put both her hands on her thighs for support. I stepped out into the road and waved. A familiar blue pickup truck came up around the bend. I didn't have to read the lettering on the side to know the familiar logo: WILKINS CONSTRUCTION.

"Hey!" I said waving frantically. "Bridge!"

Bridge slowed the truck down, squinting at me as he rolled his window down. "Portia? That you, girl? What the hell you doing out in the middle of the road?"

"She's in labor," I said, motioning across the street to where Beauji was hunched over. "Can you drive her into town?"

Bridge glanced at his passenger seat, which was filled with a large pile of hardware and tools. I looked at the bed of the pickup; it was running over with planks of wood held down with bungee cords.

"That baby'll be in school by the time I get this truck unloaded," he said. "I was on my way to the Babb farm. I'll grab Ian and we'll come back and get y'all, okay? You go tell her she's gonna be just fine."

He took off. I ran back across the road and put my arms around Beauji. "That was Bridge Wilkins."

Beauji looked up at me, her face momentarily switching from fear to disbelief. "You're kidding me."

I shook my head and smiled, happy for the momentary distraction. "What are the chances, right?"

Beauji eked out a pathetic laugh. "This town is too fucking small."

"Anyway, he's on his way to get Ian. They're going to be here in a minute and we're going to get you to the hospital."

She grabbed my hand. "Portia, it hurts. I mean, it hurts a lot. They told us it would hurt in the class, but I didn't know it would *hurt*. Not like this."

"I know, honey," I said, running my hand over her hair. Of course, I didn't know, I had no idea, but it seemed the thing to say. Her eyes watered and she grabbed my hand, squeezing it tight as she huffed through the contraction. When it was done, she looked back up at me, her eyes wide and terrified.

"I don't know if I can do this."

"You're gonna be just fine." I touched her chin and turned her head to look at me, putting on the most confident expression I could drum up. "When that baby comes, you're gonna be in a nice hospital room with Davey by your side and some terrific drugs working magic in your system. Just hang in there for me, okay?"

I put my arm around her and prayed everything would turn out as well as I just told her it would. Two of the longest minutes of my life passed, and I finally heard the sounds of a car coming. I looked up and saw both Ian's SUV and Bridge's truck slowing down and pulling to the side of the road. Ian and Bridge carried Beauji and placed her in the backseat of the SUV. Bridge tossed me his cell phone and told me to call Davey as he hopped in the truck to follow us in. I tossed myself into Ian's passenger seat; the car was moving before I got the door closed.

"Which way to the hospital?" His hands were taut on the steering wheel, his eyes focused on the road.

I gestured with the cell phone. "Take a left on Main, then just go straight until the road curves. Hospital's right there."

"Ow, ow, ow, ow, ow!" Beauji yelled from the back. I turned and dropped one hand over the back of my seat, reaching out toward her. She grabbed it, and I tried not to wince at the pain of her grip. I dialed the sheriff's office and told the girl on the line to notify Davey. Ian's eyes darted from side to side as we approached a red light on the corner of Main. He slowed a little, saw there were no other cars, and rushed through.

"How is she?" he asked.

"I'm fine!" she yelled. "Just get me to the goddamn hospital!"

"I think she's going to be okay," I said, sharing a small smile with Ian.

Davey met us at the emergency entrance. Ian and Bridge pulled Beauji out of the backseat and placed her in the waiting wheelchair. Davey hollered a "Thank you!" over his shoulder and zoomed her into the hospital. Bridge and Ian and I stood frozen at the entrance for a moment as the wave of adrenaline retreated. Finally, I turned to Bridge and smiled.

"Hey," I said, feeling the awkwardness I would have felt earlier if the situation had allowed it

He gave me a small smile. "Hey, kiddo."

Aside from a few more gray hairs in his dark beard and a marked sadness in his eyes, Bridge hadn't changed much since the last time I saw him, the day I left for college. I felt my heart squeeze tight. I'd missed him. I hadn't realized that before, although it made sense; he'd been like an uncle to me from the time I was twelve. He'd gotten me the job with Morris Babb. He'd fixed my pink bike when the tire went flat. But when he was gone, he was gone, and like all the other Miz Fallons, I'd given up on looking back. My eyes moistened, and I grabbed his hand.

"I'm glad you happened along," I said, handing him his cell phone. "I don't know what we would have done . . ."

He shook his head and gave a swift shrug.

"Ain't nothing, girl. Now, you go on in and see to Beauji." He pulled on a grin. "And you give me a call when that baby's born. If it's a boy, I want it to be called Bridge. You tell her that, now."

I smiled. "I will."

He gave a half nod, said good-bye to Ian, and left. My emotional level was in the red zone. And I still had Ian to deal with. I inhaled and turned to him.

"I'm going to go inside and see how she's doing," I said, motioning lamely over my shoulder toward the hospital. "Thank you for getting us here."

Ian gave a dismissive wave of his hand. "Not at all. I just hope she's okay."

I laughed feebly. The muscles in my arms were starting to shake. I was fifteen seconds away from either breaking out laughing or crying. The only thing I was sure of was that I didn't want Ian to see either. "Well. I'm gonna go."

Ian nodded. "Congratulate her for me, would you?"

"Sure," I said. But I didn't move. I thought about how comforting it had felt to be in his arms that one morning before everything fell to shit. There was little I wouldn't have given to feel some of that comfort right then.

Including my pride.

"Stay with me." I hadn't realized I was even thinking the words until they were out. I swallowed, forcing myself to go on. The only thing more painful than looking like an idiot was the idea of watching him walk away. I was too weak to fight needing him. "My arms are shaking. I'm a mess. There's a whole history with Bridge and Vera and I haven't seen him in years and he's probably the closest thing to a father I ever had and the whole thing with Beauji scared the hell out of me and I really need a friend right now."

He smiled. "I'd be happy to stay with you."

I exhaled. "Thank you."

"Not at all. I'm rather glad you asked, actually." He paused, took a breath, and started again. "Look, these things don't tend to happen quickly. Trust me, my sister has had three of the little beasts and they all took better than twenty-four hours to make their appearance. I'm going to have to move my car anyway, so why don't I take you back to your place and you can . . . well . . ." He motioned toward my feet. "Your shoes appear to be covered in some sort of . . . bodily fluid."

I looked down.

"Oh, God. Beauji's water broke all over my shoes. I totally forgot. Ewwww." I put one hand on Ian's shoulder and used my feet to kick them off, then hooked my toes in each sock and peeled those off as well. We stood side by side, looking at the soppy lump baking on the concrete.

I leaned in toward Ian. "I know they're my shoes, and this is more a woman's area, but I really don't think I can touch them."

Ian gave me a horrified look as he realized what I was asking, then sighed and held up one finger for me to wait. He flipped open the back of the SUV, grabbed a garbage bag, and used it to pick them up and toss them into a nearby trash can.

"Just for the record," he said as he got in the car and shut the driver's side door, "that was absolutely the most disgusting thing I have ever done for a woman."

"Thanks for waiting," I hollered through my closed bedroom door, taking the towel off my head and tossing it on the bed. "I'll be out in just a minute."

"No hurry," Ian called from the living room. I grabbed a pair of jeans and a T-shirt and put my hair up in a clip. It wasn't my hottest look, but considering that I'd started out the day with amniotic fluid on my feet, it was a step in the right direction.

"I was thinking we might stop by Sue Ann's Bakery to get some coffee and doughnuts or something. I'm starving," I said as I walked out into the living room. Ian was standing by my kitchen counter, his head bent over the ring box Peter had left there. He stepped back when he saw me, flashed a smile, and grabbed his keys off the coffee table.

"Ready to go?" he asked, motioning toward the door.

I didn't move. Ian fiddled with his keys, then raised his eyes to meet mine.

"He proposed," I said. "That's what he was doing here. After no communication for four months, he drove down here from Boston and proposed."

Ian nodded. There was a short silence in which I tried to read his expression and failed. Brits and their stiff upper lips. Finally, he spoke.

"It's really none of my business."

"I said no."

Ian looked up. Scanning my interaction with Peter I realized that I hadn't exactly said no, but I'd definitely implied it. And implications count, right? Ian's eyes traveled to the ring box and back to me, proving that implications do count. And not always in my favor.

"I haven't seen him," I said. "I plan on returning it to him when I do."

Ian was quiet for a minute, his eyes wandering around the apartment, avoiding mine.

"Portia," he said finally, still not looking at me. "I'm afraid I owe you an apology."

"No," I said, moving a step closer. "You don't. I was totally wrong and I feel horrible about what I said."

"It's all right. I understand how you would have jumped to conclusions. I overreacted and I apologize for that."

"I'm sorry, too."

He nodded. He still wasn't looking at me. I took another step closer and leaned my head into his line of vision. "What is it?"

His eyes glanced up, then away. "It's just that . . . the fact that I reacted . . . as I did . . . got me thinking . . ." He met my eye again. I had a crazy idea for a moment that he was going to kiss me.

I was mistaken.

"I think it would be best if we kept our friendship . . . just a friendship."

I bit my lip. "Oh."

He paused. "I'm going back to London as soon as I finish my book."

Ice ran down my spine as I digested this. He was fairly close to done, from what I knew. He could be leaving any day, then. He gave an uncomfortable shrug and gestured to me, his focus landing on the window past my shoulder.

"And you're going back to New York at the end of the summer. It's just . . . bad timing."

If that's all it was, you'd be looking me in the eye right now, I thought. But what was the point? There was no beating the Teflon. It was all-powerful.

"Sure. You're right. Okay."

He raised his eyes to mine. "I want you to understand. It's not that I don't . . . It's not personal."

Rejection is always personal. "Of course not. I agree, actually. I mean, things are complicated for me right now."

"Yes," he said slowly.

I swooped some hair behind my ear. "So really, what would be the point, right?"

"Right," he said. I couldn't read his expression. Sad? Relieved? A little of both? Neither? I didn't know. I hoped my expression was as unreadable for him. Fair's fair.

He jingled his keys in his hand. "Well. I do hope that you'll continue to come over in the afternoons. I rather enjoyed our time together, and I'd hate to lose it." He paused and gave a small smile. "I've missed you."

I smiled back. "Missed you, too."

We each gave a self-conscious laugh. The comfort I usually felt in his presence was replaced by a painful awkwardness.

"Right, then," he said, motioning toward the door. "Shall we?"

I stepped in front of him and headed out the door, wondering if maybe Penis Teflon was actually a physical characteristic, something in the genetic makeup of Miz Fallons that we exude, like pheromones. It would certainly explain a lot.

"Hit me." I had sixteen showing. Ian had fourteen. It was a gamble.

Ian flipped over the next card.

Five of hearts.

"Woo hoo!" I did a little shimmy as I sat Indian-style on the big block end tables we'd pushed together to create our mini-casino. Turns out Ian was right; the little beasts do take forever to make the scene. It was two in the afternoon, and still no baby. Davey and Beauji's mom were in the room with her, and they came out with updates every so often. In the meantime, Ian and I played blackjack.

"Not so fast," Ian said, holding up his hand. "I still have to take my card."

I rolled my eyes. "You're not going to get twenty-one."

He tapped the face-down card at the top of the deck. "How can you be so sure?"

"What are the odds?"

He shook his head. "I don't know, but I have a chance."

"You have no chance," I said.

"We'll see." He flipped the top card onto the table, keeping his eyes on me. I glanced down, then looked back up at him, my mouth open.

"You're a cheater," I said as he gathered the cards up, leaving the seven of clubs he'd just picked off the deck for last.

"I most certainly am not," he said, "and I resent the accusation. No matter. I win. Push goes to the dealer."

"Since when?"

He grinned. "Dealer makes the rules."

I sighed. "Fine. A bet's a bet. What do you want?"

He shuffled the cards between denim knees, his work boots tapping on the floor for a second while he thought. "Tell me the whole story about you and Peter."

"The whole story? Why do you want to know?"

"I have to admit, I'm curious." He set the deck of cards neatly between us. "It's the writer in me."

Sure. The writer.

"Okay," I said, standing up. "But it's a long story. Make yourself comfortable. I'm gonna get us some coffee."

"You do realize that this whole idea of Penis Teflon is patently absurd, don't you?" Ian leaned over me on the lumpy hospital couch and tossed his empty coffee cup into the garbage. It had taken us three cups and ninety minutes to get from the day Peter and I met three years before to the moments right before Ian came to pick me up for our date.

I shook my head. "No, I'm totally serious. I think it might be a chemical thing, like pheromones . . ."

Ian huffed. "Look, the man abandoned you with a note. Scribbled in the front page of his own novel, which tells me that he's completely self-obsessed, which in turn suggests that this sudden change of heart likely has more to do with him than it does with you."

"Oh, gee, thanks."

He let his head fall back against the couch. "Sod it. I should have known better."

I folded my arms over my stomach. "Excuse me?"

He lifted his head. "What I'm trying to say is that a person who is that self-obsessed is not likely to suddenly become otherwise. I was not making any commentary at all on whether or not you might be worthy of the change."

"I didn't say that you did." But, of course, that was the way I'd taken it. Time to get the subject back on track. "So, you don't think people can change?"

"I believe they can, yes. I don't believe they often do. But I think the real question is, is that a risk you really want to take?"

His brown eyes dug into mine, pushing for an answer. My mouth was open, but I had none. It was then that I heard a familiar voice calling my name. I looked up and saw Beauji's dad, Beau Sr., dumping some luggage on the floor and rushing over to me. His face was as red as the fringe of hair that ran around the back of his head.

"Portia," he said, pulling me into his arms for a hug. "Good to see you. Where's my baby girl?"

"She's still in labor, far as we know."

"She's okay, though? Baby's okay?"

I smiled. "Yes, both fine so far. We're just waiting for the final showdown."

He grinned. "I wasn't going to go to that conference, but Beauji's mama told me it'd be fine, babies never come on time. Shows you what women know." He gave me a nudge and a wink. "I caught the first flight out of Atlanta and damn near killed myself getting here. Can't miss my first day of being a grandpa, can I?"

"No," I said with a laugh. "Absolutely not."

He looked at Ian and held out his hand. "Beau Miles."

Ian shook it. "Ian Beckett. I'm a friend of Portia's."

Beau gave a gasp of recognition. "You're that fella writes those spy novels, aren't you? I heard you'd be in town this summer."

Ian nodded. "Yes, sir."

"Well, you and Portia are coming by for dinner before the summer's out, and I won't take no for an answer. It's not often a guy gets to show off his grandbaby to a famous author."

Ian glanced at me, then smiled and nodded at Beau Sr. "I'd be honored, Mr. Miles. Thank you."

"Oh, Mr. Miles, nothing. You're a friend of Portia's. You'll call me Beau."

Beau Sr. winked at me and I felt a blush creeping up my neck, but was saved by the sound of squeaky sneakers on the linoleum. We all turned to see Davey, red-faced and grinning, coming up behind us.

"It's a boy."

Ian and I waited an hour for Beauji and the baby to get settled in her room. She looked beautiful, if a little tired. Her face glowed. The baby was a tiny cocoon of blankets sleeping in a clear plastic bassinet next to her bed. Beau Sr. stood on one side with his arm around Beauji's mom, Wendy. Davey sat with one hip on the bed next to Beauji, cooing at his sleeping son.

Ian squeezed my hand and whispered, "Congratulate Beauji for me. I'll be in the waiting room."

As the door closed behind him, Beauji held her hand out to me.

"Come see my baby, Portia," she said. Davey stood up and moved to the side to make room for me. I walked over, took her hand, and looked. "Isn't he gorgeous?"

I peeked at the wrinkled, scrunched-up pink face poking out from the blanket cocoon and the light blue baby cap. He resembled a hairless pink pug dog, but she was right. He was beautiful.

"I am so proud of you, baby." Beau Sr. stepped over and planted a kiss on Beauji's head. There were tears in his eyes. He grabbed her other hand and pulled it to his lips. "My baby had a baby."

Davey's arm came up around my shoulders. "Don't you start crying, too," he said, knocking his head lightly against mine. I swiped at my face.

"Too late," I said, trying to smile despite the fact that I hated the reason I was crying. I leaned over and gave Beauji a kiss on the cheek.

"You get some rest. I'll come back tomorrow to visit with you and . . ." I blinked and laughed. "Hey, what'd you name him, anyway?"

Beauji looked up at her father and grinned. "Miles. Miles David Chapman."

The first thing I noticed when I opened the door to my apartment was the smell. Something was cooking. Chicken?

My eyes adjusted to the dimness. The place was littered with candles. Something was all over the floor and the couch and the furniture.

Rose petals?

Oh, God.

"You're home!" Peter, wearing an apron, popped up in the kitchenette where he'd been rummaging in the cupboards below the counter. "Did Beauji have the baby?"

He was acting like nothing was wrong, like he didn't propose only to be ignored and avoided for a week. He'd been hanging with the Mizzes for too long.

"Yeah. Boy. Miles David."

Peter smiled. "Great. I figured you'd be tired after being at the hospital all day—Davey called your mom to tell her—so I . . ." He motioned behind him, then gave me a sheepish look. "I hope you don't mind."

I sighed. I was hungry, and whatever he was cooking smelled good.

"I should mind," I said, plopping myself down on the couch. "But I'm too tired."

"Glass of wine?" he asked.

I shrugged. "Sure. Why not?"

Peter poured us each a glass of chilled chardonnay and sat down next to me. I took a sip and lolled my head back on the couch. "What are you doing, Peter?"

He grinned. "Trying to win you back."

"I'm not a carnival goldfish."

"I know that." He leaned forward, his elbows resting on his

knees as he looked into his wineglass. "And I know it might be hopeless. But I have to try or I will know I never tried."

He brought his eyes up to meet mine. I felt it, a small flicker of something that once was. I took a sip of wine to dampen it.

"So, what's cooking?" I asked.

"Vera's lemon chicken," he said.

I eyed him suspiciously. "My favorite."

He smiled. "I know."

"The Mizzes have been schooling you, have they?"

He shrugged. "I like them."

"And you're all conspiring against me?"

His smile faded. "Not against you. We all want you to be happy."

I narrowed my eyes at him but held on to a small smile. "Well, your timing is great. I'm weak and tired. You may stay for dinner, but only because you cooked it, and then you leave."

He raised his glass and clinked it to mine. "Deal."

Any idiot could have seen it coming; any idiot except me, that is. But between the wine, the exhaustion, and the residual comfort from times gone by, I was taken completely by surprise when, within an hour of finishing the meal, I found myself making out with Peter frat-party style on my couch.

"Wait," I said, pushing him away as his hand went under my shirt. I popped up off the couch and held out my hands, channeling Diana Ross. "Wait."

Peter leaned back and put his arm over his eyes. "I'm sorry."

"No, you're not," I said. "This is exactly what you wanted."

He pulled his arm down and sat forward. "That's not true.

I mean, well . . . yeah, it's true. But how you feel matters more to me. I don't want to pressure you."

"Oh, really?" I threw up my arms, gesturing around the room. "So what's this? Breaking into my apartment, covering it with candles and rose petals, cooking me dinner, plying me with wine? What is that if not pressure?"

"Technically, I didn't break in. Mags gave me a key."

I ground my teeth. "You're not doing yourself any favors by bringing Mags into this, Peter."

Peter ran his hands down his thighs and stood up. "You're right. I'm sorry. I ambushed you. That was totally unfair."

"Don't sell me this crap about fair and unfair," I said. "It's not about that. It's about you. What's with you, Peter? Who are you, Peter? Because it's for damn sure that in the two years we were living together, you never once called Aunt Vera to get the recipe for my favorite chicken."

"Maybe I've changed," he said quietly.

"Maybe," I said. We stood in a checkmate for a minute, then Peter stepped closer. I closed my eyes, and when I opened them, his mouth was just an inch from mine. I could feel the heat from his body drawing me in closer, until we were touching. His hand settled on my hip. His lips brushed mine.

And we were on the couch again.

I deserve this, I thought as his hands cupped my breasts, his fingers running lightly over the nipples and making a surge run through me. *I deserve to be touched and held and loved. I deserve a goddamn orgasm.*

"Stop," I said, pushing him back again. "Stop. I can't think. I can't . . ."

He reached up and touched my face. "Don't think. Don't worry. We'll go only as far as you want to, and if you decide tomorrow that it was all a mistake and you want no part of me, I'll accept that." He leaned into me and nibbled on my collarbone. That's the thing about exes. They know all your weak spots.

I let out a breath and tried to will my heart rate to slow down. "I don't have anything," I said. "I mean, protection."

He smiled, his hands working the button on my jeans, slowly unzipping them. "There are some things for which you don't need protection." He dipped into my collarbone again, and did something with his tongue that told me exactly what he was thinking.

"But what about you?" I gasped.

He kissed a trail down my neck, over my breasts. "Don't worry about me."

I deserve this, I thought. *He'll go away afterward if I tell him. He said so. I deserve this.*

As he slipped my panties off and lowered his face between my legs, I closed my eyes.

And thought of someone else.

chapter nine

"My feelings . . . they are so different," Elizabeth said, her hands tucked behind her as she walked with Darcy. A smile tipped the corners of her mouth. "In fact, they are quite the opposite."

I popped a cigarette into my mouth, squinting my left eye as a trail of smoke assaulted it, and reached for the remote. I paused the video on Darcy's understated expression of joy and relief as he realized that Elizabeth finally loved him back. I took a long drag on the cigarette, then put it out in the ashtray, where it joined the stubby remainders of six of its little friends. I flicked my finger over the touch pad on my laptop, banishing the annoying bouncing-ball screen saver to virtual purgatory. My dissertation was exactly as I'd left it in February, forty pages of single-spaced crap ending with a hanging sentence I'd left unfinished.

The frequent borrowing of Austen's plotlines to fuel modern literature points

I remembered having the thought, remembered getting a phone call in the middle of it, going back to my laptop, and realizing I'd forgotten where I was headed, then shutting the computer down, figuring I'd get to it the next day. The next day, however, had been Valentine's Day, the day Peter left, and I hadn't touched the dissertation since.

I refilled my wineglass from the half-empty bottle of chardonnay sitting on the coffee table. I squinted at the time on the VCR.

11:15.

In the morning.

I sighed and reached for my cigarettes. I'd smoked briefly during my sophomore year at Georgia State, but gave it up before the end of the spring semester. I hated the panic I'd felt when the pack was almost done. I figured it was better to live without them than to deal with the constant stress of wondering when I'd get my next fix. And then there was the whole cancer thing to boot.

After Peter left the night before, after I'd opened my eyes wanting to see one face and being presented with another, I'd gone out and gotten three packs, a glass ashtray, four lighters, and two bottles of wine. It may not be ideal to crave nicotine, but at least in that case I'd know exactly what I wanted and exactly how to get it, which wasn't happening in any other area of my life.

I blazed up the lighter, watched the end of the cigarette flare up and glow orange. I inhaled. *Ah.*

I had opened the windows to clear out some of the smoke, but the shades were drawn, muting the daylight and giving the room an orange glow. I picked up the remote and hit REWIND, sending Darcy and Elizabeth back to mid-walk. I hit PLAY. Darcy turned to Elizabeth, his face tortured with love and angst.

"You are too generous a person to trifle with me. Tell me, if your feelings are the same as they were last April, I will never say another word on the subject. My feelings are unchanged."

My chest tightened at Darcy's anguished face. At his obvious love. At his blatant intention to stick.

Forever.

I picked up the remote and hit the power button, shutting off the television. That was enough of the sexy Brit.

I closed my eyes and leaned back against the couch, exhaling. The truth was, I couldn't care less about Austen or the dissertation. I'd been watching six hours of one sexy Brit because all I could think about was another sexy Brit, the one I'd given myself to last night when my eyes were closed. The one who'd given me a spectacular orgasm and didn't even know he'd done it.

I sat up and tried to shrug the tension out of my shoulders. Peter's shift would be ending at noon, when Mags returned from whatever it was she was doing in the mornings. Although he hadn't tried to make plans when I ushered him out the door the night before, I knew he'd probably be coming by. I also knew I wasn't ready to make any decisions about Peter. Maybe he had changed, maybe he hadn't. I wasn't ready to figure all that out now.

I looked over at my kitchen counter, where the ring box remained, untouched since Peter had set it there. I'd been eating and cleaning around it, but I knew it wouldn't wait there forever.

I stood up, took one last drag on the cigarette, and stubbed it out. The one thing I wanted more than anything was to get some fresh air. To walk.

To pound some nails into the east wall of Morris and Trudy Babb's barn.

Why not? I thought as my heart raced. *He said he'd missed me. He said he wanted me to keep coming by.*

And he said he wanted to just be friends.

My eyes were drawn once again, almost magnetically, to the ring box. I decided a friend was exactly what I needed and went into my room to find a fresh towel.

"Ian?" I called as I stepped into the barn, holding my hand over my eyes and squinting as my vision adjusted from the bright outdoors to the dim barn where someone was moving wood around.

"Portia, girl, that you?" Bridge stood up straight and wiped his arm against his forehead.

"Yeah. I just stopped by to help Ian with the restoration. What are you doing here?"

Bridge grinned, his white teeth shining behind the sawdust-covered moustache and beard. "Pretty much the same. Didn't feel right to let him do all the work on it, considering I'm the caretaker of the property." He sat down on the pile of wood and patted the spot next to him. "Come sit with me for a minute. I was just about to take a break."

I sat next to him, facing the east wall. Most of the lower supports were in place, and some scaffolding had been set up at the second level.

"I sure wish Trudy could see this," he said after taking a long swig of his water. "I think she'd be mighty pleased."

"Yeah." I kicked my legs out and let them fall back against the wood. "You think she'll ever come back?"

Bridge sighed. "I like to think maybe. Morris Jr.'s in Fargo and Brenda's in Wichita. She mostly summers with them and winters in Sarasota with her sister." He shook his head. "She ain't been back to this place since . . . oh, must have been the August after Morris passed. She loves the place, all right, but it's just hard for her to visit, you know. Memories can be hard on people."

I stole a glance at Bridge and gave a small smile. "I know."

He nudged me slightly with his shoulder. I nudged back. He took off his gloves, leaned over, and pulled a bag of carrots out of a cooler, and we munched in silence for a minute.

"Where's Ian?" I asked after practicing my inflection in my mind so I wouldn't sound like I cared too much. "Is he writing?"

Bridge shook his head. "No. He had some business to do with Carl Raimi. Should be back before too long."

"Carl Raimi?" The words caught in my throat as I remembered how close Ian and Carl had come to duking it out in the streets of Truly. "What kind of business?"

Bridge raised one eyebrow at me. "The kind of business that's his business to tell." He shook his head. "You're just as nosy as ever, aren't you?"

I feigned offense. "You're confusing me with Mags and Vera."

I saw something in his eyes tighten when I said Vera's name, but he recovered quickly. I might not even have noticed it if I didn't know Bridge so well.

"Portia, don't you go fooling yourself," he said quietly. "You're a Miz Fallon, just like the rest of 'em. And someday you might just realize that ain't necessarily a bad thing."

I opened my mouth to say something, then closed it. I didn't want to extend a conversation that danced around Vera if it was going to make Bridge sad.

"It's good to see you again, Bridge," I said finally. "Really good."

He reached over and ruffled my hair. "You too, kiddo."

"Portia?" A jolt ran through me at the sound of Ian's voice, and I turned my head to see him entering the barn. My face started to heat up and my heart pounded so fiercely I thought sure they'd both see it right through my T-shirt.

It wasn't him last night. It was Peter. Get a grip, Portia.

"Hey," I said, hopping down off my perch. "We were just talking about you."

Ian smiled, tossing his jacket on the spot where I'd been sitting. "Nothing bad, I hope."

"No," I said. "How's Raimi?"

Ian glanced at Bridge, then back at me.

"Seems to be well." He cleared his throat. "He's dropping the charges against your mother."

"Really?" I crossed my arms and eyed him suspiciously. "I wonder why."

Ian shrugged. "I don't know. I, uh, bumped into him in the, uh, the store . . ."

"The Piggly Wiggly," Bridge offered. I glanced at him and he looked away. Men sticking together.

"Yes, the Piggly Wiggly. I asked after his cows, and we got to talking and . . . he told me he's dropping the charges." He motioned toward the scaffolding. "Good job with the scaffolding, Bridge."

I thought about pushing the subject, delving into his obvious lie, but I didn't want to put Bridge through that. The poor guy was still in love with a Miz Fallon. He'd been through enough.

Bridge cleared his throat. "Thanks. It's a specialty."

Ian smiled at him. "I'd have been happy to help if you'd waited for me."

"I waited 'bout as long as I had the patience to wait,"

Bridge said, lowering himself off the pile of wood. "Portia'll tell you, I'm not long on patience."

Ian smiled and picked up a plank of wood. "Well, then, let's get down to work, shall we?" He looked at me and nodded toward the pegs on the back wall, where a tool belt was hanging. "I suppose you should suit up, Portia." He paused and looked at me. "Assuming you're here to work?"

I smiled. "Why else would I be here?"

"All right. I'm done. My arm is going to fall off if I hammer one more nail." I pivoted my arm around in a circle and sat down, swinging my legs over the side of the scaffolding and folding my arms over the metal support pole. Warm, fading daylight filtered through the wide opening in the south wall. Bridge had left an hour before, and Ian and I had worked at a furious pace since, just now starting to slow down.

Ian put a plank of wood on the pile and looked up at me, his eyes tight on mine.

"*She is fair,*" he said softly, "*and, fairer than that word, of wondrous virtues . . . Her name is Portia . . .*"

I stared at him for a moment, speechless. "What?"

He blinked, and seemed to snap back from wherever he'd been. "*Merchant of Venice.*"

"Yeah," I said. "I know."

We locked eyes in silence for a long moment, and then he smiled. "I've been trying to remember that quote for a while. I kept meaning to look it up. Kept forgetting. But it hit me when I looked at you just now." He laughed and lowered his eyes to his hands. "It just came back to me."

There was something twisting in my chest at the way he

looked standing there, staring at his hands. A little confused. A lot vulnerable. I wanted more than anything to hop off that scaffold and wrap myself around him, but as we were mere days away from the let's-just-be-friends bit, I opted for a sympathy subject change.

"You know," I said, "someday Marlowe's gonna get proper credit for that."

Ian laughed and leaned his rear end against the pile of wood. "Oh, you're still on about Marlowe, are you?"

"Have you not read *Dr. Faustus*? Isn't it obvious the same author wrote the plays attributed to Shakespeare?"

"Frankly, no." He grinned. "Not to me, nor to five hundred years' worth of scholars, I might add."

I huffed. "You don't think it's a coincidence that an illiterate farmer started writing works of genius in 1593, the very year that Marlowe supposedly died?"

He smiled. "Coincidence is all well and good. You have no proof."

"I'll get it."

"How?"

I gave him a playful stare through narrowed eyelids. "I'll go to England and find it. And then I'll get a big plate of crow and serve it up for you nice and hot."

His grin faded a touch, replaced by a softer, more thoughtful smile. "I'll look forward to that."

This followed by intense eye contact hurtling through an electric silence. I had to say, based on appearances, we were both sucking pretty bad at this just-friends thing.

"Beau Sr. invited us to dinner next Friday," I said.

Ian's eyebrows knit for a second, and then he let loose with a wry smile. "Oh, he settled on Friday, did he?"

"Yeah, and I was thinking, since he invited us together, kinda . . ."

Ian smiled. "What time should I pick you up?"

"Seven." I felt my face flush. Gah. "I hope you don't mind. It wouldn't be like a date-date, or anything. It's strictly friend-date material."

"A friend-date," he said, one hand clamping to the scaffolding as he pulled himself up, his head popping up next to me. "I suppose I could clear my schedule for something of that nature."

I scooted to the side to make room for him as he sat down.

"On one condition," he said as he swung his legs over the side and settled next to me.

"Oh?" I gave him a sideways look, trying not to betray the fact that my heart was skipping like Shirley Temple on amphetamines. "And what would that be?"

"That you tell me what's on your mind." His expression was more serious. I looked down at my swinging feet.

"Nothing," I said.

"Oh, come on. You've been preoccupied all afternoon. I didn't want to say anything while Bridge was here, but I am now willing to officially offer you a friend-date for your thoughts." He raised one eyebrow on *friend-date*. *Skippity skip skip skip.*

"Isn't it typically a penny?"

He grinned. "I'm a generous man."

"I don't doubt it," I said, thinking of the mystery meeting with Carl Raimi. "But really, nothing's going on."

He looked away from me and stared at a point on the opposite wall. "Is it your ex?"

"What? Peter?" I watched him for signs of jealousy. I was

about to count not meeting my eye as one, but a moment later
he turned to me and did just that.

"Yes. Peter."

This time, I looked away. "He was at the apartment waiting for me last night when I got back from the hospital. He
covered the place with rose petals. Set up candles. Poured me
some wine. He got the recipe for my favorite chicken from Vera
and had it ready for me."

There was a short silence. "Do you believe he's changed?"

I shook my head. "I don't know. Maybe. He's certainly acting different."

A longer silence. Ian sighed. "Well, I hope he turns out to
be the person you want him to be."

You mean you? I looked at Ian as the thought flew through
my mind, but said nothing. He gave my knee a brief pat and
pulled himself up to a standing position on the scaffolding,
then held out his hand to help me up.

"It's getting dark," he said. "Will you let me drive you
home?"

I took his hand and pulled myself up, letting go as soon as
I could. "Sure. Thanks."

Ian walked me up to my apartment this time and poked his
head in to make sure all was well before taking off again. I
walked over to the TV, hit the power button, and pressed PLAY,
reaching for my cigarettes with my other hand.

"My feelings are so . . . different," Elizabeth said as I lit my
cigarette. "In fact, they are quite the opposite."

I walked over to the fridge, pulled out a fresh bottle of
chardonnay, and set it on the counter. I stared at it for a while

and wondered. What if Peter had changed? What if the Mizzes were right? Or, more likely, what if resistance to all their machinations was futile?

I grabbed the bottle of wine and my keys. Only one way to find out.

"Hello?" I said, poking my head inside the front door. "Anybody home?"

They were sitting at the kitchen table, playing Scrabble. I held up the bottle of wine and smiled, as if nothing was wrong. Two can play at that game.

Peter stood up, walked over to me, and kissed me on the cheek.

"I'm glad to see you," he said.

I smiled up at him. "Yeah. I brought wine."

Peter smiled. "Perfect."

Vera and Mags grinned up at me and waved me over to the table. Bev didn't glare, which was a step up from the usual. Peter came out from the kitchen with a chair for me and they all cashed in their letters and mixed them up in the center, ready for a new game.

"So," Bev said, "to what do we owe this unexpected pleasure?"

I smiled brightly. I could be a Miz Fallon with the best of 'em. "Oh, I heard that Carl Raimi dropped the charges, and I thought I'd come over to celebrate."

Mags gasped. "He dropped the charges? Who told you that?"

"Ian told me." I piled up my letter tiles and avoided Peter's eye as he poured my wine.

"I see," Bev said. "Well, that's certainly good news."

"Yes," Vera said, smiling at me and grabbing my hand. "It's so good to have you home, baby."

"Good to be home," I said with a smile, lifting my glass. "Now let's get drunk and play us some Scrabble."

- - -

I was standing on the back porch smoking a cigarette when I heard the screen door open behind me. As a group, we'd finished off three games of Scrabble and four bottles of wine, and I was feeling good and lovely.

It was Bev. She walked up behind me and took my cigarette from me, taking a long drag and handing it back.

"Bev," I said. "I thought Doctor Bobby told you—"

"Of course Doctor Bobby told me not to smoke. He tells everybody not to smoke. I'm seventy-six, damnit, I'll have a goddamn cigarette if I want one."

I couldn't argue with that. I shook my pack and offered her one. She looked over her shoulder to see if Mags and Vera were watching, then took it and lit up. We smoked in silence for a moment, and then she spoke.

"Peter's a nice young man."

"Yes," I said. "He is."

"He's doing very well at the store. He's built us a nice window display. He's good."

I nodded. "I'm sure he is."

"You should start coming in during the days again," she said. "It's not right for a young girl to be shiftless."

I was going to argue that I was working on my dissertation, but I wasn't sure if opening the file and staring at the last sentence really qualified as "working," so I let it go.

"He's a good man," she said. I looked at her, and for the

first time that summer, I saw Bev soften a bit toward me. "You could do worse."

"I know," I said softly. The screen door opened and Bev shot her cigarette to the ground. I stepped on it inconspicuously as Peter stepped outside.

"We've decided as a group that you're too drunk to drive, Portia. So, I've volunteered to walk you home."

I smiled, took a final drag off my cigarette, and stepped forward. "I'll get my jacket."

"Portia?" Peter asked. We'd gone halfway to the Page in silence. I knew he was working up to something.

"Yes?" I asked.

"I was hoping that you might let me take you out to dinner. Sometime. Maybe Friday?"

I thought about the dinner with Beauji's parents. "How about Thursday?"

"Okay." We walked a few more steps.

"Where?" I asked.

"Hmmm?"

"Where are you taking me to dinner?"

"Does it matter?"

I shrugged. "Yes."

"I hear there's a nice Italian place in Ringgold, Villa Pastoli."

I narrowed my eyes at him. "Vera been helping you do more research?"

"No. Why?"

"That's my favorite restaurant," I said warily. "You didn't find out from her?"

He shook his head and looked down at his feet. "No, actu-

ally. I just remembered that Italian was always your favorite."
He met my eye. "I did pay attention to some things, you know."

"I know," I said, too quickly.

He paused for a minute. I wrapped my arms around my
stomach as my chardonnay high started to wane.

"We don't have to go," he said. "It's not a big deal. I understand."

"No," I said. "No. I'd like to go. Really."

He gave me a small smile. "Really? It's okay? I don't want
to pressure you."

I smiled back. "No pressure. Should I meet you at the
Mizzes'?"

"No," he said, giving me a wink. "Let me come pick you up."

The last time I'd let a man do that, it had turned into something of a disaster. But since Peter and I were pretty much
steeped in disaster anyway, it seemed a reasonable gamble.

"Okay."

He grinned. "Great. Thursday it is, then. Seven okay?"

"Great." I stepped up onto the steps below the apartment.
"Thanks for walking me home."

He smiled. "No problem."

He paused for a second. "Good night, then."

"Good night."

He turned around, took a few steps, then turned back. "Oh,
I almost forgot. A woman named Rhonda called for you. I
guess she's subletting your apartment?"

"Rhonda. Yes," I said, a vision of Rhonda floating to my
mind. Blond. Mid-fifties. Secretary for the head of the English
Department at Syracuse. Will go to embarrassing lengths not
to end a sentence in a preposition. Recently left her husband,
thus the sublet. "What did she want?"

"I don't know. Just said for you to call her."

"Okay. Thanks."

Peter stood there for a minute, watching me, then said, "Okay, then. I'll see you on Thursday."

I smiled. "See you."

I watched him walk away, then leaned against the wall by the stairs, trying to focus my eyes on the stars over my head. He was a good-looking man, Peter. I had to give him that. And what harm could an innocent little dinner do? Nothing terribly significant could happen; I was coated in Penis Teflon, after all. Peter, Ian, and my father were all proof of that. As a matter of fact, I would have hardly been surprised if Peter was taking me out specifically for the purpose of retracting his proposal.

I walked up the stairs and entered the house, horrified at the mess that was my living room. I picked up the trash can and headed for the coffee table where the overflowing ashtray and empty chardonnay bottles surrounding my untouched laptop told the story of how I'd spent the last few days. I picked up the ashtray and dumped it into the trash.

"I'll bet that's exactly why he's taking me out," I said out loud, relief washing through me as I considered the idea of Peter taking it all back, saying he didn't mean it, that he intended to run off to Boston and I should just forget he ever showed up here at all.

I stood up straight, trash still in my hand, remembering how quickly he'd made his escape after our interlude the other night.

Oh, my god.

It was classic Peter; once things started going his way, he backed off. He'd done it with our relationship, he'd done it with the writing.

And he was doing it again now. It made perfect sense. He was going to retract the proposal. I could feel it in my bones.

"Bastard." I swiped an empty bottle of chardonnay off the coffee table and into the trash can, trying to work up some anger. It didn't come. I put the trash by the door and wandered into my bedroom, falling asleep to thoughts of old flames and British Flyers.

"How's that eggplant?" Peter asked. I looked down at my plate. I'd had one small bite and was still chewing.

"Mmmmm," I said, swallowing. "And your lasagna?"

Peter looked down at his plate. The lasagna was untouched. He sighed and looked up at me.

"Portia, we need to talk."

I touched both sides of my mouth with my napkin and placed it to the side of my plate. *Here we go.*

"I think I've made a mistake."

And there it was. Penis Teflon. Like magic. I should set up a sideshow act. Have a Web site with a live Web cam so people could watch it happen. For a small fee, of course. Turn Penis Teflon from a curse into the source of my livelihood. When life gives you lemons . . .

"I rushed down here with this idea in my head that you'd be happy to have me back, and I see that isn't the case." He held his hands up to silence me before I could respond. "And that's all right. It was unrealistic." He sighed. "I'd just like to know that I haven't messed everything up to the point where we can't . . . be friends."

"It's okay, Peter," I said. "I understand. The ring is back at my apartment. You can pick it up tonight." I picked up my fork and poked at my eggplant.

He deflated and sat back. "So . . . that's your decision?"

I looked up from my plate. "What? No. That's *your* decision."

He shook his head. "No, it's not."

"I'm sorry?"

He leaned forward. "I think you've misunderstood. I still want to marry you, if you'll have me. My mistake was in the way I've gone about everything."

I felt the eggplant stick in my throat and I grabbed my water. "You mean, you didn't take me out to dinner to retract your proposal?"

Peter's face fell. "Is that what you thought?"

"Well . . . yeah."

"Why?"

"Well . . ." I stammered. "You disappeared pretty quick the other night. You know, after . . ."

He blinked. "You asked me to leave. I gave you your space."

"By moving in with my family? By taking over the family business?"

"Oh, man," he said, reaching forward and taking my hand. "I'm sorry, Portia. I really am. I wasn't trying to crowd you. I was trying to show you . . ." He trailed off and rubbed his hand over his face. "I've screwed this all up."

"No, it's not that. I guess I just don't understand."

I didn't. He wasn't dumping me. He was moving from Boston to be in Truly, Georgia, where he would be running a bookstore. None of it made any sense.

"What about your writing?" I asked.

He took a drink of his wine. "Well, obviously, I'm not the kind of writer who can live without a day job. And then your mother called, offering one—"

"Offering *me*," I said, stabbing at my meal.

He sighed. "It's not like that, Portia."

I put my fork down. "What is it like, then? You tell me."

He put his fork down as well, and looked at me. "It's like a life. It's stable. A reliable income, a home. I couldn't just live off you forever, writing and making you miserable."

I blinked. "What?"

"Oh, come on, Portia. I knew I was making you unhappy. I was so absorbed in my writing. It was all about me and I didn't . . . think about you enough, I guess. You were miserable. Did you think I couldn't see that?"

"See what?"

"Oh, come on," he said. "I was a failure. You knew it. I knew it."

I felt my breath rush out of me. I knew that Peter had thought of himself as a failure. It never occurred to me that he thought I agreed.

But he did.

Peter put his fork down without taking a bite, then looked up on my silence. "Portia?"

"Did I make you feel like a failure, Peter?"

Peter shook his head. "No. No."

"Don't be polite," I said. "This is important. Did I make you feel like a failure?"

Peter sat back. "You can't *make* anyone feel anything, Portia. They have to choose to—"

"Peter. Please."

Peter leaned forward and took my hand. His eyes were sad, and as I looked at them, it was like I'd never really seen them before.

Maybe I hadn't.

"I know you didn't mean to," he said, his voice soft and conciliatory. "But you were right. I *was* a failure."

I pulled my hand away. "I never said you were a failure."

Peter shook his head. "No, of course not." He paused, started speaking to his salad. "It's just that . . . well, the fact that the book didn't sell always seemed to bother you so much."

"Well, of course," I jumped in. "It was a great book."

"Was it?" He shrugged. "Maybe. I don't know."

I felt ice go down my back. "It was."

He sighed.

"What?" I asked.

He locked his eyes on my face. "When I got a great review, you never said a word. But whenever the sales numbers came in . . ."

I blinked. I remembered going to the school computers, looking up his sales on Amazon.com, coming home incensed. I remembered reading the rave he got in *Publishers Weekly* and, instead of hailing his success, I ranted about the average reader's inability to differentiate good writing from the crap scribbled on the bathroom wall at a college bar.

I had thought I was being supportive.

Peter rubbed his fingers against his forehead. "I just didn't feel like I could do anything right. I felt myself pulling away. I felt you pulling away. And I loved you, but I didn't know how to . . ."

I swallowed, trying to get rid of the tightness in my throat. "How to what?"

Peter looked up at me. His eyes were misty. "How to be with you, I guess. I didn't know what you needed from me, and I was sure whatever it was I wouldn't be able to give it to you." He cleared his throat and blinked. "But I think I can now. And that's why I'm here. I'm going to run your family's bookstore here in Truly. And I hope you'll be here with me."

Forever. That was the subtext. I swallowed and said nothing. Peter stared at his plate.

"I don't know if that's what you want, Portia," he said after a long silence. "But since it's the only thing I haven't tried, I'm going for it."

I managed to get through the rest of the dinner and a short, lips-only kiss at the front door before I freaked out. As soon as I had the door shut behind me, I grabbed a cigarette, lit up, and began to pace the floor of my apartment.

I had made him feel like a failure.

I had pushed him away.

I had pushed *him* away.

Yes, granted, he should have told me this before he left. And I'll admit, scribbling a breakup into the front page of a book—especially his own—is seriously questionable behavior. But that stuff didn't matter as much to me anymore. What mattered was the fact that I had been so full of my own helpless victimization that it hadn't occurred to me that I'd contributed as much—if not more—to our breakup than he had.

I wasn't coated in Penis Teflon. I *was* Penis Teflon. Memories flooded in as I lit my next cigarette with the burning embers of my last one. Peter being so excited about getting published. Peter opening his box of advance copies and holding one out as if it were the Holy Grail. Peter saying that he didn't care if it sold. Afterward, when he'd retreated into silent sulks and severe avoidance, I figured he had lied about not caring.

But that wasn't it.

He cared that I cared.

I'd made him feel like a failure.

And I hadn't even known I'd done it.

I thought about Vera and Bridge. Mags and Jack. Bev and my grandfather, who had been mentioned so infrequently in my presence that I wasn't even sure his name was Henry. What if Penis Teflon wasn't a curse, or a chemical thing, but rather a learned behavior? Something the Miz Fallons passed down from one generation to the next, without even realizing it?

Without even realizing it. *I* hadn't realized it. Maybe Vera hadn't, either. Or Mags. Or Bev. Maybe we'd all learned it from each other, each of us reinforcing the behavior in each other. Invasion of the Common Sense Snatchers.

"If that's the case," I said, pointing my cigarette out between my fingers and jabbing it in the air at no one, "then we can unlearn it."

I giggled as I pressed the cigarette down in the ashtray. My heart was jerking around in my rib cage, fueled by adrenaline and fear and not a little nicotine, but mostly by hope.

I stood up and took in a deep breath.

Hope. It was like a bright shaft of light illuminating dusty corners of my mind I'd never bothered to look for.

Hope. There was hope.

I grabbed my jacket and slammed the door behind me, rushing down the stairs to get into the Page, where I planned to call the Mizzes for an emergency family meeting.

chapter ten

"Thanks for coming over so quickly," I said, picking up two mugs of coffee to hand to the Mizzes, who sat in the easy chairs circling the coffee bar at the Page. The shop was closed and lit only by the streetlights outside the front window, but none of us made a move to turn on the indoor lights.

Bev frowned and kept her hands in her lap, refusing the coffee I offered. Vera clasped her hands around her mug as her elbows rested on her knees, an expression of deep concentration on her face as she watched me. Mags smiled her typical enthusiastic smile, accepting the coffee I offered even though I knew she had no intention of actually drinking it.

Okay. I inhaled deeply and dove in.

"Look, I have something I need to talk to you guys about. Something important."

I leaned my backside against the coffee bar, my fingers grasping the edge of the counter behind me. "I think I've figured out the Penis Teflon."

Bev's eyes narrowed at me. "The *what?*"

"Penis Teflon," Mags said.

"You know, how men don't stick to Miz Fallons," Vera said. "Portia calls it Penis Teflon."

"It's not important what it's called," I said, keeping my eyes on Bev, who was hands down my toughest customer. "What's important is that I think I've figured it out. But I need your help."

The Mizzes stared at me, saying nothing. I pulled a bar stool closer to them and sat, leaning forward, talking with my hands, hoping my enthusiasm would spark some in them.

"See, all this time, I thought it was a curse driving all the men away, or some sort of . . . aura, or smell, or something . . ."

Bev raised her eyes to mine and blinked heavily. "Smell?"

"Or something," I said. "But now, I think . . . I think it's us. Our behavior. Our choices. We probably don't even realize we do it. I didn't with Peter, but after talking to him at dinner tonight, it's like—BOOM!—I suddenly understand, you know?"

Mags grinned. "How was dinner? Did you have a good time?"

"Yes," I said. "But that's not what I'm talking about. It's about how we broke up. That whole mess . . . I thought I was totally innocent, and it turns out I wasn't. I was doing things I didn't realize I was doing, and I drove him away."

I paused. They stared. I hadn't anticipated how hard it would be to ask what I was going to ask, but based on Bev's expression I'd spent whatever currency I'd made in her good graces the other night, so I didn't have much to lose by continuing.

"So, I need to know . . ." I said, my eyes connecting with each of them before I continued, "what happened. With all of you, I mean." Bev shifted in her seat. I estimated the chances at fair to middlin' that she was fixing to hand me my ass on a platter. I held my hand up to silence her.

"Look, I know you probably think this is a load of crap, but hear me out, Bev. I can't stop the pattern if I don't know how it started. I don't know anything about you and my grandfather. I'm not even entirely sure his name was Henry."

Bev's eyes iced over as I said the name. I hurried to switch my attention to Mags. "And Mags, I know you don't want to tell me, but you and Jack . . . I need to know what happened."

Mags focused on smoothing her skirt over her legs. I turned to Vera, who was watching me intently.

"And Vera . . . What about you and Bridge?"

Vera kept eye contact but didn't say anything. I felt a cold sweat break out on my neck. All wrong. I was handling this all wrong. I got up and began to pace the floor in front of them, searching my mind for another tactic, something that would work, some secret handshake that would allow me into their world, that would help me understand. All these years, we'd never discussed these things, and it was scary territory. For me as much as them. But I needed to know, damnit.

I needed to know.

I stopped pacing and slowly moved my eyes from Miz to Miz.

"Look," I said, "y'all are always saying that you want me to be happy. If I'm gonna be happy, with Peter or with anyone, I need to know what I've been doing that's been making me unhappy. You can help me. Just tell me your stories. It was all a long time ago, but I'm going through this now, and I need your help."

There was a pin-drop silence. Finally, Bev stood up, her eyes swimming in fury, her index finger pointed at me like a gun.

"Let me tell you something," she said, her voice scratching the muddy bottom of her range, "just because you can't make a relationship work, do not turn around and blame it on us. Peter wants to marry you and care for you, and you keep putting him off, and then you have the nerve to come to us talking about Penis Teflon?"

I didn't know what to say. I'd pissed Bev off a fair amount

in my day, but I'd never seen her this angry. Her lips trembled.
Her jaw clenched. She lowered her shaky index finger and took
a step toward me. I half expected her to slap me across the face.
Instead, she just locked her steely blue eyes on mine.

"And don't you dare ever mention your grandfather's name
in my presence again. You hear me, child?"

I nodded, feeling like a terrified six-year-old. She tightened
her grip on her sweater and walked out, slamming the door
behind her, the bells jangling nervously in her wake. I stared at
the door, heat shimmering in my eyes. I swiped my hand over
my face and looked at Mags and Vera.

"Well. What about you two?"

Mags hesitated for a moment, then stood up. Her eyes were
watery and her smile was gone. Without a word, she walked out,
her unholy red pumps making almost no sound as she made her
way out of the Page. I watched as the door closed behind her,
waiting for the bells to stop jingling before I spoke again.

"Go on, Vera," I said. "I'll make sure everything's locked up."

She was quiet for a minute, then said, "You were right, you
know."

"Me? Right? When?"

"When you said I should know better. You were right. I do
know better." She inhaled and looked up at me. "But Mags and
Bev don't, and their stories are their stories. But, if it would help
you to know what happened with Bridge and me, then I'll tell
you."

"It would help, Vera," I said as I settled myself in the chair
next to hers. "It really, really, really would."

She gave me a sad smile. "But first you've got to tell me why."

I rubbed my fingers over my eyes, feeling suddenly drained
to exhaustion. "What?"

Vera watched me for a moment. "Why is this so important?"

"Because," I said, choosing the first reason that came to mind, "Peter told me that he left because I made him feel like a failure."

She shook her head. "That's not the reason."

I blinked. Looked up at the ceiling. Shrugged. Looked back at Vera. "Because I don't really want a cat?"

She rolled her eyes. "Aw, girl, you're not even trying."

"Good God, Vera. Why don't you just tell me what answer you want because I don't know what it is."

Vera leaned over the side of her chair and stared me down. "I think you do."

I felt light shed on a thought that had been hovering in a dark corner of my mind. "Because if I don't understand what the Penis Teflon is all about, I'll lose him, and I don't want to lose him."

She nodded knowingly. "That's the one."

She didn't ask me who I was talking about. Either she assumed I meant Peter, or it didn't matter. Either way, I was grateful for the stay of execution. I wasn't entirely sure myself.

"I've known Bridge since high school," Vera said, leaning back in her chair and settling her delicate hands over her stomach, "but we didn't start seeing each other until Bev hired him to install the shelves in the back of the store."

"I remember," I said. I'd been in the sixth grade at the time and had thought it funny how Bridge kept coming back to make sure the shelves were level.

"Yes," she said. "Anyway, not long after you went away to college, he asked me to marry him."

I blinked. "He what?" No one had told me this part.

"Anyway, I wasn't sure what to do," Vera said. "So, I did a Tarot card reading, and the reading said no. And I told Bridge I couldn't marry him."

Her voice was starting to waver. I stayed quiet until she was ready to go on.

"He asked me why not, and when I told him about the reading, he got angry. We didn't speak for years, and now, when we see each other . . . Well. We're civil."

I waited a minute before asking my next question.

"Did you love him?"

She smiled a faraway smile, as if reliving an old memory. "Yes."

"Then why did you pay attention to the Tarot reading? Why didn't you just marry him anyway?"

"Listen, honey, if you go into it with intent, the Tarot will read whatever way you want it to. That Tarot reading didn't say no. I did." She sighed and leaned her head back on the chair, staring at the ceiling. "I was scared. When Bridge and I fought, I could never feel right again until we'd made up. It scared me, needing one person so much that if they ever up and left . . ." She gave a small laugh. "I guess you weren't the only one who'd noticed the Penis Teflon."

I sat back in my chair. "Do you think that's what I did with Peter? Pushed him away because I was scared?"

Vera shrugged. "Only you know that for sure. What do you think?"

I sighed. "I don't know."

"Well," Vera said, pushing herself up from her easy chair. "I'll leave you to yourself to figure that out."

I got up and pulled her into a hug, resting my cheek on her shoulder like a little girl.

"Thanks, Vera."

She patted my back, pulled away, and cupped my chin in her hand. "You tell me what you find out, okay?"

I smiled. "Okay."

I watched her leave, shutting the door carefully behind her and tucking her hands into the crooks of her elbows as she headed back in the direction of the house. I waited a few minutes, then followed her out, closing and locking the door behind me before dragging myself up the outside stairs to my apartment. I brushed my teeth, thinking about Bridge and Vera and how I was almost sure they both still loved each other, and how Bridge's pride and Vera's fear had cost them eleven years that might have otherwise been happy.

Or that could have led to pain and loss and heartbreak anyway, like Mags and Jack.

I spit and rinsed and looked at myself in the mirror

"It's all a big, stupid crapshoot," I said to my reflection. My reflection didn't seem to be buying that line.

"Oh, what the hell do you know?" I said, turning out the light in the bathroom and heading for bed.

"Portia! Ian!" Beauji's mom, Wendy, clapped her hands after opening the front door. "We're so glad you could make it!" She took Ian's bottle of wine and the baby gift basket I'd brought and grinned up at us.

"Oh, you didn't have to bring anything, honey, but thank you." She motioned with her head toward the living room. "Everyone's in there. I'll be right with y'all."

I felt Ian's hand on the small of my back as we moved into the house, and I was glad I decided against jeans and went with the sheer blue summer dress the Mizzes had given me when I got into town. I had to admit it was gratifying when I caught Ian tugging at his collar after he picked me up.

Beau Sr., Davey, and Beauji were in the living room, all

crouched over the bassinet where, judging by the relative quiet, baby Miles was sleeping.

"Well, hello, you two." Beau Sr. popped up when he saw us. He engulfed me in a hug, kissing me on the cheek and lifting me off my feet, then reached out to shake Ian's hand.

"I have to thank you two again for taking care of my baby." He glanced over at Beauji and winked, then turned back to Ian and me.

"Not at all," Ian said. "Glad we could help."

"Bridge couldn't make it tonight, so Daddy sent him five pounds of peaches," Beauji said, waving us over to the empty spaces on the couch next to her. "I think y'all got the better end of the deal."

Davey grabbed Ian's arm as he was about to sit down. "I have to warn you, man," he said, glancing quickly over his shoulder toward the kitchen, "Wendy's a huge fan. She's read all your books and she actually changed her dress four times in the last half hour."

"Really?" Ian said, quirking an eyebrow at me.

"Don't look at me," I said, smiling back at him. "I had no idea."

Beau Sr. stepped forward and clapped Ian on the shoulder. "She's promised to behave herself, but my lovely bride is known for behaving however she damn well pleases."

My lovely bride. Hearing Beau Sr. talk about his wife was like standing next to a blazing hearth in winter. I smiled at Beauji, who rolled her eyes affectionately.

"So it's a decent bet she'll be making you sign a pile of books," Davey said.

"Or posing for endless Polaroid pictures she can show off in town tomorrow," Beauji added.

"My bride," Beau Sr. said, leaning in toward Ian, "is an enthusiastic woman."

That was an understatement. Wendy had been famous for doing the cheers from the bleachers along with Beauji and the rest of the squad at all the home football games. And some of the aways.

Ian grinned. "It's no problem. I'm terribly flattered, really."

Wendy entered the room at that moment with a tray of hors d'oeuvres. She watched Ian as she toured the room with the platter, finally breaking after he complimented her on the stuffed mushrooms. She put the platter down and placed one hand on his arm.

"I'm just such a huge fan," she gushed. "I read *Clean Sweep* at least five times, and I just think you're one of the most talented writers I've ever read."

"Thank you, Wendy," he said, putting his hand over hers. "You're very kind to say so. I do hope you'll allow me to sign your copy while I'm here."

"Copies," Davey coughed into his hand. Beauji smacked his leg. Wendy grinned and clasped her hands together.

"Oh, really? Would you?" she squealed, practically hopping up and down. "That would be oh so wonderful! They're right down here, in the den."

Ian started down the hallway and Wendy practically skipped after him, turning back to squeal in excitement at us before following him. I didn't realize how big my smile was until I turned to Beauji and saw hers. Davey and Beau Sr. looked at each other.

"I don't know about you, son," Beau Sr. said. "But I need me a drink."

"Right behind you. Portia?"

"Gin and tonic," I said.

He blew a quick kiss at Beauji. "And I'll be bringing the nursing mother the stiffest ginger ale in the house."

As the men left, I stood up and looked down over Miles, sleeping in his portable bassinet. Beauji got up and stood next to me.

"Is he or is he not the most beautiful baby ever?" she asked.

"He is," I said. Although it had only been two weeks, he was distinctly less puggish looking. That had to be a good sign.

Beauji bit her lower lip and spoke quietly. "I got Jack's phone number and home address."

I straightened up and turned to her. "You're kidding."

Beauji shook her head.

"I found him in the online white pages. He's living in Tuscaloosa." She leaned over the bassinet and picked up Miles's baby bag, pulling a little yellow piece of paper from the front pocket.

"You don't have to call him, but if you decide you want to, which I predict you will, it's there."

I stared at her, all the warm fuzziness of the last few minutes practically obliterated by the small square of yellow paper in my hand. Beauji clasped her hand over mine and looked into my eyes.

"You're going to be just fine, darlin'," she said. "Now put that in your pocket and don't you think about it again until you're ready. We're going to have a good time tonight."

I gave her a small smile as the rest of the party flooded back into the room on cue. Davey pressed my drink into my hand and I sipped it gratefully.

"You seemed a little quiet at dinner," Ian said as he shut the car door behind him. "Is everything all right?"

"Yeah," I said. "You were great with Wendy. I think you made her year."

He started up the engine and shrugged. "It was nothing."

"Not to her, it wasn't." I watched the trees and the houses float by as Ian drove us out of the neighborhood and toward town. "You don't like attention, do you?"

"What makes you say that?"

"Well, for starters, you don't write under your own name." I leaned my head against the window. "And you didn't tell me who you were at first."

"That's because I'm not anybody."

I pulled my head up and looked over at him. "Sure you are. You're a famous millionaire writer."

He raised an eyebrow at me. "Who told you that?"

"Everybody knows it."

He laughed. "Writers don't make as much money as you'd think."

"But the movies . . ."

"I'm a comfortable, moderately well-known writer, that's all. And weren't we talking about you?"

"We're always talking about me. I want to talk about you."

I could see the muscles working in his jaw as he made the turn onto Main. He pulled up in front of the Page. I made no move to get out of the car. He shut off the engine and we sat in the pool of light coming from the streetlamp.

"I'm not sure what you'd like to know," he said finally.

"I want to know why you don't like the attention you get for being a famous millionaire—"

He held up one hand. I nodded concession.

"A comfortable, moderately well-known writer."

He sighed, staring out at the empty street in front of him. "I guess I've always felt somewhat . . . apologetic for what I write."

"Why?" I asked, but I knew damn well why. He'd told me his father had been a lit professor, and I knew what the typical lit prof felt about genre fiction. It had been my own reaction, at first.

I put my hand on his shoulder.

"If it helps at all," I said, "I'm as snobby as anyone, and I think your books are great."

He smiled at me. "Well, we're friends. You like me, so you like my writing."

I shook my head. "It's not that—"

He shrugged, and my hand fell off his shoulder, trailing down to his elbow. He smiled and squeezed my hand.

"You're very kind."

"I think your father would have been proud of you," I said, surprised when I heard the thought come out in real words. Having been without a father my entire life, I knew how powerful a comment like that could be when a parent wasn't around to say it themselves. And typically, how unwelcome.

"I'm sorry," I said. "I'm tired and I don't know what I'm saying. I'm going to go."

I opened the car door and had one foot out the door when Ian spoke again.

"Thank you, Portia."

I turned back to see him watching me, his eyes intense with . . . something. Something private. Something his own. I scooted back into the car, leaned over, and pressed my lips lightly to his for a second, using all my will to pull back before it went any further.

"You're welcome."

We stared at each other for a moment. His chin moved toward me, and then he pulled back. Just a touch, just enough for me to see that we were both sharing the same conflict. I put my finger to his lips.

"It's okay. You were right, about us. About it not making sense. Bad timing, yadda yadda yadda. But I can't have a comfortable, moderately well-known writer in town for a whole summer and not kiss him at least once, right? I'm a Miz Fallon. I have a reputation to protect."

I pulled my eyes away and got out, deliberately not looking at him as I crossed in front of the car and headed toward my apartment. If I'd looked at him, I would have gone home with him. And I was pretty sure he would have taken me.

And then he would leave, and there's only so much Penis Teflon a girl can stand in one lifetime.

"Hey, Rhonda, it's Portia." I leaned over the back office desk, my hand playing with the pen jar in the little pool of light from the green library lamp. I glanced out the open office door. It was a quarter after eight, and the Mizzes didn't typically stop by after closing at seven, but I was still a little nervous. I'd had the little yellow piece of paper with Jack's name on it for a week, and had snuck down every night to call. Every night I went to bed without doing it.

The night before, I'd picked up the phone and listened to the dial tone before hanging up.

Tonight I called Rhonda, the English department secretary who'd sublet my apartment in Syracuse. Hey, progress is still progress, right?

"Portia!" Rhonda said. "How are you?"

"Great," I lied. Well, it wasn't entirely a lie. If you discounted romance, family, and career, things were just peachy. "How about you?"

"Okay," she said. "I haven't found a new apartment yet, but

the judge ordered the Rotten Bastard to pay me eight hundred a month to cover it, so that's good."

Rhonda's husband, before the divorce, had been named John.

"I heard you tried to call me," I said.

"Oh, yes, you have a message." I heard some papers ruffling in the background. "Where is it . . . Where is it . . . ? I have to apologize, Portia, things here are a bit of a mess. I promise I'll get it cleaned up before you get home, though. Oh, here it is. Jack called."

I sat up straight. "Jack? Jack who?"

Rhonda hummed for a moment as she thought. "I want to say Triplesec, but I don't think that's it."

I swallowed. "Tripplehorn?"

"Yes!" I could hear the slap of Rhonda's hand against my kitchen counter. "Thank you. That was driving me crazy. Anyway, I didn't tell him where you were. You know, in case he was a stalker or something." I heard her take a bite of something crunchy. I envisioned carrots. "He left a number. Do you want it?"

"No," I said. "Thanks. I have it. Were there any other messages for me?"

Rhonda hummed again. "Nothing I can think of."

"Okay. Great. Thanks, Rhonda."

I hung up and walked over to the office door, staring out into the Page. The sun was setting, glazing everything in an orange glow. I stepped out into the shop and walked between the shelves, holding my fingers out to graze both sides at once, the way I had when I was a little girl. It was easier to do now.

It was a hell of a coincidence, chickening out of calling my father only to get a message from him. It was a convergence, as Vera would say.

It was a sign.

And I was a coward.

"Are you busy?" I held up a bottle of wine as Ian opened the front door. "I need to drink and Beauji's nursing, so . . ."

I gave him my most winning smile. He laughed and stepped aside, letting me in. I headed into the kitchen and began opening drawers, looking for a corkscrew.

"How's the book coming?"

Ian leaned against the kitchen doorway, watching me with a small smile. "Excellent, actually. Almost done."

I focused my attention on rummaging through a drawer. "And when you're done . . ."

I trailed off. He looked away.

"I go back to England."

"Yeah," I said, trying to reason away the icy panic that shot through me at the thought. I mean, it's not like I didn't know he'd be going back. So there was no reason why my hands should suddenly be shaking.

No reason at all.

"Well." I shut the drawer with my hip. "That makes sense."

We looked at each other for a moment. I felt a desperate thirst for wine. I opened another drawer, blinking furiously as I rifled through it. No corkscrew. I forced a laugh as the panic rose. "Please tell me I'm not going to have to open this wine with my teeth."

Ian stepped forward, moved me out of the way, and slid open a drawer to my left. He pulled out a corkscrew and straightened up, looking down at me as he slowly shut the drawer with his knee. A smile played on one side of his mouth. I could feel a sheen of sweat forming on the back of my neck as my heart rate kicked up.

"Hey, hey," Ian said softly, his eyebrows knitting in concern as tears fell down my cheeks. He dropped the corkscrew onto the counter and put his hands on my shoulders. I lowered my head. Ian tucked a finger up under my chin and pulled my face up to look at him, his eyes searching mine.

"You must think I'm the weepiest person on the planet," I said, swiping at my face.

"Oh, not at all." His smile quirked up at one side. "I'm certain in a world of over six billion people that there are likely hundreds out there weepier than you. Possibly thousands, even."

My small laugh turned into a series of staccato sobs. Ian ran his hand over my hair and settled it on the back of my neck, his thumb rubbing into my shoulder, calming me.

"My father called me," I gurgled finally. "I got the message today. I haven't talked to him yet, but . . ."

"But you will, and it'll be fine."

I looked up at him. "It will?"

He smiled. "I promise."

More tears rained down. Ian lowered his head to look into my eyes. "I take it there's more?"

"Yes," I said, the tears coming with ferocity now. "Bev hates me."

"I'm sure that's not true," he said.

"It's true," I sniffled. "I asked her about the Penis Teflon and she yelled at me and stormed out. She hasn't spoken to me in a week."

Ian put his hands on either side of my face, using his thumbs to wipe my cheeks. "She loves you. She'll recover."

I felt a hitch in my breathing as I looked into his eyes. His smile faded a touch, his thumbs slowing as they moved over my cheeks. I could hear his heart hammering in his chest. Or maybe that was mine. We were so close I couldn't be sure. One of his hands moved over and tucked a strand of hair behind my ear.

Oh, God.

"And then there's . . . Peter," I said, the words tumbling over each other to get out, as though they couldn't wait to screw things up. Ian paused for a moment, then lowered his hands and stepped away from me, reaching for the corkscrew.

"What about Peter?" he asked, his voice cool and even.

"We . . . we had dinner," I stammered, wishing to God and all the saints that I had just kept my big, stupid mouth shut.

"How did that go?" he asked, his voice flat.

"Okay, actually." I took a deep breath and swiped the last of the wetness from my face. "Although it turns out our breakup was really all my fault."

Ian popped the cork. "How so?"

"I sabotaged him. I made him feel like a failure."

I could see his jaw tighten as he poured the wine. "He told you that, did he?"

"Well, not in so many words, but it's true. I remember now, the things I did, and it makes so much sense. I can't believe I didn't see it before."

Ian handed me a glass and shook his head. "He's quite the fellow, isn't he?"

I took a gulp of wine. It cut through my throat, but the instant softening afterward was worth it. "What's that supposed to mean?"

"You don't find it interesting, how he shirks all responsibility for the collapse of the relationship, simultaneously making you grateful to take the blame?"

"He didn't . . . shirk." I said, trying to regain my hold on what had seemed so logical only moments before. "But it sheds some light on the whole Penis Teflon thing, don't you think?"

"Frankly, no." Ian downed half his glass and gave me a sharp look. "It certainly sheds some light on Peter, though."

"Oh, yeah?" I crossed my arms over my chest. "How so?"

He looked at me like I was the stupidest person on the planet. "He abandons you with a note, scribbled in—of all places—his own book. You hear not a word from him for four months, and then he's proposing on your doorstep, as though you should be happy to have him back. Then he takes you to dinner and convinces you the breakup was all your fault. And you don't see anything wrong with any of this?"

"Well," I stammered, not sure if I was defending Peter or myself. "It's complicated. There's more . . . involved than what you know about. We have . . . a history . . ."

Ian rolled his eyes and gave a cynical laugh.

"Just what exactly is your problem, anyway?"

"I don't have a problem," he said through clenched teeth. "I'm just asking reasonable questions. It might behoove you to do the same."

"It might *behoove* me?" I said. "What the hell is that supposed to mean?"

"It means it would be in your best interests—"

"You know that's not what I meant!" My voice was loud enough now to bounce off the hard kitchen surfaces.

"I *know* what you meant," he said, matching my decibel level, "and if I must explain myself, it means that Peter is a narcissistic asshole and perhaps you should take that into consideration before you run off and bloody marry him!"

He stopped. His breathing was uneven, and there were red patches on his cheeks. He rubbed his forehead with one hand, and his voice was soft when he spoke again.

"Excuse me for a moment, will you?"

He headed out, leaving the kitchen door swinging behind him. I closed my eyes, not knowing what to do. Follow him? Wait there? Sneak out the back and run home and duck under the covers, refusing to come out until everything made sense or I was too old to care?

I pushed through the swinging door. The dining room and living room were empty. I poked my head out the front door and saw Ian sitting on the porch swing, lit only by the soft glow coming through the window. I closed the door behind me, and waited for him to say something. When he didn't, I spoke.

"I'm not going to marry him," I said.

Ian didn't move. "Have you given him the ring back?"

I didn't say anything. Ian stared out at the trees flanking the property and twirled his wineglass absently in his fingers. "Then you haven't exactly declined, now have you?"

"What does that have to do with anything, Ian?"

He glanced up at me, and then looked away. "You're my friend. I see you making what I think is a tremendous mistake. I find it hard to believe you'd want me to keep quiet on something like that."

"I wouldn't." I paused and took a deep breath. "I wouldn't want you to keep quiet about anything."

I could feel my heart rate kick up as I said the words. I couldn't tell what he was thinking, only that whatever it was, he wasn't going to share it with me.

"Good night, Ian." I set my wineglass down on the porch railing and headed toward the steps.

"Wait."

I stopped.

Ian's eyes raised to mine. "Please."

We stared at each other for a moment, then he motioned

toward the space next to him on the porch swing. I walked over and sat down, staring ahead as the trees turned into a blackened silhouette against the darkening sky.

"I'm sorry, Portia. I shouldn't have reacted that way. I was completely out of line."

"It's okay," I said.

"It's not," he said. "But I thank you for your generosity."

We exchanged simple smiles, neither of us able to maintain the eye contact for too long before we stared back out at the trees.

"Take your time finishing that novel, okay?" I hung my head as the heat rose behind my eyes. "Who am I going to run to when I'm all weepy and stupid if you're not around?"

I nudged my knee playfully against his. He nudged back, then looked up at me with a smile that quickly faded.

"Hey, no," he said, reaching up and wiping a stray tear from my cheek. His voice was barely above a whisper. "Now what's that about?"

I forced myself to meet his eye. His hand snaked around to the back of my neck, and he pulled me toward him, kissing me on my forehead.

"We'll stay in touch," he said. "We'll be transatlantic pen pals. You can tell me stories of your barmy family . . ."

I chuckled and leaned my head against his shoulder. He put his arm around me and rested his head on mine.

". . . and I'll send you proper tea and biscuits. It'll all be quite lovely, actually. Don't you think?"

I didn't think. I couldn't think. I just sat there, taking comfort in his touch as his hand stroked from my shoulder to my elbow and back again. We rocked on the swing in silence for a while until I finally got up to go home, and he let me, neither one of us saying a word.

chapter eleven

At midnight, I went into the office at the Page and flicked on the lights, then walked over to the desk and grabbed a trash can to prop the door open, letting the office light flow into the store. I gasped for a second, thinking Mags was in the office, and then I realized it was just her red cardigan, draped over the back of the office chair. I had an impulse to pick it up and smell it for her perfume, the way I had on occasion when I was little, but instead I turned and walked out into the store.

I inhaled the earthy scents of books and old wood, and felt some of my jagged pieces flow back together. I walked between the rows of shelves, running my fingers over the spines of the books. The old squeaky floorboard welcomed me in Nonfiction Bestsellers. I rubbed my thumb over the chunk of white showing through the green wall, where I'd rammed it with a cart after an argument with Mags when I was in high school.

I put a kettle of water on the hot plate at the coffee bar and grabbed my itty bitty book light out from behind the counter. I wandered to the fiction section and picked *Flyover*, the first novel in the Tan Carpenter series, off the shelf. I'd read it, but I wanted to read it again. I tossed it and the book light on one of the big easy chairs, then went back and grabbed Mags's sweater, pulling it around my shoulders, inhaling the scent of her perfume, and remembering how great she'd been when I was in crisis as a kid. Whatever it was—bike injury, broken heart—Mags would always wrap her arms around me and I'd take in her scent and I'd know everything was going to be okay. Between that and the smell of the Page, I was calmed enough by the time I sat down that I fell asleep almost instantly, hugging the book to my chest and dreaming of spies and red sweaters.

"Portia?"

I felt a hand on my shoulder. I looked up.

Peter.

"Hey," I said. "Sorry. Guess I fell asleep."

He grinned. "Ya think?" He tilted his head, looking at the back of *Flyover,* which I was still hugging to my chest. His smile faded. He pointed to the book.

"You're reading a spy novel?"

I shut the book and stood up. "Yeah."

I could see his smile took effort. "Is it good?"

"Yeah." I walked to the front counter and set the book down. He snorted.

"What?"

"You hate genre fiction."

"No, I don't."

"Yes, you do."

"Only because I never read it."

"So why are you reading it now?"

I didn't say anything. Peter reached over, picked up the book, and looked at the picture, then set it down again.

"Never mind. I can guess why."

"What is your problem? You know Ian and I are friends."

"Yeah. Well." He walked over to the coffee bar. "This is a really stupid argument. I'm gonna make some coffee. You want some?"

I nodded, three parts guilty, one part indignant.

"Portia, honey!" Vera's voice rang through the store accompanied by the jangling bells on the door handle. "Are you helping out today?"

"No, actually," I said. "I was in here reading last night and I guess I fell asleep."

"Too bad," she said, glancing at Peter and then tossing a smile my way. "Peter and I were just talking about updating the window display with the summer beach reads. You know, put up a lawn chair and a towel and maybe a beach ball, then set all the books around it."

I raised an eyebrow at Peter. "Your idea?"

Peter stared at me, saying nothing.

"Of course it was his idea," Vera said, patting him on the arm. "He's brilliant. He's a godsend to this place."

She winked at me and walked back to the office, chattering about placing an order for the children's section. I smiled at Peter.

"I'd like to go upstairs and shower, but I could come back if you really need the help."

Finally, he smiled. "I'd like that."

"Hey, that looks great!" Vera said as she checked out the window display, filled with beach-style paraphernalia and about twenty breezy paperbacks. She grinned at Peter and me. "You two make a great team."

Peter touched the small of my back lightly, then pulled his hand away. "I've always thought so."

I tucked my hand into my pocket and felt the little piece of paper I'd been carrying around with me for days. It was as good an excuse to get away as any, and maybe if I picked up the phone during the day rather than at night, I'd actually go through with it and dial.

"Hey, Vera, do you think I might be able to use the phone in the office for about fifteen minutes?" I caught her eye. "Privately."

"Sure, honey," she said. "Go on back. Peter and I will sit with some coffee and admire your handiwork."

Peter squeezed my elbow. "See you soon."

I stepped away, tightening my grip on Mags's red sweater, and headed toward the back office.

I shut and locked the door behind me, then sat down at the desk. I picked up the phone. Hung it up. Picked it up, dialed three numbers. Slammed it down. I stood up, stretched my arms, and sat down again.

"Oh, for Christ's sake, Portia, just do it," I said, dialing the entire number with shaking fingers and then turning around in the seat to discourage myself from hanging up.

Ring. Ring.

Ring.

If it's the answering machine, I'll just hang up, I thought, a sense of refreshing relief washing through me.

"Hello?" A woman's voice, light and Southern with a hint of honey. A lot like Mags's.

My throat closed. My eyes watered.

"I'm calling for Jack Tripplehorn?" My voice sounded childlike. I cleared my throat. "Is he at home?"

"No, he's at work right now. May I take a message?" I heard water running in the background. Dishes clanking.

I cleared my throat. "Do you know when he'll be back?"

The water stopped. "This is his wife. May I ask who's calling?"

His wife. His *wife*.

My stepmother.

Oh, god. Would she even know who I was? Would she even know I existed?

"This is his daughter."

I heard a gasp and what sounded like the clatter of a glass hitting a countertop.

"Portia?" My name came through the line in an incredulous whisper.

He'd told her about me. My eyes started to tear up.

"Um, is there a better time for me to call?" My heart was battering against my chest and I was sure it would burst through if I didn't hang up soon.

"Oh, honey, yes, he'll be home tonight." Her voice gave a little squeak, and then came through again, an octave higher. "I can't believe it's you. Jack has missed you so."

My heart stopped its battering. "What?"

"He's missed you, honey. He's just a big, stupid, stubborn, stupid man is all. Oh, I'm so glad you called. I've been after him to call you forever." She sniffled, and I heard her blow her nose.

"He did call me," I said, feeling as though someone else was talking. Detached.

"He did?" She huffed. "Well, he didn't tell me. But that doesn't matter. What matters is that you two reconnect. Can we see you?"

I started to reattach, and the anger flowed in like lava.

"If he's missed me so much, why did you have to bug him to call me?"

"I told you, because he's a big stupid man." She paused, sighed. "I don't mean that, baby. Your daddy's a good man. It's just that after your mama threw him out and returned all the letters he wrote you, he kinda bought into all that pardon-my-French crap about you being better off without him—"

"What?" My heart was doing double-beats now, and my hands were going cold.

"He understands now how a girl needs her daddy, but by the time he figured it out it had been so long—"

"My mother threw him out?"

There was a long pause. "You didn't know that?"

"He wrote me letters?"

Silence.

"I'm so sorry," she said finally. "I shouldn't have said anything. That's between you and your mama, honey. Oh, this is a horrible way for us to start our relationship, me causing you trouble in your family. I just assumed you knew the whole story."

I could hear the earnestness in her voice, the understanding, the compassion I'd always wanted from Mags.

Mags. Fury raged in my gut.

"I've never gotten the whole story," I said after a minute.

"I'm sorry, baby."

"I have to go. Thank you, uh . . ." I paused, realizing I didn't even know her name.

"Marianne," she said quietly. "My name is Marianne."

"I have to go, Marianne," I said.

"Portia?" I could hear the tears welling in her voice.

"I'm sorry I've upset you," I said.

She sniffled. "Oh, don't you worry about me. I cry when the peas overcook." She laughed. I wished I could laugh with her. "I just . . . Can I tell Jack you'll call again? Or is there a number where he can reach you?"

Only with the Mizzes, at home or at the Page, and I didn't want them messing with this anymore. "I'll be in touch. I promise."

"Okay," she said. "You take care now, Portia."

I nodded without realizing that would mean nothing to her and hung up the phone. I felt dizzy. I clenched my hands into fists and pushed them into my legs, trying to find something solid I could cling to.

I heard the bells jingle on the door. Mags's tinkling laugh floated through to the back of the store, followed by Bev's deeper tones. I stood up and walked with heavy feet toward the door of the office, pulling it open.

Mags was standing across from Vera at the front counter, wearing a light blue Donna Reed dress, every brown hair perfectly placed. Lips flawlessly lined. She saw me approach and was about to speak, but stopped as I came close enough for her to see my expression.

"You threw him out?"

I could see Bev stiffen in my peripheral vision, but I kept my focus on Mags.

"You sent back the letters he wrote me?"

Mags looked around the store. No one else was there but Peter, and he was busying himself at the coffee bar, pretending not to listen.

"Do you want to tell me where the hell you got the right to return *my letters*?"

Bev took a step forward. I held my hand up.

"So help me God, Bev, if you tell me this has nothing to do with me—"

"Don't you dare speak to me in that tone, young lady," she hissed.

"No," I said, pulling up to my full height. "Don't *you* dare, Bev. Don't you dare pretend this is okay. This has less to do with you than it does with me, so why don't you just stay the hell out of it?"

Bev's face burned red. Vera stepped out from behind the counter and put her arm on my shoulders. "Portia, you're upset, maybe you should go upstairs for a while and—"

"No, Vera," I said through clenched teeth. "Thank you. I'd like to stay here and have this out."

Peter and Vera exchanged looks, and Peter wordlessly headed to the front door, quietly flipping the OPEN/CLOSED sign and locking the door. I turned my eyes back on Mags.

"Are you going to give me an answer, Mags?"

She turned her head to the side. There was a tear running down her cheek, but her shoulders were still as stone.

Bev stepped forward. "I think you should go upstairs and cool off for a while, Portia."

"Stay out of it." I leveled my eyes on her. Her hand, which was about to touch my arm, froze in midair.

"Excuse me?" she said, lowering her hand slowly. If I had been in any other state of mind, I would have crumbled under her iron stare. As it was, I took a step closer to her.

"This is none of your business, Grandma." Bev's eyes flashed. I knew they would. "That's what you are, right? Why the hell do I call you Bev, anyway?"

"Because that's my name."

"Because you didn't want to be a grandmother. Or a mother.

You wanted everything to be a good time, like we're all a bunch of buddies. Well, you know what? I didn't need a buddy. I needed a grandmother." I turned my focus on Mags, who hadn't moved an inch. "I needed a mother."

I pulled the cardigan away from my shoulders and gripped it in my fingers, staring at the vibrant red for a moment before handing it to Mags.

"You never told me he wanted a relationship with me." She raised her eyes to mine and I met them, cold with rage. "I take back what I said about being a buddy. You're not even that."

She said nothing. I spun around and stormed out the side door, banging it into the wall as I flew out, enraged. I didn't realize Peter had followed me until I almost slammed the door on him as I flung myself into my apartment.

"Go back downstairs, Peter."

"No," he said, following me into my bedroom, standing in the doorway with his arms folded over his chest "I'm not going to leave you when you're in this state."

"What?" I said. "Georgia? Don't worry. I won't be here for long."

His eyebrows knit together for a second as I tossed my duffel bag onto the bed. "Where are you going, Portia?"

"I'm going to Tuscaloosa," I said, throwing a small pile of T-shirts in the bag, then standing up and pointing one finger at Peter. "All this time, all this time she had me believing that he'd left. And she *threw* him out. It was her, it was her choice the whole time."

"I understand you're upset," Peter began.

"Upset? I don't have a relationship with my father because of her lies and her . . . her . . . her *lies*." I threw up my hands and gave up trying to find the words for what I was feeling. Screw words. I turned and pulled open another drawer, grabbing some jeans.

"You shouldn't drive like this," Peter said.

"I'll be fine, Peter." He watched me with soft concern. I tried to swallow my annoyance. "I'm fine."

He held his hand out. "Wait for a half hour. It won't take me long to pack."

"Thanks, Peter, but no thanks. Tell Vera not to worry." I swiped my hand over the top of my dresser, tossing hair stuff and deodorant into my bag. "I'll be back tomorrow."

Peter shook his head. "We'll call when we get to the hotel."

I slammed a drawer shut with my hip. "Don't you know when you're not wanted?"

He smiled. "No. And so far, it's working for me."

He walked over to me, took the bag from my shoulder and tossed it on the bed.

"Peter, I'm not playing games here."

I made a move toward the bed. He grabbed me by my shoulders and moved me back.

"Me, neither. I don't want you driving in this state of mind, and you shouldn't be alone when you see your father. Now, I'm gonna go and I'm gonna pack and either you're going to be here or you're not when I get back. But I don't think it would kill you to wait thirty fucking minutes and let somebody help you for once."

I crossed my arms over my abdomen and stared him down. Was this the same mild-mannered Peter who'd let me push him out of my life without saying anything? Had he really changed?

There was only one way to find out.

"Okay. Thirty minutes."

He smiled. "Thank you. I'll be right back." He headed out the bedroom door and I reached into my duffel bag, then rushed out after him.

"Peter!" I called. He turned as he pulled open the front

door. I grabbed a piece of paper off the counter and scribbled some instructions on it. "I need you to get me something from the house."

"She's fine," I heard Peter say as I stepped out of the hotel bathroom. We'd gotten one room with two double beds. I just couldn't see being prudish about sleeping arrangements with a guy who'd seen me naked every day for two years. We were adults and there were two beds, so I wasn't going to worry about it.

"Yeah, we're just about to go see him." He pointed to the receiver and mouthed "Vera" at me, then spoke back into the phone. "I'll watch out for her. Don't worry. How are Mags and Bev?"

I bristled at the sound of their names. I didn't want to think about Mags and Bev. I was too angry and too hurt to think about either of them without feeling physical pain.

"Uh-huh," Peter said, and looked at me, but didn't give any clues as to what Vera was saying on the other end.

"We're planning on heading back early tomorrow morning, so I should be able to help out in the store . . ." He stopped. I didn't have to listen in to know that Vera was telling him not to worry about it. He smiled and made a motion to me, asking if I wanted to speak. I shook my head.

"No, she's still in the shower," he said. "But I'll tell her."

He hung up and looked at me.

"They're worried about you," he said finally.

I looked at my watch. "It's almost eight o'clock," I said. "Are you ready?"

He stood up. "Are you?"

I nodded. "Ready as I'll ever be."

That was true enough. Part of me wanted to run home and hide under the covers. But I'd come all this way, dragged Peter through my drama, and it was time to get it over with.

Peter put his hand on the small of my back and ushered me out the door.

"Let's do it, then."

Jack's house was a big, white sprawling ranch-style on the outskirts of town. Peter pulled up in front and stopped the car, then turned to me.

"You want me to come in with you?" he asked.

I stared at the lights in the house. I saw a figure float past one of the windows. Looked like a woman. Must be Marianne.

"Portia?" Peter craned his head into my line of vision. "You okay?"

"Yeah," I said, unbuckling my seat belt and clutching the box in my lap. "I don't know how long this is going to take."

Peter smiled. "I'll wait."

I looked at him, and the irritation I'd felt earlier melted away. "Peter, thank you for—"

"It's nothing. Really. I'll be here when you're ready."

I squeezed his hand and hopped out of the car. The night air felt heavy and wet, and gravity seemed to get stronger the closer my feet brought me to Jack's house. When I got up to the porch, my heartbeat was quick and light, and I thought I might faint. I pushed the doorbell.

"I'll get it," a man's voice boomed from inside. My gut did a flip. The porch light turned on, glaring in my face. The door opened.

I froze. I thought about running away, but couldn't move.

There he was. My father, the man who had picked me up and danced with me when I was a little girl. The man who, as it turned out, had loved me after all. His hair was graying at the temples, and he looked heavier than the man I remembered, but I knew it was the same man.

And I didn't know him at all.

He smiled at me politely for a moment, then his smile faded.

"Well, I'll be," he whispered. "Don't you look just like her?"

I blinked. It took me a second to realize he was talking about Mags.

"I'm sorry for not calling," I said, my voice wavering in and out like a bad radio. "I should have called first."

"No," he said. "No, it's okay. I'm . . ." He paused and I could see the muscles working in his jaw. "I'm real glad you're here."

"Okay," I said. I held out the shoebox in my hands. "This is for you."

He took it tentatively and pulled the top off.

"I wrote you letters, through the years," I said. "There are some pictures of me growing up."

He picked my sixth-grade picture off the top and smiled. "You had braces."

"Yeah."

He looked from the picture to me, his eyes shining. "You're beautiful."

I tried to blink the tears away, but they came too fast. I put my hand over my face and sobbed. I heard him put the box down on a deck chair and felt him pull me into his arms.

"Now don't tell me no one's ever told you that before," he said, his voice crackling with the effort of his humor, running his hands over my head. "I wouldn't believe it for a second."

The floodgates opened, and thirty years of hurt and anger and confusion came out in enough tears to drown a small city. I couldn't have stopped it if my life depended on it. Through it all, he held me tight to him, running his hands over my hair, telling me he was sorry.

"It's okay," I choked finally, pulling back and swiping the back of my hand over my soppy face. "It's not your fault. But I didn't know . . . I didn't know until . . ."

He struggled to pull on a small smile. I could see that his eyes were shiny and that it was taking a lot out of him to hold them at shiny. "I know. Marianne told me."

I pulled my shirtsleeve down over my hand and mopped at my face, letting go with a feeble laugh. "Great first impression, huh?"

He smiled. "You made your first impression on me at the hospital." I raised my eyes to his. He let out a stuttered sigh, watching me with the same loving expression he'd had the day he picked me up in his arms and waltzed me around the room. Another surge of emotion overtook me, and I could feel my eyes welling up with fresh tears.

"Baby, I'm so sorry." He coughed and pinched his fingers over his eyelids. "I should have never let this go so long. I was just scared."

I swiped at my face. "Scared of what?"

"That you'd be so mad at me for taking so long, you wouldn't want me in your life," he said.

I felt my face crumple again and I shook my head. "I'm not mad."

His face contorted for a moment and then he pulled on a smile. "Well, you should be."

"Jack?" A woman's voice came through as the screen door

squeaked. Jack stepped aside and turned around to face a short, pudgy woman with blond hair wiping her hands on a dish towel. She looked from me to Jack, then put her hand to her mouth with a gasp. "Is this . . . ?"

Jack nodded. "Portia, this is my wife, Marianne."

Marianne waved her hand in front of her face as her eyes filled up.

"I'm sorry," she said, her voice tight and high with emotion. She looked at Jack and grabbed his hand, squeezing it and raising it to her heart.

"I'm going to get y'all something to drink," she said, stepping back toward the door. "Portia? What's your drink?"

"Water would be great," I said.

"You bet." She looked at Jack, smiled, and disappeared into the house.

Jack raised his hand to the Adirondack chairs on the porch and we both sat. We were quiet until Marianne brought us each a glass of ice water, and then once she went into the house again, Jack began to speak.

"Did you talk to your mother?"

"No," I said. "I mean, I confronted her. But she didn't say anything."

He gave a sad laugh. "That's Mags for you."

He took a sip of his water. I stared into my melting ice.

"I can't believe she did that," I said. "She had no right to send those letters back. She had no right to throw you out and not tell you why."

I could see his head turn in my direction out of the corner of my eye, but I continued to stare into my glass.

"Don't be angry with her."

My head shot up. "What? How can I not be angry?"

"I'm not saying you don't have a right to be angry," he said. "As my daddy used to say, just because you have a right to be angry doesn't mean you should be."

"How can you say that? Aren't you mad?"

He shook his head. "I used to be. But, truth is, maybe she was right. Maybe we would have just drove each other crazy in the long run. And I knew where you were. I could have come and beat down the door until she let me see you. You're gonna be mad at one of us, you're gonna have to be mad at both. And you already said you're not mad with me, so . . ."

"I don't know how you're not furious," I said. "I'm furious. I'm so angry right now I could spit."

"Well, I've known the whole story a lot longer than you."

I took a sip of water and sat back in the chair. Jack sat back in his chair as well, and we both looked at the sky. When he spoke again, his voice was soft and thoughtful.

"There's no other person on the planet as true to her own self as your mama is," he said. "There's a cost that comes with loving someone like that. They march to the beat of their own drum, and a person can make himself crazy trying to figure out that rhythm." I didn't say anything. He sighed. "I guess what I'm saying is that your mama is who your mama is, and once you accept that, you'll love her so much your heart's gonna be fit to burst."

I looked at him, watched him staring at the sky with a faraway smile on his face.

"Do you still love her?" I asked. I hadn't meant to voice the thought out loud, but I was in no state to be coy.

Jack raised his eyebrows at me. "My heart burst over Mags a long time ago."

That was enough of an answer for me. I looked back out at the sky, clear and deep blue and glittering with stars.

"I know she's talked to you about visiting in September." I waited for him to speak. When he didn't, I nudged. "Are you going to see her? Like she asked?"

He paused for a while before speaking. "I don't know. I assumed it must have been about you. That's why I put her off until September, to give me some time to track you down."

I shook my head. "She says it has nothing to do with me."

"Well, if it doesn't concern you, I'm not sure it'd be right. I've got Marianne to think of now. Seeing Mags again . . ." He looked down at his hands, then back up at me. "Well, I'm just not sure it'd be right."

I nodded. "What does Marianne have to say about it?"

He gave a small laugh. "Oh, she's been buggin' me to go. She thinks it might help me gain *closure*." He took a drink and laughed again. "That's an Oprah word, isn't it?"

I laughed. "Sounds like Marianne is a good woman."

"She is. She's excited about getting to know you. She wanted me to invite you here for Thanksgiving, matter of fact."

I smiled. "Really?"

"She makes the best homemade cranberry sauce you ever tasted," he said, winking at me.

"I'd like that," I said. I put my glass down and stood up. Jack did the same. I looked out toward the street, where I could see the moonlight reflecting off the Hyundai's hood.

"I have a friend waiting for me."

Jack looked out to the car, then back at me. "Oh, sure. Well." He looked at me and smiled. "You need anything, you call me, you hear?"

"Sure," I said, smiling.

"No, no, don't you 'sure' me, young lady." He reached over and gave my shoulder a squeeze. "I mean it. I got a lot of time to make up for. I don't care what it is. I started me up a lumberyard in town does pretty well. You ever need a job . . ."

I laughed. "I'm an English Ph.D. candidate. I'll definitely be needing a job."

He smiled. "No kidding? Ph.D., huh?"

"Yeah, but I don't know if it's what I want to do anymore."

He grinned. "You finish that Ph.D., and if you ever want a job at the lumberyard, we'll talk."

I grinned back. I doubted I'd be moving to Tuscaloosa, but he'd offered. And that mattered.

"Well, then," he said, motioning his head toward the car. "Your friend is waiting. It was good to see you. Don't be a stranger."

"I won't."

"Okay, then," he said, stuffing his hands in the pockets of his trousers. "You go on with your friend now."

"Say good-bye to Marianne for me," I said.

He smiled. "I will."

I took a step toward him and he pulled me into a hug.

"Don't you be too hard on your mama, now," he said. "She's just a human person like the rest of us, and we all get things wrong every now and again."

I held on to him for a bit longer, waiting for the hug to fill in all the little empty pockets I felt in my heart. He got a lot of them.

But not all.

chapter twelve

"Are you sure we're not going to get in trouble?" I asked as Peter put his hands on my waist and boosted me up. The chain-link fence looked eerily bluish in the moonlight and glittered as I stuck my foot in and grabbed hold.

"No," he said. "Now, hurl yourself over the top. And don't drop the beer."

I adjusted the backpack over my shoulders and tossed myself down on the other side of the fence, landing in a cloud of dust at the bottom. Peter hopped down beside me.

"I'm not sure this is a good idea," I said.

Peter laughed and wiped his hands on his jeans. "You asked to do something stupid and fun. That comes with a little risk."

I looked behind me at the swing sets and slides. "Right. Besides, it's a public school. My taxes pay for this, right?"

"Well, technically, your father's taxes paid for this one, but good enough." Peter took my backpack and slung it over his shoulder, where it collided with the pack he was carrying. His arm slid around my waist and guided me toward a grassy sloping hill under cover of trees. He put both packs on the ground and began unloading. He laid a large blanket, borrowed from the hotel, over the slope and set out a six-pack of beer, opening a bottle for each of us. We clinked the necks and drank.

"I also got something else for you," he said, reaching into his pocket and pulling out a pack of cigarettes.

"Yay!" I said, and grabbed the pack from him and started slamming it against my palm. "I know you don't approve, but thank you. I really need these tonight."

We sat and I lit up and inhaled deep. I stared at the squat, one-story brick school. Peter stared at me.

"What are you thinking about?" he asked.

"Trying not to think," I lied. "Counting bricks in that wall there."

I pointed. He looked.

"How many are there?"

"I don't know," I said, taking a drink from my beer. "I lost count at twelve. So, tell me you're not really going to manage the Page, Peter."

"I'm not really going to manage the Page," he said with a wry smile.

"I mean it," I said. "It would be all wrong. You're a wonderful writer. You should be writing."

He lifted his beer at me. "But I'm no Alistair Barnes, am I?"

I let out a huge breath. "Why are you obsessing over him? What does he have to do with any of this, anyway?"

He looked at me. "I don't know. You tell me."

"Oh, God," I said, falling back on the blanket and wincing as my spine connected with a large stone. "I can't deal with this right now."

"You're right," Peter said. "I'm sorry."

We were quiet for a while. I tried to count the leaves on the tree over my head.

I lost count at twelve.

"What did you mean when you wrote Eloise?" I said finally. "Why couldn't she walk in a northerly direction?"

Peter gave a tiny laugh. "Oh, man. I haven't thought about that in a while."

I pushed myself up on my elbows and watched him. "She was based on me, wasn't she?"

Peter looked at me over his shoulder, then turned back to face the school. "She's an amalgam of many women I've—"

"But mostly me, right?"

Peter was silent.

"I know you've told me before," I said, "but I want you to really tell me. What did it mean?"

Peter sighed. "Do you really want to have this discussion right now?"

"Yes," I said. "I really do."

"All right." He shifted around to face me. "It means that you would gladly walk south for the circumference of the earth rather than turn north and walk two steps."

I sat up. "That's not true. And I still don't understand what that means."

Peter laughed. "It means you're stubborn. It means you see things a certain way and you refuse to see anything else."

"You think I'm stubborn?"

Peter laughed again. "Am I the first person to tell you this?"

I took a drink from my beer, thinking about what Jack had said. "Do you think there are things in Mags I don't see?"

"To be fair, if she was my mother, I don't know if I'd see them either."

"What do you see?"

Peter took a deep breath and was quiet for a moment. "She has an interesting walk."

"An interesting walk?"

"So do you," he said, "but not in exactly the same way. She walks like someone who's paying attention to every step, you know? It's like she doesn't want to miss anything."

"And how do I walk?"

"Like someone with a destination in mind."

I huffed. "As long as it's south."

He ran his hand over his hair. "I'm never going to live that down, am I?"

"Not until you write your next book," I said. His smile faded. I hugged my knees to my chest. "I hate the idea of you giving up your writing because you think it's what I want."

"I hate the idea of you and Alistair Barnes," he said.

I opened my mouth to say something, but a light flashed in my eyes.

"Hey!" a voice called out. "Damn kids!"

In a flash, Peter was up. I tried to clean up the cigarette butts—this was a kids' playground—but Peter grabbed my arm.

"No time!" he said, hurrying me to the fence.

"But . . . all this stuff—"

"No time!" He pulled me with him, practically hurling me over the fence as the flash of light bounced wildly over the play-ground to the rhythm of pounding feet. I landed on the asphalt in the parking lot and ran for the car.

"You got the keys?" Peter hollered from behind me.

"Yes!" I said.

"Stop right there . . . you damn . . . kids," we heard the secu-rity guard yelling. He was slowing, out of breath, and by the time

Peter hopped in the car and we tore out of there, he'd stopped running and settled for flipping us off from inside the fence.

"Well, you wanted fun and stupid," Peter said, laughing.

"And I got it," I said. My heart was racing and I was smiling and it felt good to smile. I grabbed Peter's hand and squeezed it. "Thank you."

He pulled my hand up to his lips and kissed it.

"Anytime, sweetheart. Anytime."

We stopped at a red light and made eye contact for a long moment. For that moment, I could visualize myself married to him. Forever.

The light turned green and I drove on to the hotel, where we fell asleep in separate double beds.

We left the hotel early the next morning to drive the three and a half hours back so Peter could be in time to help Vera at the Page. Peter drove while I napped in the passenger seat. When he pulled up in front of the Page, he woke me with a soft kiss on the forehead.

I smiled. "Here already?"

He grinned. "Here already."

I stretched and reached in the backseat for my duffel bag. "Thanks, Peter. For driving, for going with me. I appreciate it."

Peter kept his eyes on mine. "No problem."

I smiled, leaned my head against the headrest, and said what I was thinking. "Peter, if it wasn't for me, would you want to be here?"

He inhaled deeply. "What do you mean?"

"I mean, if it wasn't for me, would you want to manage a small bookstore in northwest Georgia for the rest of your life?"

He shrugged. "I don't know. Maybe. But it doesn't matter, because I am here for you." He turned toward me, picked up my hand, and kissed my palm. "And I'll stay here until you tell me to leave."

"Why?" I asked. "I don't understand. Why do you want to throw away your life on me?"

He released my hand. "I don't think of it as throwing my life away."

I looked down at my hands and said nothing. After a moment, Peter sighed.

"I wish I knew what you wanted, Portia."

"That makes two of us," I said quietly. I leaned over and kissed him on the cheek, then got out of the car and headed up to my apartment. I turned on the light and sat down on the couch, squinting at the clock on the VCR.

8:02.

I rested my head back on the couch. Thoughts bumped into each other as they wandered through my tired mind. Jack and the letters I'd never gotten. Mags and her never-miss-a-thing walk. Peter offering me forever. Ian offering me nothing. Vera still loving Bridge, after all this time. Bridge still loving Vera. Bev and her anger.

I heard the door bells jingle below, signaling that Peter was inside the store. I grabbed my car keys and headed out, taking the Mazda out the back of the alley so that Peter wouldn't see me driving past through the windows at the Page. I wanted to remain undetected, at least for a little while.

I'd pulled onto our street just in time to see Mags getting into the Jeep. Big and red and loud, it was easy to follow. I tried to keep a few cars back, but I didn't worry too much about Mags catching me. I didn't care much. I just wanted to know where she was going.

About fifteen minutes later, we arrived at an elementary school in Ringgold. Mags pulled into the lot, parked and headed through the front door. I waited, watched her walk.

Peter was right about her walk.

Five minutes later, I walked in the same door. The halls were empty. To my left was a glass fishbowl office with a counter and a woman behind it. I pushed through the door and an older woman with a head of the brightest bottle-red hair I'd ever seen smiled up at me.

"Are you Cecilia's mom?" she asked. I looked over her shoulder at a pathetic-looking little girl with red eyes almost as bright as the receptionist's hair.

"No," I said, smiling at the little girl and then down at Big Red. "What's the matter with her?"

Big Red shook her head compassionately. "Pinkeye, poor thing. Forgot her eyedrops."

"Oh." I smiled again at Cecilia, who stopped kicking her legs in and out under the chair long enough to smile back.

"Can I help you with something else, then?" Big Red asked, smiling brightly.

"Yeah. I'm looking for Mags Fallon."

"Oh, Mags!" Big Red laughed. "Isn't she a wonder?"

"Yes, she is. Might I speak with her?"

Big Red walked over to a schedule tacked on the wall that read "Little Bears Summer Day Camp—August." Her finger trailed through the calendar and landed on today.

"She should be out on the playground doing the imagination workshop with the seven-to-nines," she said. "Do you have a child in the class?"

"No," I said, holding out my hand. "I'm her daughter, Portia."

Big Red laughed and pushed my hand away, going for a hug. "Oh, I should have known. You look just like her." She released me and pointed out the office and down a hallway. "Follow that hall to the end, and it'll open out to the playground. You'll find her in the back with twenty or so children just adoring her to pieces."

I thanked Big Red, waved to poor Cecilia, and headed out to the playground. I spotted Mags immediately. She stood in front of the kids, circling around in an exaggerated stomp. The children were laughing and doing the same. I walked around the edge of the playground until I got to the swing sets, which were off to the side a bit where Mags didn't notice me, but close enough for me to hear what she was saying.

"Now, imagine," she said, her voice sweeping in broad, sweet strokes, a voice made to talk to children, "that you are a big, *ugly* bear. I mean, you are the *ugliest* bear that ever did walk the planet."

The kids giggled. I smiled.

"I mean it. Make your *ugly* face."

The kids all contorted their faces into horrendous expressions. Tongues lolling out of mouths, hands pulling down cheeks until the under eyelids showed.

"Oh, that's good," she said, walking among the children, checking out their faces. "Oh, Sarah, for such a pretty girl you sure can be one *ugly* bear."

She patted a little blond girl on the shoulder and resumed her place in front of the children.

"Now," she said, "you are all terrifyingly ugly bears, and I'm so proud of you. But—now quiet—I need to tell you something."

All the children quieted down and moved closer to Mags. Their faces, while some were still contorted, were wrapped up in her every word.

"You are an *ugly* bear, but imagine now that you love one thing." She held up an index finger. "Just one thing. It could be a flower. It could be your mama. It could be the person standing next to you. I want y'all to close your eyes and think about the one thing you love more than anything else."

Mags closed her eyes, then peeked out and pointed at Sarah.

"I said close 'em. I wasn't kidding." Sarah giggled and closed her eyes. When Mags seemed assured all the kids had their eyes closed, she closed hers again.

I did the same.

"Now," Mags said, "keep that picture of that one thing you love more than anything else in your mind, and open your eyes."

I opened my eyes. Mags was looking right at me. She smiled and turned her attention back to the kids.

"Now, look at everything and everyone around you." Mags said. "Go on. Look around at all you ugly bears. Did any of you notice how y'all are beautiful again?"

The kids, faces all smiles and not a contorted one in the bunch, oohed and aahed at each other, at the magnitude of their glorious transformation. Mags watched them, her face alight. I caught her eye again and she blew me a kiss. I grabbed it in the air and touched it to my face.

A man about my age walked up and called the kids over, informing them it was time for arts and crafts. Mags spoke to him briefly, hugged a few of the stragglers, and sent them on their way, then walked over and sat down in a swing next to me.

"I was wondering what was taking you so long," she said. "I

can't believe any daughter of mine would take this long to hunt me down."

I laughed. "What can I say? I'm slow."

A group of children, slightly older than the group Mags just had, were assembling in the kickball field. We watched the kids settle in to the game, and then I spoke.

"I saw Jack last night."

Mags kept her eyes on the game, but I saw her grip on the swing chains tighten.

"Really?" she said, her voice almost too light. "How is he?"

"He's fine. Good, actually."

Mags gave me a fleeting smile, then turned her attention back to the kids. "I'm glad to hear it. He told you, then. What happened with us?"

"Not really," I said. "All I know is that you threw him out."

She nodded. "Yes. I did that."

"Okay," I said. "I don't care."

She turned her head, and brought her eyes up to meet mine. "You're not mad?"

"What's the point?" I sighed, kicking dust clouds up with my feet. "I've been mad at you for so long and it never gets me anywhere. Just because I have a right to be mad . . ."

". . . doesn't mean you should be." Mags laughed. "You *have* been talking to Jack."

"I won't lie and say I'm not curious, but I didn't come here today to beat it out of you."

"Well, that begs the question . . ." she said.

"Why *did* I come out here? I don't know. I just know I don't want to fight you anymore." I reached out and grabbed her hand. "I want my mom."

She smiled at me and squeezed my hand, and I was amazed

at how easy it was to sit there with Mags. For the first time in my life, I wasn't expecting her to disappoint me. I wasn't expecting anything.

Who knew it could be that simple?

"I loved him," she said after a moment, her eyes returning to the kickball game. "I always have. I still do."

I sucked in a deep breath, trying not to sound too shocked by her openness about Jack. "Then why did you kick him out?"

"Because I loved him."

I waited, saying nothing, just holding her hand in mine. Finally, she spoke again.

"Bev and your grandpa were married. Did you know that?"

I shook my head. Fallon had been Bev's maiden name, and she'd passed it down to all of us. It had never occurred to me that she'd ever been married. Then again, I'd never asked.

"Vera was too young to remember when he left, but I remember. I still don't know why. Just one day, he was gone. Bev was devastated. She stayed in her room for a year and didn't come out until Gladys Cheever dragged Reverend Billy to the house to minister to her."

I felt my mouth drop open. "Bev? Bev stayed in her room for a year? Over a *man*?" I couldn't picture it, although it sure did explain a lot.

"Well, I don't know what it was all about, exactly. I was only six and Bev's never talked about it. She broke out of it, mortgaged the house, and opened the Page. And we've been together, the three Miz Fallons, ever since." She squeezed my hand. "Until you came along. Then there were four."

I smiled at her. After a short silence, Mags continued.

"Anyway, I didn't want that to happen to me. I didn't want it to be a surprise. So, I told Jack to leave and he left." She let go of my hand and curled her fingers around the metal chains, swinging a bit as she talked. "I didn't know anything about the letters you mentioned, but I don't think he'd lie about something like that. I half suspect Bev might have been the one to send them back. I don't remember looking at the mail or doing much of anything for a long time after I sent him away. It's all a big blur for me." She looked at me, her eyes anxious. "So, you really went to see him?"

I nodded. "Yes."

"And he's doing well?"

"Yes."

She smiled and looked out at the kickball game.

"That's good. Jack's a good man." She took a deep breath. "I was okay for a long time, but things started to change after you left for college. It was like, I didn't have any part of Jack left to love and I just felt . . . empty. I started getting . . . I don't know. Mopey, I guess. Vera and Bev sat me down last winter and told me to go find whatever was gonna make me happy."

"You always seemed happy to me," I said. "Absurdly happy."

Mags smiled. "When you were around, I was. You always filled my heart. But when you were gone . . ."

I couldn't believe what I was hearing. I filled Mags's heart? The possibility had never occurred to me. "I'm sorry, Mags. I had no idea."

"Of course not," she said. "A child isn't supposed to know that sort of thing." She gave me another weak smile before going on. "Anyway, Bev and Vera told me to go do something that made me happy. I tried everything. I made cakes and bagels with Sue Ann at the bakery. I was a cashier at the Wal-Mart in Fort Oglethorpe for a very short while. Finally, I found this place." She motioned toward the kids playing. "How can your heart not be full with these precious things to stare at all day?"

I thought of Mags's big, ugly bears, which led me to another train of thought. "I don't understand what that has to do with freeing all the cows on Carl Raimi's farm."

"Oh," she said with a good-humored scowl. "That was Vera's idea. She thought I had bad karma from using animal-tested makeup products, and she was sure that my chakras would clear right up if I did something to help the animals."

I laughed. "Vera told you to set all Raimi's cows free?"

Mags laughed, too. "Not specifically, no. Afterward she said that wasn't the kind of 'helping the animals' she was talking about. I think she expected something along the lines of a donation to People for the Ethical Treatment of Animals, but those folks are just too crazy for me."

I had a thought about pots and kettles, but I kept it to myself.

"And how are your chakras?" I asked.

"Murky as ever." She giggled, then her smile faded a bit. "Until I found this place. You know, darlin', I think I'm really happy here. I was talking to one of the kindergarten teachers, and she asked me to apply to be a teacher's aide during the school year. Can you imagine?"

"Yes," I said. "I think you'd be great."

She smiled. "Thank you, baby."

We swung lazily in the sun for another minute until I could gather up the courage to say what I had to say next.

"Jack's married."

Mags's swinging slowed to a stop. "Really?"

"He didn't tell you? When you talked to him?"

Mags shook her head. "No. We only spoke briefly. He said he'd be able to make a visit in September, and I hung up. I figured it could wait." She paused for a second, then asked, "Is he happy?"

I nodded. "I think so."

She was quiet for a minute, then gave me a bright Mags smile. "That's good. I'm glad. Will you do something for me, darlin'?"

"Sure," I said.

"Will you tell him that I don't need to talk to him after all? That I just wanted to say I was sorry, and that was all it was?" Her eyes were shiny. I smiled at her.

"I think he'll be glad to hear that," I said. I stood up and reached my hand out to Mags, pulling her up. She tucked her arm in mine and we walked across the playground. Right as we were about to enter the building, a man in a suit with graying hair and bright blue eyes rushed over to get the door for us.

"Gary," Mags said, "I want you to meet my daughter, Portia. Portia, this is Gary. He's the school superintendent."

Gary reached over and gave me a firm handshake. "Your mother is an incredible asset here. I don't know what we'd do without her."

"Thank you," I said. "I'm very proud."

He smiled and held the door, shutting it gently behind us as we entered the building. Mags tucked her hand in my arm and pulled me to her for a conspiratorial whisper. "I think that man would make an excellent Flyer, don't you?"

I rolled my eyes. "Mags, I don't need—"

Mags nudged me with her elbow. "I wasn't talking about you, darlin'."

I looked behind me as the superintendent made his way down to the opposite end of the hall. He had a masterful walk, full of energy and presence. I turned back to Mags and winked at her.

"If it ever happens, I want a full report, immediately."

She laughed. "Why, of course, darlin'. I wouldn't have it any other way."

chapter thirteen

I barely had my hand off the buzzer when Ian answered the door. I raised the chilled bottle of chardonnay in my other hand.

"Shall we try this again?"

He smiled and stepped aside. "By all means."

He walked ahead of me into the kitchen, grabbed the corkscrew, and got to business.

"Your timing's perfect. I have something I want to show you."

I smiled, trying to quell the nerves in my stomach. I'd come on a mission and was determined that nothing would stop me. Penis Teflon was nothing mysterious; it was just everyday fear masquerading as something bigger. It had caused Mags to lose Jack, and Vera to lose Bridge. On the drive back home after seeing Mags, I decided that if I lost Ian, it wasn't going to be because of fear.

Not mine, anyway.

Ian gave me a glass, then grabbed my hand and led me out the front door. We walked quietly toward the barn, but even in the darkening shadows as the sun set behind the clouds, I could see the brightness of the red. The entire exterior had been painted.

"Ian," I said. "Oh, my god, how did you . . . ?"

"Bridge and some people from his construction company volunteered to paint," he said. "But wait . . . there's more."

He pulled the door open and I stepped inside.

It was done. The entire east wall had fresh, golden supports. The scaffolding was gone, and everything had been cleared out.

"We didn't have time to rebuild the stalls," he said, "but if Trudy ever decides to sell it, the new owners can do what they like with it. The frame should last a good while, at least."

"It's very kind of you," I said. "I think Trudy would be really pleased. I hope she gets to see it."

He shrugged and smiled. "Thank you for all your help."

"I didn't do anything." I took a sip of my wine and smiled up at him. "You're quite the secret benefactor, aren't you?"

His eyebrows knit together for a second and he lifted his glass to his lips. "I'm not sure what you mean."

It wasn't what I had come to talk about, but it had been on my mind all the same, and as long as the topic had been raised . . . "How much did you pay Carl Raimi to drop the charges against Mags?"

Ian stopped in mid-sip. "Who told you that?"

"No one," I said, watching Ian for a reaction. "Carl Raimi is the biggest asshole in Catoosa County. He hasn't asked us for a dime of reimbursement, and there's no way he'd drop the charges just out of the goodness of his heart."

Ian was silent for a minute, then shrugged. "It wasn't much."

I watched him in silence until he shifted uncomfortably on his feet.

"Does it matter?" he asked. "It wasn't much, really, and it's over with. Can't we just forget it?"

"We'll have to pay you back," I said, feeling barbs of good ol' Southern pride start to kick in now that my suspicions had been confirmed.

"That's ridiculous. You're a grad student. Your family owns an independent bookstore. I'm quite well off. I have no children, no wife . . ." He paused for a moment. "It's my money and this is how I've chosen to spend some of it. I wish you would just forget about it."

"How much did you pay him?" I asked.

He shook his head. "I'm not going to tell you that."

"You might as well. One bottle of scotch and Raimi'll be bragging about how much he took you for all over town."

"You'll just have to ply him with liquor and ask him, then, won't you?" He took another sip, exhaled a long breath, and ran one hand through his hair. "Look, let's not argue. If you really must pay me back, although I hope you'll give me the opportunity to talk you out of it, we can work out those details later. Please. Don't be angry."

He put his hand on my shoulder and gave a gentle squeeze. It was then that I sensed something was different. There was a hint of urgency in his manner that hadn't been there before. It made me nervous.

Well, *more* nervous.

"Okay," I said, smiling. "We'll talk about it later."

"Thank you." He let his hand trail down my arm and took another drink. "Tell me about your trip to Tuscaloosa."

"How did you know about that?"

"I stopped by the Page last night. Vera told me."

"Oh," I said. He never went by the Page. Something was

definitely up. "It was good. Jack's a nice guy. I'm going to see him at Thanksgiving."

"Really?" He grabbed my hand then and gave it a squeeze. "That's wonderful. I'm so happy for you."

"Did Vera tell you that Peter went with me?"

Ian's face tightened. "No, actually. How did that go?"

"It was good. He was really great. Very kind. Very sweet."

Ian gave a brief nod. "Good. Glad to hear it."

I took a deep breath, prepared myself for takeoff. "He plans on staying here. He wants me to stay with him."

Ian landed icy eyes on me. "You're not going to, are you?"

"Can you give me any reason why I shouldn't?"

He huffed. "I believe I've already given you quite a few."

"No," I said, taking a deep breath and forcing myself to push through, "can you give me a reason not to be with Peter?"

I felt like all the air in the barn whooshed out while he stared at me. After a long moment, he looked away.

"I'm not sure I know what you're asking me."

"I think you do."

"I've finished my book." The words came out in a rush, almost bulldozing mine. Still not meeting my eye, he drained the last of his wine. "My plane leaves on Saturday night."

Oh, God. My heart began to hammer and skip, and my stomach rolled over. "Saturday?"

I watched him as he stared at a spot just over my shoulder. Thunder rumbled in the distance, accentuating our painful silence. I drained the last of my wine and handed him the glass.

"Have a nice flight," I said, and turned on my heel to escape, cursing myself with each step that I hadn't yet done what I'd come there to do. But what difference would it really make, anyway? It wasn't a curse. It wasn't anything mystical. It was just stupid fear and I was drowning in it. So what? Big deal. I could grow old and gray alone with the Mizzes. There were worse fates.

Ian's hand clamped around my arm and pulled me to a stop. A drop of rain plunked down on my head.

"Portia." His breath was ragged from running after me. His eyes were darting back and forth, searching mine. "Will I see you again before I go?"

"Why?" I asked. "Why not just get it over with? What's the difference between now and Saturday?"

His grip loosened on my elbow, and his hand slid up my arm, over my shoulder. He tucked a strand of hair behind my ear, and it almost killed me. When he spoke, it came out in a ragged whisper.

"Five days."

He stepped in closer, entwined his fingers in the hair at the back of my head, and pulled me close to him. His lips grazed my cheek, then trailed downward until they fell onto mine. He curled his other arm around my waist, lifting me up to him. He tasted like wine and he smelled like paint and his warmth radiated through every part of me. We finally separated to take a breath and I reeled back and slammed the flat of my hand against his shoulder, knocking him back a step.

"Ow!" he said, putting his palm to his shoulder. "What did you do that for?"

"Because you're a butthead!"

He blinked. "Did you just call me a *butthead?*"

"What the hell, Ian?" I said. "We wasted the whole summer doing this stupid dance, and you wait to kiss me *now,* right when you're about to leave?"

"Admittedly, yes, this is bad timing—"

"Bad *timing*? You've had all summer!" I tried not to think about the fact that I'd danced as much as he had. But I'd come there that night to tell him all, to bare my soul. That had to count for something.

We stared at each other for a moment, both of us breathing hard, and gradually moving closer, although I'm not sure if either of us was doing it deliberately.

"Portia . . ." He placed his hand on my cheek, his fingertips grazing my hairline. His eyes were half-closed and he brought his lips down to mine again. If not for that moment, I would have never known it was possible to feel so wonderful and so awful all at once.

"I've tried not to do this," he said, putting his hands on either side of my neck, his forehead pressed to mine. "I can't do it anymore. I don't care if it makes sense. I don't bloody care about anything but having these next five days . . ."

He kissed me again, all warmth and persistence, and all I could think about was taking him into the barn and Flying until I forgot he was leaving.

Only I couldn't forget.

"I can't, Ian. I need . . ."

"What?" he said, pulling his hands away, his voice rising as the rain gained more momentum. "Forever? What makes you think anyone can promise you that? Even Peter?"

I shook my head, but didn't say anything. He took another step toward me.

"Trust me, Portia. Someone promised me forever once and it didn't add up to anything. I won't do that to you."

"No," I said. "You won't do anything."

"Damnit," he said, frustration tightening his voice. "What am I supposed to do? Give up my life? Ask you to give up yours?

Over a few weeks of . . ." He stopped, ran his fingers over his hair, swiped the rain away from his face. "The most anyone can ever promise you is the hope of staying around indefinitely, and anyone who says differently is either lying or fooling themselves. There are no guarantees"

"That is so cynical."

"No," he said. "It's honest. It's the truth."

I stared at him. The truth. Wasn't that why I was here in the first place?

It's time, I thought. *It's now or never.*

"Ian, I came here tonight to tell you something." I stared at the car keys in my hand and forced myself to say what I'd come there to say. "I care about you. A lot. More than I probably should. The reason I kept visiting you wasn't just to work on the barn. It was to see you. To be close to you. I want . . . I want to be with you. Every day." I pulled on a weak smile. "Indefinitely."

Silence. He was staring at me, his face blank. I summoned up the rest of my courage. "I don't care if it makes sense, or even if you feel the same way. Well, that's a load of crap, of course I care if you feel the same way. I just don't want to make the same mistakes . . ." I could feel the muscles in my legs start to shake. *Time to wrap it up.* "I don't want to live the rest of my life knowing I let you go without having told you."

He simply stared as the rain beat down on his face. He'd heard me. I knew he'd heard me.

But he wasn't saying anything.

"It doesn't matter," I said quickly, grateful for the rain making my tears less obvious. "You're going away and I can't see you anymore."

"Portia . . ."

I forced myself to meet his eye, waited for him to say . . . something. But he didn't. There was no "I want to be with you, too." Just my name, because apparently there was nothing else to say.

I pulled on a smile. "It's okay. Really. No big deal. It's been fun. A great time. Good job on the barn. I'll be first in line to get your next book."

I walked over to my car. He didn't try to stop me. The rain began to pour with force. I pulled the driver's side door open and paused, forcing myself to look at him one last time. We stared at each other for a minute. I stepped into the car. I didn't look in the rearview mirror until I'd almost reached the road. He was still standing there in the rain, watching me drive away.

I busted through the front door of the house, dripping big fat drops on the hardwood floor. The rain was beating out a primal rhythm on the roof. In my imagination, Ian was still standing outside where I'd left him. In reality, he was probably packing, glad it was over.

"Mags?" I called out. "Vera?"

There was no answer. My muscles were still shaking with cold and emotional fatigue. I sat on the arm of the old easy chair and called out again.

"Bev? Peter?"

I heard steps on the staircase, followed by Mags's honeyed voice.

"Portia, baby, is that you?"

"Yeah," I said, swallowing hard, trying to keep it together. Mags froze at the bottom of the steps when she saw me. Vera and Bev stood behind her.

"Baby, are you okay?" Vera asked.

"Where's Peter?" I didn't want him to be a part of this.

"He's sleeping," Bev said. "Do you want us to wake him?"

I shook my head and burst into a fresh round of sobs. Mags hurried over to me and put her arms around me, guiding me to the couch and pulling a blanket over my shoulders.

"Oh, baby," she said. "What happened?"

I swiped at my nose with the back of my hand. "Penis Teflon. I tried to face it, tell him that I wanted to be with him, because I thought maybe if I wasn't afraid like you and Vera had been, that maybe that would work, you know, break the curse, but . . ."

Vera grabbed a box of tissues from the end table and handed them to me. Mags guided my head to her shoulder. I inhaled her smell and felt a rush of healing go through me.

"Oh, baby," Mags said. "Did you go and fall for that Flyer?"

"Yes," I sobbed. "He's going back to London on Saturday and he doesn't want me and I'm all covered in Penis Teflon and no one is ever going to stick to me, ever."

"Oh, now, I'm fairly sure that's not true." She paused for a moment, running her hand over my hair. "Did you tell him how you feel?"

I nodded.

"And what did he say?"

"Nothing," I squeaked. Mags pulled her head back. I looked up at her. She smiled at me.

"Congratulations, darlin'."

I rubbed my face and sat forward. "For what?"

She grabbed my hand. "Because you did it, and that matters."

I sniffled. "It does?"

"Of course," Vera said, kneeling by my feet. "You can't control what he does or how he feels. That's not for you."

"Most people don't have the courage to do what you did," Mags piped in, putting one hand on my face. "I'm proud of you, baby."

"Really?"

"Yes." She patted my knee and got up, surreptitiously snatching a tissue and dabbing at the corners of her eyes. Vera stood up and looked to Bev. Bev looked down at me, her eyes as hard and inscrutable as always. Then, slowly, a kind smile tinged the edges of her lips.

"I'll get the fondue pot," she said, and headed toward the kitchen. Vera and Mags put their arms around me and leaned their heads against mine, muttering words of comfort. I smiled. It was good to be home.

"I don't care what he said or didn't say." Beauji pushed the stroller down River Road and I had to speed up to keep pace with her. Even pushing a stroller, she was faster than me. "I've seen him look at you. That boy's crazy about you."

"It doesn't matter," I said. "It's over. He's as good as gone and I don't want to talk about it anymore."

I could see Beauji watching me through my peripheral vision, but I kept my eyes straight ahead.

"What about Peter?" she said after a minute.

I shook my head. "I don't know. He sure looks great on paper, though, doesn't he?"

"I think the fact that he moved in with the Mizzes just to get you back is more than good on paper," she said with a sigh. "That's just plain ol' good."

"I know." I shrugged. "I'm beginning to think that whether he's a good guy or not isn't the problem, though."

"Right. So what's the problem?"

I shook my head and shrugged. I had an idea that the problem wasn't Peter at all, but I wasn't ready to say so out loud. Miles gave a short cry and Beauji lifted up the shade on the stroller to peek at him. "Isn't he just the most beautiful thing you ever did see?"

I smiled into the stroller. He was looking more and more like a real baby every day, and I had to admit, he was a looker. Beauji reached in and lifted him out of the stroller, walking over to a grassy patch off the road.

"Feel free to keep going and come back for me," she said, lifting one side of her shirt with her free hand as she sat down. "He's a notoriously slow eater. This might take a while."

I held my hand over my eyes to shade the sun and looked around. There was nothing, except a dirt road by a sign that read WILKINS CONSTRUCTION. The idea popped into my head fully formed, as if it had been waiting for me, and I latched onto it. After all, misery loves distraction.

"I'll be right back, Beau," I said. She waved me on and I headed down the road to the trailer office next to the huge, square warehouse that had housed Wilkins Construction since I could remember. I stepped up to the door and knocked, then walked in.

"Can I help you?" Betty Jo Allen shut a filing cabinet drawer with her hip, then looked up from the file in her hand and smiled. "Well, I'll be damned. Portia Fallon. Ain't seen you out here for . . . gosh, ten years?"

"About that, yeah."

She grinned and tossed the file on her desk. "You here to see Bridge?"

"Yes, is he in?"

"Bridge!" she yelled toward the office door, open just a crack. "You in for Portia Fallon?"

I heard some movement in the office, then Bridge's face poked out of the door. He smiled.

"You bet," he said, waving me in. "Come on in, Portia."

I walked into his office and shut the door behind me. Bridge motioned to the chair opposite his desk.

"Have a seat, darlin'," he said. "Have you seen the barn? I took some pictures for Trudy. I think she's going to be really pleased."

"I can't stay," I said. Bridge tilted his head at me and leaned against the edge of his desk.

"Everything all right out there with . . . your family?"

I smiled. "Yes. Fine. Actually, we're having a party on Saturday night. Just a casual get-together. I was hoping you might come."

Bridge looked down at his feet, then back at me. "I'm not sure that would be a good idea, Portia."

"Vera would like it very much if you came," I said quickly. It wasn't exactly a lie. I was fairly sure if I dosed her with truth serum and shined a light in her face, she'd admit to wanting to see Bridge again.

Bridge crossed his arms over his chest. "She tell you that?"

I smiled. "Seven o'clock. Saturday. If you're not there, I'll hunt you down, hog-tie you, and drag you there myself."

Bridge laughed, then was quiet for a long minute. Finally, he gave a brief nod.

"Should I bring anything?"

I grinned. "No, we've got it covered. See you then."

I left the office and waved a quick good-bye to Betty Jo, who pretended she wasn't calling everyone in town to tell them a Miz Fallon had just shown up in Bridge Wilkins's office. I stepped out into the sunshine and ran all the way back to Beauji, who was just packing little Miles into his stroller.

"Did you just go see Bridge?" she asked.

"Yeah," I said. "I've gotta get to the Page and tell the Mizzes we're having a party on Saturday night."

I started speed-walking back toward town. Beauji turned the stroller around and jogged to catch up.

"What did you do?" she asked, her voice a mix of surprise and suspicion.

I grinned at her. "I just graduated. I'm officially a Miz Fallon now."

"Well, Beauji and Davey, of course," I said as Peter scribbled down the names. "And Beau Sr. and Wendy."

Mags stepped into the dining room and put her address book on the table next to Bev. "I just got off the phone with Marge Whitfield. That Betty Jo Allen has told half the town you were in Bridge's office this morning."

"Was she listening?" Bev asked. "Did she say anything about the party?"

Mags shook her head. "No. I'm pretty sure if she knew, she'd have mentioned it to Marge."

I put my index finger on the sheet Peter was writing on. "Put Marge Whitfield and Betty Jo Allen and her husband, Alan."

Peter looked up with a smirk. "Alan Allen?"

I waved my hand at him. "Long story. But let's make sure they all get invited so no one gets suspicious." I looked up at Mags. "Have you decided what we're going to tell Vera?"

"It's your good-bye party," Bev said quietly. I looked up.

"My good-bye party?"

Mags waved her hand at me dismissively. "Or something. We're Miz Fallons. If we can't find an excuse for a party, who can?"

"You're leaving in, what, two weeks?" Bev asked. "Why not have the party now?"

I swallowed. I hadn't looked at a calendar in ages. I looked down at the list Peter'd been jotting down. "Sure. Why not?"

"Fine, then," Bev said, getting up. "It's settled."

She stalked out of the dining room. Mags and Peter exchanged looks.

"What?" I said.

"You know what?" Peter said, standing up. "I'm gonna go get my jacket so I can walk you home, Portia."

He slid out of the room. I looked at Mags.

"What, Mags? What am I missing?"

"Well," she said slowly, "I think it might be a good idea if you spent a little time with Bev and talked."

"About what?"

"You may not have noticed because Bev is so good at hiding it," Mags said, going light with her sarcasm, "but she's a little upset about you being away so much."

I blinked as the obvious began to dawn on me. "Are you kidding me? That's why she's been so pissy with me all summer? Because I'm going back to Syracuse?"

Mags reached over and patted my hand. "She just thinks children should come home after college, that's all. I've tried to explain it to her, but . . . well. You know Bev. Maybe you should try to talk to her yourself."

Peter stepped back into the room. "Ready, Portia?"

I kissed Mags on the cheek and smiled. "I'll talk to her. Later."

I smiled at Peter. At the moment, I had bigger fish to fry.

Peter and I were quiet for most of the walk home, commenting only on the honeysuckle in the air or the guest list for the party. I didn't gather up the courage to say what I wanted to say until we'd reached the front door of the Page, and he was about to turn around and head back.

"Peter," I said. "I think we need to talk."

He gave me a tight-lipped smile. "I don't think there's ever been a pleasant conversation that started out that way."

"I'm sorry," I said.

He nodded. "About?"

I sighed, and pulled the ring box out of my jacket pocket. I'd been carrying it around with me for days, waiting. "I think you know."

He reached out and took the box, staring down at it in his hand. "I see."

"No," I said. "You don't. Neither did I, really, not until recently."

Finally, he looked at me. "Care to enlighten me?"

No. But I owed it to him. I took a deep breath and started in on the speech I'd been preparing since we came back from Tuscaloosa.

"You are perfect. You always were. You were always kind. You were always there for me. There's nothing wrong with you."

He pulled on a weak smile. "So far, so good. Keep going."

I sighed. "I thought a lot about what you said. About me making you feel like a failure. And you were right."

He shook his head. "No, Portia, that was totally unfair of me to pin it all on you—"

"No, it wasn't." I blinked. Damnit. Shouldn't a person just run out of tears after a while? "I did it deliberately."

He was quiet for a bit, then, "What do you mean?"

"I mean, I was a coward." I swallowed. This hurt worse than I thought it was going to, mostly because of the extent to which Peter deserved better. "I mean, I wasn't in love and I didn't want to admit that the problem was me. So I drove you away. On purpose. Well, subconsciously on purpose."

He stared past my shoulder into the window display we'd built together. "I'm not sure I understand what you're saying. Are you saying you didn't love me? *Ever?*"

I wanted to tell him I had, as much to make him feel better as to make me look better, but he'd earned the truth. "I wanted to. I tried. I should have. There's no reason not to love you, Peter."

He held up his hand and I could see his face harden. "Oh, please don't give me the 'it's not you, it's me' crap."

"I'm sorry," I said. "I didn't know any better. I didn't know what it meant to love someone. I felt strongly for you, and I thought it was love, but I didn't know. I didn't have anything to compare it to."

He nodded slowly. "And now you do?"

I didn't say anything.

"And how long have you known this?"

"How long have I known?" I laughed feebly. "Or how long have I been willing to admit it to myself?"

"I'm glad you can find humor in this," he said. I could hear the bitterness in his voice, and while it hurt, I could hardly blame him.

"I'm sorry," I said again.

"Yeah," he said. "Me, too."

We stood there in silence for a long time, then he turned and walked back toward the Mizzes'. I watched until he walked out of my sight, then I turned and headed up the stairs toward my apartment.

chapter fourteen

I stepped out from the back door onto the lawn and the stiletto heels on my strappy shoes immediately sank an inch into the ground. I stood up on tippy toe and peered over the heads of the partygoers, smiling as I saw Mags in the back talking to Bridge. The week had been full of scheming and conspiracy, and while that typically wasn't my thing, it served as a fine distraction from all the men fleeing Truly, Georgia—Peter for Boston and Ian for London. Peter's departure was sad, but all agreed it was necessary. Ian's was not spoken of, and we all pretended it was just a blip on the radar, soon to be forgotten.

That was the hope, anyway. The truth was, any moment in which my thoughts weren't properly diverted, they turned to Ian. I imagined him on the plane, flying over the Atlantic, memories of me fading with every first-class cocktail. The only thing for me to do was throw myself into figuring out my future, deceiving my most beloved aunt, and planning the party.

Not necessarily in that order.

The door opened behind me and Bev stepped out, smoothing her hands over her blue cardigan sweater.

"Has she figured it out yet?" I asked.

"She knows something's going on," Bev said. "She's doing a Tarot reading right now trying to figure out what it is."

I smiled. You gotta love Vera.

"Okay, then. Are you ready?"

"Ready," she said, holding up the Love Kit. We each headed out to our positions—she at the liquor table, me on the other side of Bridge.

"Bridge!" I said, raising my arms and throwing them around his neck. "I'm so glad you came."

Bridge hugged me back, but I caught an uncomfortable expression on his face when I pulled away. I put my arm through his.

"Don't look so scared, darlin'," I said in honeyed tones. "The night is lovely, the drinks are cold, and the party's just getting started."

"You can hardly ask for better," Mags commented.

"I ain't scared," he grumbled, raising an eyebrow at Mags. "But I have a feeling I'm being worked on pretty good."

I gave him a playful smack on the arm and started to say something when his face went slack. I looked up.

Vera stood frozen at the back door. She looked beautiful, wearing a long blue dress which, unlike most of her drapery-style clothes, clung in all the right places. Her eyes were locked on Bridge, and his on her. I leaned over and grabbed Mags's arm, pulling her close.

"You better go get her or she's gonna run," I whispered. Mags grabbed Bridge's almost-full beer.

"Let me get you a fresh one, Bridge."

Bridge didn't even notice. Mags hurried toward the house. When she was about halfway through the throng of partygoers,

Vera took a step forward. Mags froze and looked at me. I exchanged glances with Bev, who was smiling.

"Vera," I said when she reached us. "Look who decided to show up for my going-away party."

"What a surprise," she said, giving me a long look. Finally, she raised her eyes to Bridge, and smiled. "Hello, Bridge."

"Vera." Bridge lifted his hand as if to take a drink, but there was nothing there. He stared at his empty hand for a second, then lowered it.

"Where is Mags with that beer?" I said, moving away. "Honestly, that woman would lose her head if it wasn't attached. I'll be right back. You two . . . talk."

I rushed away, waving Mags over to the liquor table.

"I don't want to be too obvious," I said when I reached Bev, keeping my back to Bridge and Vera. "How does it look?"

Bev leaned to the side, peering around me, then returned and gave me a smile. Mags scurried over.

"What do you think? Success?"

Bev gave a serene smile. "We'll have to wait and see."

"Give him his beer back," I said to Mags. "He's gonna need it."

"Oh! Yes, of course," Mags said, hurrying off.

"And report back!" I called after her. She gave me a thumbs-up and headed over to where Bridge and Vera were talking, each of them wearing a tentative smile. I turned back to Bev.

"I think this might actually work," I said.

"It just might," she said.

I sat back and crossed my arms over my chest, staring at Bev. She glanced at me sideways.

"Stop eyeballing me, child. You got something on your mind, speak up."

I smiled, suddenly overwhelmed with love for the cranky old bat.

"I was going to give you a big lecture, actually," I said. "All about how I have to live my own life, do my own thing, and you can't hold that against me."

She raised an eyebrow, but was no closer to a smile. "You been talkin' to Mags, I see."

I leaned forward. "I'd be right to give you that lecture. You've been acting like a pissy little kid this whole summer."

Her eyes flared and she turned to face me. I held up my hand.

"But, as it turns out, I'm not going back to Syracuse. Not right away, anyway. And it's not because of you being a big brat, so don't go thinking I'll let you get away with this kind of crap in the future."

Finally. There it was. A small smile. She turned her eyes back to Bridge and Vera, who seemed to be relaxing as they talked.

"So, what are your plans, then?"

"Vague. I'm changing my dissertation topic, so I'll never finish in time for the faculty job. I called Rhonda and she's going to assume my lease in Syracuse."

"I see," Bev said.

I paused for a moment, then went on. "I heard y'all were in the market for a business manager, so if it's okay with you, I thought I might do that for a while. Maybe live in the apartment over the Page. Figure out my life. Have some fondue." I wagged a warning finger at her. "But it's not a promise of forever, so if I end up leaving again, you'd better take it like a lady and be gracious. I don't want any more of this cranky shit between us, you hear?"

Bev nodded slowly and leaned back in her chair. She was quiet for a long time, and I was about to give her a good nudge to her ribs when she nodded toward the gin bottle sitting to my left.

"Sounds like a drink is in order," she said.

I smiled and got two glasses, scooped ice into them, and covered them with gin and a splash of tonic.

"To the Miz Fallons," I said, holding up my drink. Bev smiled, picked hers up, and clinked it to mine.

"May we reign forever."

I put my arm around her shoulders and kissed her cheek.

"I love you, Grandma," I said.

She gave a good-humored scowl and held up her drink to me in a warning fashion. "Who you callin' Grandma, child?"

It was two in the morning by the time we finished preliminary post-party cleanup. Although Bridge and Vera hadn't fallen into each other's arms and made immediate use of the Love Kit, we did get a promise from him that he would join us for dinner on Sunday night. And Vera had been smiling when she tottered off to bed. That was something.

It was more than something.

After declaring the evening an unqualified success, Mags and Bev talked me into crashing at the house for the night, and we all went to bed. Despite the good feelings I had from our victory, I tossed and turned all night, my head filled with visions of Ian on his way to London. It was wrong. Didn't he know that? Was he really that stupid? But then, who was I to be pointing fingers about stupid? Memories of working on the barn, of that first night when we'd stayed up in bed talking over two bottles of wine, of the kiss in the rain, crowded my mind no matter how hard I tried to push them out. Finally, at about five-thirty, I gave up. There would be no sleep. There would be no Ian. But at least I had the Page. I got up, got dressed, and stepped carefully over every crack in the sidewalk for the six blocks to the Page.

I was so wrapped up in my thoughts that I didn't notice Ian's SUV parked out front until after I'd walked in and started the coffee, at which point it hit me. I turned around just as the bells on the door jingled.

And there he was. His jacket was crumpled, his hair was a mess, and his eyes were red. He'd never looked more adorable.

"I heard the bell," he said. "I hoped it was you."

"It's six in the morning." I couldn't think of anything else to say, and just focused on trying to calm the wild tap dance my heart was performing.

"I know." He motioned vaguely toward the alley, then ran his fingers through his disheveled hair. "I've been sitting on your steps since eleven last night."

I blinked. It appeared he hadn't gotten any more sleep than I had. At least we were on an even playing field. His face was taut as he watched me. Finally, he looked away.

"I'm glad you're all right. I was a little worried when you didn't show up." He looked back up at me, his eyes questioning.

"I was at the Mizzes'," I said. "We had my good-bye party."

He nodded. "And Peter . . . ?"

"Gone. He left two days ago."

A small, relieved smile broke on his face. He took a step forward. I took a step back.

"Your plane," I said quickly.

"Yes," he said, stopping where he was. "It left."

"Without you."

"Without me."

I shook my head. "I'm not sure I understand."

His eyes held on mine. "Don't you?"

"No." My brain was still foggy from lack of sleep and too much thinking. "Why weren't you on your plane, Ian?"

He stuffed his hands in his pockets and rocked back on his heels, looking like a guilty kid being called to the principal's office. "I was all packed. I was on my way out the door. But then I realized I had . . . unfinished business."

He watched me quietly for a moment. I guessed it was my turn to say something.

"I have no idea what that means." That was a lie. I was beginning to get some idea. But he was going to have to spell it out for me. No way was I putting myself out there again. There weren't enough fondue makin's in the state of Georgia to get me through another rejection from Ian Beckett.

"Well," he said, pulling his hands out of his pockets, "I realized that we never did that book signing."

I blinked, surprised. "I'm sorry, what?"

"The book signing. I committed to it and then never followed up on it. It was horribly unprofessional of me." He took another step closer, his eyes growing more serious. "I should have said something earlier. I'm so sorry, Portia."

"I see." I walked over to the coffee bar and poured us two mugs, handing him one. I settled on one of the bar stools and swiveled outward, facing him as he stood in front of me.

"So," he said slowly, putting his coffee mug down and leaning one arm on the bar behind me, his face hovering near mine, "if you could find it in your heart to forgive me, I was hoping we might, you know, schedule one."

I smiled. "A book signing?"

He nodded. His face was so close I could feel his breath on my neck. "Yes. I was hoping we could schedule it soon. I'm not sure how long I can wait."

His lips grazed my cheek. I put my hand on his face and moved him until our eyes were level. "And how long will you be available for this . . . book signing?"

He pulled my fingers away from his face and kissed them.

"Well, I do have some commitments in England. A public appearance. A university lecture. I will have to leave, Monday morning at the latest, but I can be back in a week. Two weeks, at the most." He lowered his hand, intertwining my fingers with his. "Will you still be here then? Because I'm very selective about who I sign books with."

I smiled. "I will be here as a matter of fact. I've committed to stay. Indefinitely."

He raised an eyebrow. "You're not going back to Syracuse?"

I shook my head. "No. I'm taking some time off. Changing my dissertation topic."

He pulled back a bit and smiled. "Don't tell me. The Marlowe thing?"

I grinned. He laughed, then his face flashed brilliance and he tightened his grip on my hand.

"Then come with me. To London. I'm sure your family can spare you for a few weeks." He leaned in and kissed my lips softly before pulling back again. "You can do some research. Prove me wrong."

"Then we'll come back here and do the book signing?"

He gave a salacious grin. "We can do the book signing anywhere."

I shook my head. "I need to know what happens next."

He laughed. "You're rather into plans, aren't you?"

"I'm a first-timer," I said. "Humor me."

He leaned down and kissed me below my left ear. "Well, the Babb farm is available for rent. Indefinitely, I'm told."

"So, it could be . . . indefinite?"

He kissed a trail over my jaw and hovered, so close I could feel his breath on my lips as he spoke.

"Excruciatingly indefinite."

That was the moment. I could almost hear it, like an audible crack in the energy in the room. The Penis Teflon was gone. He was going to stick. I put my arms around his shoulders and wove my fingers through the soft hair at the back of his neck. I guided his face down to mine and I kissed him softly, knowing for the first time in my life that there would be plenty more where that came from.

So I took my time.

about the author

Hi, there! Thanks so much for reading my book! I adore you for that, and as a reward, I'm going to limit my bio to only the things about me that are mildly interesting. Because, really, you don't care where I went to college, do you? Didn't think so. So here we go:

I once called "Car Talk" and confessed to my terrible backseat driving on national radio because my husband and I were too broke to afford anniversary gifts.

I have an unnatural celebrity crush on Colin Firth. As a matter of fact, the character of Ian in *Ex and the Single Girl* was totally based on Colin. You probably already figured that out, but if you didn't, it's worth another read to go back and picture Colin Firth delivering all of Ian's lines. Trust me.

I once touched Michael Landon's pants. Sadly, he wasn't in them at the time. I was working wardrobe at Old Tucson Studios and there was a pair of pants with a tag stating Michael Landon wore them while filming scenes for *Little House on the Prairie* there. Looking back, I kinda wish I'd stolen them. This would've been a rockin' bio if I could have said, "I have Michael Landon's pants in my closet . . ."

I wore Rollerblades to work for two years and didn't get fired. FYI, if you ever get the chance to work at a place that values quirky people, do it.

All right. That just about covers it. If I come up with anything else interesting, I'll put it on my Web site at www.lanidianerich.com, so come find me there! Thanks for reading!

lani diane rich's top five lame break-up excuses (and what they really mean)

TOP 5

1. It's not you, it's me. (It's you.)

2. You deserve better. (Is your sister available?)

3. I'm not attracted to you physically. (Just because I'm balding doesn't mean I can't be picky.)

4. I love you, but as a friend. (I may need to borrow money from you in the future.)

5. I'm not comfortable in a monogamous relationship. (However, if you'd consider a threesome, we might have something to talk about. Is your sister available?)